MW01645005

New Beginnings

BEN & BECKY, BED & BREAKFAST TRILOGY

BOOK ONE

Deloris Packard

First Edition—2025

FICTION, CONTEMPORARY WOMENS

ACKNOWLEDGMENTS

This book is for my faithful readers, who asked for more from the Delanie sisters.

Thanks to my editor, Marilyn Boake (author of, Water Over the Bridge). Thank you, for your guidance and insight. You have polished my words, and made them shine.

Thanks also to my very talented friend, Michelle Scott, for painting my beautiful cover. Your talent is truly a gift, to us all.

OTHER BOOKS BY DELORIS PACKARD

FICTION:

The Cedar Grove Resort Trilogy:

The Inheritance of the Cedar Grove Resort

The Nuptials at the Cedar Grove Resort

The Sale of the Cedar Grove Resort

NON-FICTION:

Anticipatory Grief

Anticipating the passing of a loved one

ONE

Debbie watched as the twins got onto the little bus for their first day of school. As the bus drove out of sight, she let herself have a good cry. The tears were streaming down her face as she walked back to the house, chastising herself for being so emotional. She knew they'd be home later, with all kinds of tales of what they had done at school, but she still couldn't account for her own sadness at seeing them go off on their adventure. Her babies were growing up so fast. They were giddy with excitement, while Debbie was very sad. She had been dreading this day, and now that it was here, she was conflicted with a sense of pride and a sense of utter dread.

With Brad gone to work and Ben and Becky off to school, the house felt unusually quiet. Debbie suddenly felt lost, and out of place. Her usual morning bluster was replaced with total silence. She could even hear the clock ticking on the kitchen wall. She had never noticed that before.

Black coffee in hand, Debbie wandered through the living room and sat down in the big bay window. She had made a cushion for the seat and two big throw pillows to match. This had quickly become her favorite spot in the house. She could sit there for hours and watch the ever-changing view. As she sat there, overlooking the lake, she was feeling a bit melancholy. She looked beyond the beautiful scene before her: the manicured lawn, the road, the water rippling on the lake, and the beautifully colored trees. Her mind wandered, reminiscing about the last five years since she was forced to sell her resort.

She was proud to be Mrs. Bradley Mumford and proud to be a good mother. The twins, Rebecca and Benjamin, were a lot of work but oh so worth it. Debbie loved them both unconditionally, as only a mother could. And then there was the '*bun in the oven*' as her mom used to say.

Debbie could still remember the sound of her mom's voice inside her head, and she was happy she was still able to hold onto her good memories. Her mom would have been ecstatic to be a grandmother and meet the twins. Debbie smiled to herself when she realized she rubbed her baby bump every time she thought of her mom, which was often.

She knew her mom would have also been happy to know that she had finally married Brad, the love of her life, and that she was truly happy enjoying her marriage and her family. Her mom had always liked Brad, and used to find excuses to invite him over to the resort, even when he was married to his first wife.

Brad was the most honest, reliable man that she knew. He always had a smile on his face and Debbie couldn't help but admire him. He worked hard, but he always put his family first. He was her king, she was his queen, and life was good. So why was she feeling so sad and depressed? She felt like she just needed time to stop for a minute so she could catch up.

And here she was pregnant again, and at her age, what a cruel joke. They hadn't even discussed having another baby, but life happens. They were being careful, but obviously, not careful enough. The proof was in her belly.

For the past five years, Brad promised he was going to build her a bed-and-breakfast, once the kids were in school. Just the other day he asked if she would prefer it to be attached to their existing house with the pool beside it or have the bed-and-breakfast on the other side of the pool as a separate building. Debbie thought about it halfheartedly, her mind caught between her old life and the new one she was building with Brad and the kids.

Her husband and her family were, at the moment, her only job, and she was good at spoiling them all, including Chef George. Chef had really slowed down, and although he now sometimes used a walker, he could still dance around a kitchen. At Debbie's request, Brad had added a ramp at the front door to accommodate walkers and baby strollers, and Chef came over every Monday and did some baking for them. Chef was also teaching Debbie some of the cooking tricks he had learned over the years. He enjoyed teaching, she enjoyed learning, and they enjoyed each other's company.

Debbie smiled as she thought about her sisters Susan and Janice who both had a habit of showing up Monday afternoons and always went home with a goody bag from Chef.

Susan and Keith were both doing well. Keith had been promoted to head teacher of the English department at his school. Katie and Joshua were both now attending the same university. Katie was in her third year to become a teacher, just like her dad, and Joshua was in his first year studying to be an engineer. Susan was doing very well in her real estate business. Debbie knew how much Susan was enjoying having her biological father, Jefferson, living with them. According to Susan, he was a great help with the housework and the cooking, and they all loved and respected him. Susan didn't know how lucky she was to have a live-in maid and cook.

And then there was Janice, who had just confessed that she was in love, again. Debbie was surprised that Janice jumped right back in, after her short, ugly marriage to Tony had ended. She did get her son, Zackery, from the marriage, but it had gotten ugly when Tony and his mother filed for custody. It had been quite the battle, but Janice ended up with full custody and Tony had supervised visits. Since Tony had lost his license due to drinking and driving, Janice had to take Zack to see his father every other weekend, which Zack hated. It all kept Janice in a constant state of stress. She wished Tony would just give up. It would be so much easier on her and Zack. Thank goodness Janice still had her manager's job at the resort, to keep her busy and distracted from all the Tony drama.

Sometimes her sisters could be a real pain, but she loved and respected them both. She had been totally impressed when Susan had stepped in and had made sure Tony did not get any of Janice's inheritance. Susan saved the day, and because of that, Janice and Zack were doing just fine. And now, Janice thought she was in love again. Debbie decided that Janice loved being in love. They would have to lock her in a dungeon, to keep her from falling for every guy she met.

The ringing of the telephone brought Debbie out of her daydream. As she stood up to answer it, she glanced down at the empty coffee cup in her hand and wondered how long she'd been sitting there. She had a habit of losing track of time when she was sitting in her favorite spot in her bay window.

Debbie kept an eye out for Chef's arrival. He used his walker now to get from the car to the house, and she liked to be ready to open the door to make it easier for him.

"Chef, hi, come on in."

"Morning, child. Here, I brought you all some apple strudel."

"That was nice of you. You will need to teach me how to make them one day."

As Chef hung up his jacket, he told her, "They are made from puff pastry, and yes, I can certainly teach you how to make them."

"I've never worked with puff pastry much. But I would like to learn. I just put on a fresh pot of coffee for you. Would you like a cup?"

Chef followed her into the kitchen and pulled up a stool at the breakfast nook. "A coffee would be nice. So, besides bread, what else are we baking today?"

"You mentioned last time about making me a raspberry pie. I have the berries thawing out in the sink as we speak."

"Well, I guess we should get started." Debbie handed him his apron and they lost track of time as they worked side by side baking breads and making raspberry pies for her family.

TWO

The kettle whistled on the stove and Debbie made herself a tea. She had decided to give up on coffee, at least for now. She loved coffee and drank it all day long, but now, every time she tried to drink it, she would end up throwing up. She had just taken a tray of cookies from the oven when the phone rang.

Debbie knew from call display that it was the resort calling, but it could be anyone from there. It could be Nancy, or Janice, but Janice usually called from her cell phone, unless it was business-related.

"Hi, Debbie. It's Nancy. Did I catch you at a bad time?"

"No, not at all. I just finished baking cookies for the kids' lunches."

"I am on a break and thought I would give you a call."

"Is everything alright? How are things going over there?"

"Oh fine. The golfing is winding down and the ski hill hasn't opened just yet. Phil suggested I invite you and your family for dinner one night to catch up. How does that sound?"

"Sounds wonderful to me. I am sure Brad will agree. What night is best for you guys?"

"Any night through the week should be good."

"Do you still have the chicken and ribs on the menu?" Debbie asked. "I know that is Brad's favorite. He likes it even better than a good char-broiled steak."

"Yep, sure do. We used to run it as the Saturday night special, but it was so popular, mostly with the local people, that we just decided to add it to the menu."

"Makes sense. So, you have had a good summer then?" Debbie couldn't help but ask. Although she didn't own the resort anymore, she was still curious about how it was doing.

"Yes, we did. We even debated about doing the Home and Cottage Show because we were ninety percent booked already."

"We used to wrestle with that decision every year," Debbie said, "but we always ended up doing it. Personally, I think it is good to support local events like the show and the parades."

"I agree wholeheartedly. We ended up going mainly for that reason alone. And it did pay off with bookings," Nancy said with pride in her voice.

"That a girl. You guys are getting to be old pros at being resort owners. Would you say you're enjoying it as much as you thought you would?"

"Honestly, I would have to say it's a lot of hard work, but we have the best resort we could possibly have, and although somedays I'd give anything for an hour to myself, it's all worth it when the day is over and I tally up the sales."

"I used to take the bank deposits in and stop at the local café in town to have a moment to myself. Ah, the good old days. I remember them fondly."

"So, when arc you going to get that bed-and-breakfast built?"

"Soon, I expect. We were always planning to do it when the kids started school, and they are in school now. Brad asked me just the other day if I thought I wanted the extra rooms added to this house or in a separate building altogether."

"What did you tell him?"

"I don't know. I am thinking it should be attached, then the guests will just need to come downstairs for breakfast. Know what I mean?"

"That makes sense, and all the extra laundry will be easier to deal with too."

Debbie smiled at the realization that Nancy was becoming quite the little entrepreneur, understanding the logistics of doing business. "Exactly what I was thinking."

"Well, I hope you get it built and up and running soon. I will send you all the extra customers that I can't accommodate here, because we are always full."

"I'm counting on that! Guess I should let you go. I'm sure you are busy. I'll ask Brad what night he wants to come for dinner and let you know."

"That sounds good. Any day next week would be just fine for us."

"Thanks, Nancy. You take care and say hi to Phil and the girls for me."

Debbie had cleaned up the kitchen from the cookie baking and was now chopping vegetables for dinner when Brad came sailing through the door.

"Hey, hun, come check this out. I had rough drawings done for the B&B. Come see what you think." Brad unrolled the blueprints onto the dining room table.

Debbie dried her hands and joined him. "You'll have to explain them to me. I don't understand what I am looking at."

"See here, this is the front view of the new house with

the B&B attached, and this one is with the B&B as its own building. Which one do you like better?"

"I have been thinking it would be easier if it is attached, if it doesn't change the look of the house too much."

Brad rolled up the other set of blueprints. "I agree. And see here, if we add onto this existing hallway, we can have the office and the laundry room with doors on both sides for us and the guests to use."

"That makes sense. I like that idea." Debbie truly only understood half of what she was looking at.

Brad flipped over to another page of the drawings. "This is the side view to show the side and back with the proposed addition added on. See, we will extend the existing roof line back and up here."

"Looks good. So, the six new rooms are all upstairs, right? Then what is under them on the ground floor?" Debbie asked.

"I was thinking storage and perhaps two small apartments. Or one apartment for rent and a small guest room for anyone that can't handle the stairs, and a linen closet for storage."

Debbie smiled at him. "You have given this a lot of thought. Thank you, hun. You are truly the best husband a girl could ever ask for."

"Alright then, decision is made. I will get the architect to start on the official drawings. You should also know that there are some logistics involved. First, we need to get the rezoning done and then the building permits."

Debbie looked puzzled. "Rezoning? What do you mean?"

"Currently this house is zoned residential, and it will need to be rezoned as commercial property, if we are going to run a business from it. Legally, I should not even have my office here, but I am such a small business, no one notices. I meet most of my clients in town, or on-site, so there's not a lot of strange vehicles coming and going from here. But a full-size addition, and an in-ground pool could draw some unwanted attention. I think we need to make it legal and get the rezoning issue resolved before we spend any money."

"How exactly do we do that?" Debbie frowned.

"We have to apply for a rezoning permit, and probably go to a meeting about it. The neighbors will all be notified, and if there are no objections, it is just a formality, and no big deal," Brad told her as he rolled up the blueprints.

"What happens if there are objections from the neighbors?"

"Then we will address their concerns, and do whatever is necessary to make them all happy," Brad said in his reassuring business voice. "Don't you worry about it. Let's not stress over problems that may never even happen."

"I am glad you know what to do. I wouldn't even know where to start."

"I know what we have to do. I'll take care of it." Brad sniffed the air. "Am I mistaken, or do I smell chocolate chip cookies?"

"You have the nose of an old hound dog, Mr. Mumford. Yes, you smell cookies. I just took the pan out of the oven when you came flying in."

"Could I have a couple? I am starving, and lunch is still so far away."

"I suppose you could," Debbie said as Brad followed her into the kitchen.

Brad let out a heartfelt moan when he bit into the still-warm cookie. "Babe, these are the best cookies I have ever had. Don't tell Mom, but they are even better than hers."

"Thanks, hun. Speaking of your mom, I was thinking we should have them over for dinner one night real soon."

"Yes, they would love that. But we should wait till we know officially that you are pregnant. I am quite likely to blurt it out. I know she wants more grandkids, and I don't think my dear sister will ever get around to it."

"You never know, she may surprise you. Have you spoken to Barb lately? When is the last time you called your sister?"

"I talked to her two weeks ago. Remember I told you that she just got some kind of promotion and a bigger office. You know those marketing executive types, always climbing the corporate ladder," Brad said as he bit into his second cookie.

"Oh yeah, I forgot. You did mention that. Well, as for Barb ever having a baby, we are living proof that you never know when unexpected things can happen."

"How are you feeling? Are you still getting sick in the mornings?" Brad asked as he pulled her into his arms for a kiss.

"Yes, as soon as I have a coffee. I remember I had to give it up when we had the twins. Well, here I am living without it again. Every time I try to have one, it's a colossal failure."

Brad's cell phone rang, and he looked to see who was calling but didn't answer. "Just a supplier calling. I'll call him back later." Brad kissed her again. "You know, pretty lady, I have some free time right now. Could I interest you in some lovin' time before I have to go back to work?"

"Listen here, cowboy, I will have to take a rain check. I

have a list of chores that still need to be done, before the kids get home from school. Just because you have a job where you can goof off doesn't mean I do. Now go on, get back to work." Debbie gave him a gentle push.

"I guess if I can't get any lovin', I might as well go make some money." Brad pouted. "But I'll take one more cookie for the road."

"You know I baked those cookies for the kids, right?" Debbie chuckled at the guilty expression on his face.

"See you for supper." Brad retrieved his blueprints, gave her a quick kiss, and was gone again.

She sat and thought about whether she really wanted a bed-and-breakfast now. Five years ago, when she was forced to sell her resort, she wanted it badly, but now she really wasn't so sure. As soon as she and Brad had married, they got pregnant, so they put the plans for the B&B on hold. And she was already busy, being a full-time wife and mother, and now, there was another baby on the way. Did she really want to commit to a B&B for the rest of her life? She admitted to herself that she wasn't really sure, but there was also Brad to consider. He was so excited to build it for her, and she didn't want to disappoint him. She needed some sisterly advice.

Debbie picked up the phone and speed-dialed Susan's cell phone.

"Hey, sis. What's up?" Susan answered cheerfully.

"Oh, nothing. I was just thinking about you. Brad just stopped in to show me the blueprints for the new bed-and-breakfast."

"How exciting. You've been waiting for this for a long time."

"Yeah, I guess so." Debbie sighed. "The thing is, I'm not so sure I want it anymore."

"What? I thought this was all you ever wanted," Susan said in her serious business tone.

"Five years ago, when we sold the resort, yeah, it was all I wanted. But a lot of things have changed since then."

Susan was quiet for a moment. "Look, Brad loves you, and he would understand if you've changed your mind. Talk to him about what you are feeling."

"You're right. But at this point he is excited about building it for me. I wouldn't want to let him down."

"Sounds like you will need to decide quickly. The last thing you want is to be running a business you resent, just because you don't want to let him down."

"I know. You are right. I'll talk to Brad tonight. Thanks. I guess I just needed some sisterly advice. Talk soon."

Debbie sat finishing her cold tea. *Sue is absolutely right. I need to make a decision and make it quickly.* On the one hand, Debbie knew she would enjoy the variety of people who would be guests. She still missed that aspect from her days managing the resort. But, on the other hand, she had a husband and two kids to look after and a baby on the way. She wasn't looking forward to the two a.m. feedings, all the poopy diapers, the teething, or the potty training. So, why was she hesitating? Maybe if she wasn't pregnant again, she'd be more interested.

She wasn't sure how, but she would bring it up to Brad; she had to find a way. He should know how she was feeling. He was such a loving, supportive husband, and she knew he would understand. She just wished she had more conviction in her own feelings about it all before she talked to him.

THREE

Saturday morning, Brad had gone to check on one of his buildings and the kids were playing in the living room while Debbie tidied up the kitchen from breakfast. Brad always gave his workers the choice to work on Saturdays. Most of the guys took the day off, but some would choose to work. No one worked on Sundays.

Debbie heard a little knock on the door and saw Timothy and Valerie rounding the corner. Timmy headed straight into the living room to play with Ben and Becky, and Val helped herself to a coffee.

"Morning, Deb. How're things going over here? James is working today so Timmy and I are on a mission. We get to go grocery shopping today. Isn't that exciting?" Val took her usual seat at the breakfast nook. Debbie was glad that her best friend felt comfortable enough to make herself at home, but she sensed that Val was in a strange mood.

"Sounds like fun. I did that yesterday while the kids were in school. It's a real treat for me to not have four little hands helping me put things into the cart."

"I look forward to the day when I can grocery shop by myself. How pathetic can my life get?"

"It's just part of life, Val. You know, the good and the boring stuff too. It can't be all rainbows and glitter."

"Don't I know it. Most days I think Timmy doesn't even like me that much. If he can choose, he always chooses to go to James."

Maybe you should spend some more mommy time with him. "Timmy adores you. I know he does. Don't be so hard on yourself. He will always love you. You will always be his mother."

"Hell, I think he even likes Patty, the nanny, more than he likes me." Val sipped at her coffee. "I am so glad I decided to keep working. It is, at least, an escape from my domestic life. I have discovered that I still like adult conversation."

"I know what you mean. I spend all day with the kids, and when Brad gets home at night, he almost always has paperwork to do. We have Sundays off to spend together, and that helps. We spend Sundays together as a family. Perhaps you and James should adopt that idea."

"Sunday, James usually goes fishing, and if I am really lucky, he takes Timmy with him, so I can catch up on the housework and prepare dinner for my guys. Gosh my life is just so exciting." Val shrugged. "But on a happier note, I just got a raise at work. Steve even bought me lunch to celebrate. When I told James, he looked up from the TV just long enough to mumble congratulations."

Debbie wondered why Val always complained. "Who's this Steve guy you are always mentioning? Sounds like you and Steve go out to lunch a lot. What's that all about?" Debbie asked.

"It's not about anything. Steve and I happen to have the same lunch hour. It's just a friendly lunch with a coworker, and some adult conversation."

"But you've never mentioned having lunch with any other coworkers, only this Steve guy. Tell me more about him."

"He's a super nice man. He's handsome and charming

and a real good listener. He is a reporter, a good reporter, and I really like him. If you met him, I am sure you would like him."

Debbie couldn't help but notice how Val's eyes sparkled when she was talking about Steve. "Sounds innocent enough, but you know how people talk. Be careful, Val. You're playing with fire."

"I'm not doing anything wrong. But this small town's busybodies are probably watching me like a hawk."

"I'm sure they are. Small towns are like that. There is good and bad in every town. It's just that in a smaller town, everyone knows all your business."

"Well, I think everyone should mind their own business, and stay out of mine!" Val said in a slightly raised voice.

"Are you referring to anyone specific, or just all people in general? I didn't mean to offend you; I am just checking that you're alright."

"No, not you. People in general. I see the looks that Steve and I get when we are out to lunch together. It's nobody's business. We are not doing anything wrong. All we are doing is eating lunch together, and having a nice conversation."

"I believe you. But you know people only see what they want to see, and often come to the wrong conclusions. Just be cautious. Maybe go out to lunch with someone else, or even go by yourself. I could meet you for lunch on Wednesdays as the kids are in school all day."

"That would be nice. I would like that very much. Well, I guess we should get going. Come on, Timmy, it's time for grocery shopping," Val called out while she put her dirty cup in the sink. "Are we still on for dinner tomorrow night?"

"Yes, I am looking forward to it. I haven't been to the resort in quite a while."

Debbie questioned whether she should have offered to let Timmy stay and play until Val got back from shopping, but Val didn't spend enough time with her son as it was. Kids aren't stupid. They pick up on things. Timmy likely sensed that his mother's heart just wasn't in it. She's just not that interested in being a wife and mother. But Val had to make her own choices, and Debbie hoped taking things too far with Steve wasn't one of them. Val could be very head strong at times. She had always been a charge in, head-first-and-think-later, kind of gal. It had gotten her into trouble, more than once.

Debbie had just finished tidying up the kitchen and loading the dishwasher when Susan stopped in. "Hey, sis, you guys home?"

"In the kitchen. Come on in," Debbie called out. "You're not at the office today?"

"No, I have an open house this afternoon just down the road, so I figured there wasn't much sense going all the way into Clifford."

"Makes sense. Time for a coffee then?"

Susan took a seat at the breakfast nook. "Thanks. I need one. We had such a strange night last night. Dad wasn't feeling well, and I heard him up, so I went to check on him. He was all sweaty and fevered. He seems to be feeling better this morning. Probably just picked up a bug or something."

"Glad he's alright. You'll have to keep an eye on him. How're the kids?" Debbie asked.

"They are good. When Katie is home on the weekends, she spends every possible moment with Jeremy. He's a really nice kid, very well-mannered and considerate. If my baby girl wants to have a boyfriend, at least she made a good choice in Jeremy. Josh is always busy. He spends his spare time out in the woodshop. He's currently building bookshelves for his room. And, Keith is so proud to be teaching him woodworking skills. They are like two peas in a pod," Susan said with pride in her voice.

"I'm surprised that Joshua doesn't have a girlfriend yet. He's a good-looking young man."

"He goes out on dates, mostly just first dates. I think he's going to be very fussy about choosing a girlfriend. He keeps saying that the girls at college are too childish for his taste. Maybe he'll end up like my dad, a reformed bachelor."

"Oh, he'll find a girl sooner or later. There's nothing wrong with taking your time and picking the right one. Just look at me and Brad. We dated briefly in high school, but it wasn't until he married the wrong woman that he realized I was the one he wanted. I always knew Brad was the one for me, even back then. I just had to be patient, and let me tell you, it was definitely worth the wait."

"Oh, I know. I expect any day now he'll be bringing a girl home for us to meet. But for now, he is staying focused on his studies and enjoying woodworking with his dad."

Debbie offered Susan a cookie. "You just missed Val. She and Timmy were going grocery shopping."

"How's she doing? I saw her in town yesterday. She goes out to lunch with that same guy a lot. Is there anything going on there? They always seem so cozy, touching each other's arms and hands all the time."

"I just asked her about that, and she assured me that it was just lunch, with some adult conversation."

"Well, keep your eye on her. I would hate to see her do something she may live to regret."

How was she supposed to keep an eye on her? Val was a strong independent woman who would do whatever she pleased. Debbie got up to answer the telephone. It was Janice, so she put it on speaker.

"Hi, Janice. Susan and I are just having a coffee. What's up?"

"Deb, I hate to ask, but could you possibly watch Zack for me today? I just drove all the way to Grandma's house and Tony was passed out drunk. At ten o'clock in the friggin' morning. The court-appointed supervisor was about as impressed as I was. I told her straight out that Grandma couldn't take care of Zack and Tony wasn't able to, so I was taking Zack home. She didn't even argue with me. So now, I have Zack, and because he was to be at his dad's, I don't have a babysitter. She has gone away this weekend, so now I am stuck. Can you help me out?"

"Sure, bring him over. I plan to be at home all day with the kids anyway," Debbie assured her.

"Thanks, sis. I'll see you shortly," Janice said before she hung up.

"Poor kid," Susan stated. "Tony is such a fool. Hopefully the supervisor will have to report this. Who do you know that is passed out drunk at ten in the morning?"

"Nobody I know." Debbie refilled her sister's coffee.

When Brad came home later, he was surprised to see Zack. Debbie had to explain what had happened, and why Zack was there.

"I can't believe the hell that Tony is putting that girl

through," Brad said quietly. "Tony has no interest in being a father to that boy, and it's a damn shame that Janice has to put up with this nonsense. I think, if I was her, I'd take him back to court and appeal for no more visitations. I suspect it's the grandma that's pushing Tony. That would be like pushing a wheelbarrow with a flat tire."

Debbie chuckled at Brad's analysis of the Tony situation. "I agree wholeheartedly."

"How long till dinner?" Brad asked.

"About fifteen minutes. Yes, you have time for a shower."

"Thanks, babe. What are we having? It sure smells good."

"Zack's favorite, spaghetti."

"That's everyone's favorite." Brad gave her a quick kiss before he headed upstairs.

A few minutes later, they all sat down and had a nice dinner. The kids told their dad about the big building they had built that morning, and how Zack had bumped into it, and it all fell down. Brad's silly shocked expression made them all laugh.

Ben had asked his dad if he could show him how to build it stronger so it wouldn't fall down so easily, and Debbie's heart melted. *I am so lucky to have such a great man and such great kids. Their lives are certainly different than Zack's was.*

After dinner, Debbie put a movie in for the kids and helped Brad clean off the table. As she passed him between the kitchen and dining room, he said, "I have some estimates I need to get done for Sharon. She's coming tomorrow morning for a few hours."

"Just give me a minute to wipe the table. And don't

forget we are going out for dinner tomorrow night with Val and James, and Sharon has agreed to babysit the kids."

"It'll be good to see them. I haven't seen James in over a month," Brad said as he took the towel from her, and dried the table she had just finished wiping.

As Debbie tidied up the kitchen, she debated about sharing her concerns about Val with Brad. If she told him, she knew he would be upset. If there was a possibility that Val could hurt his best friend, James, Brad would not deal with it well. She quickly glanced into the dining room and saw that he was focused on the papers in front of him.

As Debbie sat down in the recliner to watch the cartoons with the kids, she couldn't help but think about the Val situation. She decided that if she didn't tell him, and he found out later that she knew and kept it a secret, he'd be terribly upset with her. Since Val had assured her that it was just a harmless lunch with a coworker, she decided to keep it to herself for now. But she was still annoyed that Val, once again, had pulled her unwillingly into her drama. Being Valerie's friend was sometimes a lot of work.

FOUR

Debbie was in the kitchen preparing a tossed salad for supper when Brad came in. He pulled her into his arms for his usual kiss.

"Whatever you are cooking sure smells good. I hope you know how much I appreciate that you cook dinner for me every night. Deb, I love you so much."

"Flattery will get you everywhere, cowboy. How is your day going?"

"Oh, you know, the usual. Before I forget, we have to go to a meeting about the rezoning on Tuesday night. Can you make arrangements for a babysitter? Maybe I could even enjoy a dinner out with my wife afterward."

"Are you concerned about the neighbors objecting to the rezoning?" Debbie asked. She was feeling anxious but tried to hide her concerns from Brad.

"No, not necessarily. Because I had the foresight to build in the middle of my eight acres, I am not that close to any neighbors, but I do have Jerry across the road. He doesn't like the fact that I have waterfront access adjoining his property, even though I planted a row of cedar trees along the edge to allow him some privacy. I hope he remembers I did that for him."

"He seems to like you. He is always over here borrowing tools from you. And his wife, Sheila, is friendly enough. She always waves when we see each other." But what about the other neighbors? Although they were not located too close together, they were still there. Brad and Debbie only knew them to see them. They weren't friends, only neighbors. They may have negative feelings about Brad turning his eight acres into commercial property. Debbie had this pit in the bottom of her stomach, this nagging doubt that things could go very wrong, and very quickly at this meeting.

"I'm sure it will be fine. No sense worrying. We will know on Tuesday night. I am going to run up and grab my shower before dinner. What are we having, anyway?"

"Meatloaf. Hun, before you go, I also have some news to tell you, and you're not gonna like it. We have a meeting on Monday night at the school," Debbie said in her most serious tone.

Brad looked at her in total surprise. "At the school! What for?"

"Seems that your son, Benjamin, got into a bit of a scuffle with a kid on the playground this morning at recess. Sounds like it was just a shoving match, but the principal and teacher want to meet with us, to discuss their no-bullying policy."

Brad furrowed his brow. "Should we punish him here at home? Maybe ground him or something?"

"I don't know. I wanted to discuss it with you first. According to the teacher, Ben said the other boy was picking on Becky, and he was just defending his sister." Debbie shrugged.

"Let's talk about it with him over dinner. I do think we should take away his toys or some sort of punishment to prevent this kind of behavior from happening again, don't you?"

"Let's ask him what happened, but after we eat dinner,

we can decide what the punishment should be. How does that sound?"

"Fine with me. Maybe we could take away any video games for the weekend."

"I will leave the punishment up to you. I want to know what the teacher who saw it happen has to say." Debbie shrugged. "Now go have your shower. Dinner will be ready in about ten minutes."

As Debbie finished putting the meal together and setting the table, she couldn't help but feel an overwhelming sense of dread. Monday night she had a meeting about her son bullying another boy on the playground, and Tuesday she had another meeting about rezoning issues.

"Dinner's ready, kids. Go wash your hands, please," Debbie called out.

They had planned on talking to Ben after dinner, but Becky blurted out, "Ben got in trouble at school today for pushing a boy on the playground."

Ben responded, "Shut up Becky."

"Ben, we don't tell people to shut up. Would you like to tell us what happened?" Brad asked.

"This boy Ricky was teasing Becky. He pulled her pigtails, so I shoved him and told him to leave her alone. He is a bully and always being a big tough guy. No one likes him, not even the teacher," Ben explained with a quivering lip.

"So, you only pushed him once?" Brad asked.

"No, he pushed me back so I pushed him again and then the teacher stepped in and stopped us." Ben had tears running down his cheeks now because he knew he was in trouble. "Ricky is a bully, and he pushes everyone around."

"Do you not think it would have been better to just tell

the teacher that Ricky was pulling Becky's hair?" Brad asked.

"I didn't see the teacher, and he was hurting my sister. I just wanted him to stop." Ben was sobbing now.

"Alright now, let's finish supper and we can talk about this after," Debbie said. "Ben, just so you know, your teacher called, and your daddy and I have to go to a meeting Monday after school."

Ben looked at her with terror in his tear-stained eyes. "All I did was stop him from pulling Becky's hair." He sobbed.

Debbie's heart was breaking, watching Ben. She glanced over to Brad for some support.

"Becky, do you have anything to add?" Brad asked.

"No, what Ben said is right. Ricky was teasing me and pulling on my pigtails. He pulled really hard, and it hurt. I yelled at him to stop, and then Ben pushed him away from me," Becky explained.

"Alright then. Ben, you know you were wrong in pushing Ricky. You know you should have gone and told your teacher. You know it is better to settle disagreements with your words. So, although your intentions to protect your sister were good, your actions weren't so good, and you should be punished." Brad was all business as he looked at his son. "I think you should have to give up video games for the weekend. Do you agree that is a fair punishment? Benjamin, do you agree?"

"Yes, Daddy," Ben said through sobs. "May I be excused now?"

"Yes, you may." Brad looked over at Debbie. She gave him a halfhearted smile and a shrug.

"Can I still play my games?" Becky asked.

"Yes, you can," Debbie answered. "But since Ben is in trouble for defending you, maybe you should think about not playing video games, to show your support and love for your brother." She watched as Becky debated what to do.

"I guess we could find other things to play with for the weekend then," Becky said and nodded.

"That's my girl." Brad smiled at her. "You are so smart and kind."

"Oh, Daddy. May I be excused?" Becky was already climbing out of her chair.

"Yes, go check on Ben." Debbie looked at Brad. "Well, that went about as well as could be expected."

"We'll see." Brad pushed his chair back from the table. "Dinner was good, hun. What do we have for dessert?"

"I still have some chocolate cake and ice cream. Would you like some?"

"Yes please. I'll go ask the kids if they want dessert."

That night after the kids were in bed, and Brad was lost in his mountain of paperwork, Debbie sat quietly in her bay window staring out into the darkness. The house was quiet, but her mind was anything but.

She was thinking back over dinner and how her heart broke when Ben was sobbing. After all, he was only sticking up for his sister.

She was worried about these upcoming meetings. Monday at the school and Tuesday in front of the zoning committee. Brad seemed to just take all these things in stride. As confident as he was, she was just as anxious. She was trying to hold onto his optimism, but the sense of dread was stronger.

Brad was a businessman and looked at all problems in

the same way. Ben was in trouble, so he wanted to find out the details, do what he could to rectify the problem, and move on to the next. Debbie admired his business mind, but kids' problems weren't always that straightforward. She just hoped that Ben learned that actions have consequences.

FIVE

Wednesday morning Debbie quietly sat with her conflicting thoughts, sipping at her tea. She wasn't this emotional when she was expecting the twins, but lately, her feelings were all over the map. What she wouldn't give for a cup of coffee. She knew Brad was excited at the possibility of another set of twins, but she really hoped it was just one baby this time.

She was thinking about the meeting at the school. The teacher admitted that she had not seen Ricky pulling Becky's hair, only the ensuing pushing match. Once Brad had explained what Ben had said, the teacher stated that she would just have to take Ben's word. Brad quickly assured her that Ben had been taught not to tell any lies and that he believed his son. And, Becky had confirmed what Ben had told them.

Debbie decided the teacher was being a bit confrontational. Just because she didn't see it didn't mean it didn't happen. But Brad had set her straight, quickly enough.

The principal had seemed pleased that Ben had been punished at home, and stated how happy she was that they were working together as a team, both his school and his home.

It had been decided that no further action would be taken at this time, but they all needed to be vigilant with their no-bullying policy.

Debbie had been so proud of Rebecca. True to her

word, she didn't play any video games all weekend. That was her choice, to support her brother, and Debbie was so proud of her.

Debbie took a sip of her tea. She was doubting herself, wondering about her future. *Can I really do all this, have another baby, take care of the twins, and get a new B&B up and running? Am I able to take care of my family and run a business?* She did manage to raise the twins, but she wasn't as young as she used to be. Some days, she just got tired of the daily grind. As her mom used to say, '*Pull up your big girl panties, and get it done.*' She missed her mom, especially when she was out of sorts. Her mom was the most logical, sincerely caring person she had ever known, and she missed having her to talk things through with. She missed her mom every day, but today, she was aching for her loss.

The night before, they had gone to the rezoning meeting. That had been a little daunting for Debbie, sitting in front of the five committee members who were all strangers to her. She did get the feeling that they knew, or at least knew of, Brad. One member commented that his reputation preceded him. Brad had just smiled confidently and said thanks.

They explained that they had done their due diligence, including reviewing the case, doing a title search, and putting the required notification in the local newspaper, as well as notifying all the neighbors with a registered letter. The deadline had passed, and there were no objections, so Brad's eight acres were now clear to be zoned as commercial property.

As she sat there watching the proceedings, Debbie was feeling so proud of Brad. He was all business in the meeting. He knew what he was doing and wasn't nervous at all, while she, on the other hand, had been a bundle of nerves.

There was one concern, however. About the existing septic. Debbie had thought that since none of the neighbors complained, they would find some other reason to put a kibosh into the works. Brad assured them that the existing system would be upgraded, and new tiles installed for the addition.

One councilor mentioned that Brad's taxes would increase substantially because of this decision, which Brad acknowledged that he was aware of.

Brad is so confident and so in charge, and I love that about him. She smiled to herself thinking about the dinner they'd had after the zoning meeting. Brad assured her that everything was fine. Now that they had their property rezoned, they were free and clear to do whatever they wanted. When she'd discussed taking the payments out in trade, Brad actually blushed, and Debbie had laughed out loud at him.

She'd better stop daydreaming as she had things to do. Debbie remembered to make the doctor's appointment. Brad, the loving, caring father, wanted to go with her. She picked up the phone and pushed the speed dial for the doctor's office and made an appointment for Friday morning. She wondered what Doctor Barnes would say when she asked for a pregnancy test. She was sure he'd be just as surprised as they were.

Checking the time, Debbie found her purse, her sweater, and her car keys. She needed to get a move on, or she'd be late for her lunch with Val.

Half an hour later Debbie was surprised at how busy the downtown was. She circled twice to find a parking space.

As she walked into the restaurant, she was surprised to see Val sitting with a man she presumed to be Steve. *Did she have to bring him?*

"Hey, Debbie, come join us," Val called out.

"I made it!" Debbie said as she slid down into a chair.

"Debbie, this is my friend Steve. Steve, this is my best friend, Debbie."

"Hello," Steve offered. "I have heard a lot about you. It is nice to finally put a face to the name."

"All good things, I hope. I thought it would just be the two of us for lunch, Val. But it's nice to meet you, Steve." Debbie smiled. "What's good here? I am starving."

"They have homemade burgers, and they also make a nice Caesar salad," Steve suggested.

"Homemade burgers, that sounds good today." Debbie noticed the waitress standing at her side. "I'll have a cheeseburger and fries, please, with a Coke. Thanks!"

The waitress left so Debbie asked, "Have you guys already ordered then?"

"We both come here so often we have standing orders," Val explained.

"Oh, I see. Don't you ever change it up or bring lunch from home?" Debbie asked.

"I go out for lunch every day. I need the break from the office," Val told her.

"And I am the same," Steve said.

"So, Steve, I have known Valerie all my life, so I know all about her. Why don't you tell me a bit about yourself?"

"Not much to tell, really. I am an army brat. My dad was military, so I moved around a lot growing up. I envy you, having a friend that you have known all your life. You don't know how lucky you are."

There was an awkward silence. *He's not getting off that easy*. He was handsome, and Val was absolutely glowing. She was leaning into him and kept touching his arm. If she didn't know better, Debbie would think Val was in love with this guy. "How long have you worked here and where did you move here from?" Debbie asked.

"Let's see, I have been a reporter with this paper for three years almost, and I moved here from Scarborough."

"Bet that was a bit of a shock to the system, coming from a city to this small town." Debbie smiled. They had that in common. Val had also moved from the city to here. They were both big city people lost in a small-town world.

"Yes, it was a shock. Still not sure that I'm even used to it yet. I find reporting stories in a small town is more challenging, because everyone knows all the gossip and details before the paper even comes out. It is only a weekly edition, so by the time it makes it to print, it is already old news," Steve explained.

"Yes, I was born and raised here, so I know all about waiting for the paper to confirm the details of anything juicy," Debbie added.

While they ate lunch, they chatted about life in general, and then it was time for Val and Steve to get back to work.

"Deb, it was so nice of you to join us for lunch today. We'll have to do this again another time." Val gave her a hug.

"I was expecting we would be eating alone. There were things I wanted to discuss with you privately. But they can wait for another day," Debbie said quietly as she hugged Val back. "Talk soon."

"Steve, it was nice to meet you. Maybe I'll see you around sometime," Debbie said as they were leaving.

As she drove home, she thought about how comfortable they both seemed with each other. She decided that if you didn't know better, you would think they were an old married couple, or at least lovers. Val even finished his sentences! Debbie knew she did that to Brad sometimes, but she had never done that with anyone she had ever worked with. That seemed very intimate, with a lunch buddy.

She felt totally torn about Val and Steve. Val was married to James, the nicest guy any girl could ever ask for. Why would she be messing around with this Steve guy? Everything she wanted and needed was waiting at home. Sure, maybe James wasn't all that exciting, but he was definitely stable and reliable. And then there was Timmy. He was such a sweet little guy. What the hell was Val thinking? Debbie decided Val needed a little reality check before she took this thing with Steve too far, if she hadn't already.

She questioned whether to tell Brad about this. She could use his opinion on what, if anything, she should do. Val and James seemed happy enough, the last time they were out for dinner. Brad would probably say that she was overreacting, because he hadn't ever met Steve. And what, if anything, could Brad do about it? Debbie decided to talk to Val first and then decide whether to tell Brad. Val was struggling with her feelings between two men, and Debbie was struggling with her feelings about having a new baby and a new business. *Why does life have to get so complicated?*

SIX

Debbie had just waved goodbye to the twins as they got on their school bus. She always had a tug at her heartstrings to watch them depart for a day of fun and games with all their new friends.

As she walked up the driveway, she tightened the sweater she had around her. There was a chill to the morning air. It wouldn't be long before the leaves started turning color and falling, and then the dreaded winter. She used to like winter when she was a resort owner, but now that it didn't affect her life so much, she could admit that winter was definitely not her favorite season.

As she hung up her sweater, the phone rang and pulled Debbie from her thoughts. It was Brad. "Hi, hun. Just wondering if I could bring a guy home for dinner tonight. I would like you to meet him. You know I trust your instincts about new people, better than I trust my own."

"Sure, that won't be a problem. What is his name and what is he going to be doing?"

"Jamie. I just hired him as a laborer to start, but I am thinking I may make him my assistant supervisor if he can do all the things he has said he can do. He has lots of experience and has been foreman on several big projects."

"We are only having shepherd's pie with salad. Is that alright?"

"Sounds good to me."

As Debbie hung up, she smiled as she thought about how Brad valued her opinion. As well, he should. After all, she had found Sharon, who turned out to be both a great secretary and a great babysitter. Hopefully Jamie would also be a good fit. Brad had yet to replace Phil, who had been his assistant supervisor for a while, but was now busy running his new resort. It was getting easier, but if Debbie was being honest with herself, she still missed her resort. Janice had told her that Phil was doing a good job, but still not as good as Debbie had done.

"Is anybody home?" Henry asked as he stuck his head through the door.

"Henry, hello! Come on in. What brings you by today?" Debbie asked as she gave him a hug. "Have you got time for a coffee? I haven't seen you in a long time."

"Coffee would be fine." Henry followed Debbie into the kitchen. "Do I smell cookies, perhaps chocolate chip? How are those twins doing? Bet they are growing like little weeds."

"Would you like a fresh cookie? In fact, why don't you stay for lunch? I am making our favorite, tomato soup and grilled cheese." Debbie poured him a coffee. "The kids are both good. They like school for the most part. Ben got in trouble for pushing another boy who was pulling Becky's pigtails."

"It's good to know that he will stand up for his sister, though."

"Yes, but we got called into the principal's office because of it. They have a no-bullying policy so now Ben is on their radar," Debbie explained as she warmed the soup and grilled the sandwiches.

"Back in my day, if that had of happened to me, I would

have met the bully after school and settled it like men." Henry chuckled at himself.

"Things are much different nowadays, my friend." Debbie patted his hand. "It's so nice to see you. How have you been feeling? Has your heart been behaving?"

"Yes, I go in and out of this A-fib off and on, but the medication is helping. I have slowed down a lot now that I don't work at the resort anymore. But I have been doing some work for the ski hill. Robert and Nancy have me sprucing up the place a bit."

"How are they doing? I haven't heard from them since they got back from their trip." Debbie set his soup and sandwich in front of him.

"They are both good. Robert keeps busy puttering around outside and Nancy putters inside. They are very nice people, and I am helping with minor repairs, painting and that sort of thing."

Debbie joined Henry at the counter and tested her soup. "And you are loving every minute of it." Debbie had worried about Henry, not having anything to keep him busy after they'd sold the resort and Phil let him go. She was happy to hear that he had found something else to do.

"Yeah, I guess I am. You know me, I do like to stay busy. They are gone to town today so I have the afternoon off and thought I should pop in and see how you folks are." Henry smiled as he ate his soup.

"If you are needing any more work, you should talk to Thomas Townsend over at the golf course. Once it closes for the season, he may have some painting and things that need fixing." Debbie refilled their coffee cups and returned with two cookies.

"Yes, thanks." Henry bit into his cookie with a grin. "I

will stop in and see him. Glad to see you are still full of your good ideas. Before I forget, I need to borrow Brad's weedwhacker. Mine just died, and I still have a job to finish. I'll pick up a new one, next time I am in town."

"No problem. You know where it is. Help yourself. Brad won't be using it till this weekend anyway."

"Great, at least I'll be able to finish the backyard." Henry took his empty dishes over to the sink. "Well, thanks for lunch. Say hi to Brad and the kids for me. I'll drop the weedwhacker off tomorrow on my way to town."

Debbie walked him to the door. "It's been so nice to see you, Henry. You must plan on coming over for dinner some night soon. Is lasagna still your favorite? I'll let you know the next time I make it, and you can come have dinner with us."

"Now that sounds like another good idea." Henry gave Debbie a hug.

Later, when Brad and Jamie arrived, the kids were watching a cartoon in the living room and Debbie was in the process of setting the table for dinner.

Brad came over, kissed Debbie, and then introduced Jamie. "This beautiful lady is my wife, Debbie. Deb, this is Jamie."

Jamie stepped forward and extended his hand. "It is nice to meet you, Mrs. Mumford. Thanks for having me for dinner."

At least he's polite. We're off to a good start. Debbie liked his firm handshake. "Please call me Debbie."

Brad added, "These two curious munchkins are Benjamin and Rebecca, better known as Ben and Becky." Brad rumpled Ben's hair.

"Nice to meet you both," Jamie said.

Once the kids' curiosity had been satisfied, they went back to their cartoons. Debbie returned to the kitchen and Jamie followed Brad to the office to have a cold beer.

A short time later, Debbie announced loudly that dinner was ready. During dinner, Jamie and Brad discussed current buildings they were constructing. Debbie observed Jamie, and as she listened to him, she got an uneasy feeling. Brad seemed impressed, but her gut feeling was telling her that Jamie was full of himself, and she trusted her gut. Her first impressions were usually right and had served her well enough when she used to run the resort. People are so predictable if you care to look.

Jamie seemed too good to be true. He was bragging about some of the projects he had managed in the past. As Debbie observed, she could see that Brad was impressed with his new hire. Her, not so much.

After Jamie left, Brad asked, "So, what did you think of Jamie? What was your first impression?"

"Honestly, I think he is nice, but a bit full of himself, almost to the point of being arrogant." Debbie instantly saw the total look of disbelief all over Brad's face.

"Really, I didn't see that at all. He did give me a list of references." Brad took the list from his pocket and handed it to her. "You really didn't like him? I thought you would. Maybe his references will improve your opinion of him. Do you think you could make the calls for me?"

"Yes, I could do that tomorrow while the kids are at school." Debbie took the list and the kiss that she knew was coming.

"I have an estimate to work on tonight, so let me help you clean off the table." Brad started picking up dirty dishes.

"I still think it's funny that you have that big desk in your office, but still prefer to work on the dining room table," Debbie said as she loaded the dishwasher.

"I prefer it. I like to be close to you and the kids, even if I am working," Brad explained. "I like my office just fine, but it's lonely, and honestly, it's too quiet, especially when Sharon is not in there with me."

"Well, you won't get much quiet out here." Debbie smiled as the kids came running past. They were playing tag, and both squealing with delight as they ran through the kitchen and on into the hallway.

"I see what you mean." Brad laughed out loud which made Debbie laugh at him.

Brad spent the next hour doing paperwork. She always liked this time of day. The dinner was over, the kitchen was cleaned up, the dishwasher was loaded, and this was her quality time to spend with the kids. Tonight, they had chosen to watch a movie. She sat in the middle of the couch with Ben on one side of her and Becky on the other. After the movie, it was time for their baths and then bed. Brad came upstairs in time to read a story to Ben, while Debbie read to Becky.

Later, as Debbie lay beside Brad, trying to fall asleep, she couldn't help but think about Jamie. She couldn't explain it in words, but she had an uneasy feeling that Jamie wasn't all that he said he was. Only time would tell if her feelings were justified.

SEVEN

While the kids were at school, Debbie took the list of Jamie's references and sat down with pen and paper to call them. She reminded herself that these were people that Jamie trusted to give him a good reference. Across the top of her page, she made herself a note to ask it they knew of any other contacts or places where Jamie had worked.

She smiled at herself for making the note. She used to do that all the time at the resort. She always had papers with little notes and reminders on them. *Guess old habits do die hard.* Nowadays, all she had was a grocery list, attached to the side of the fridge.

She dialed the first of the five numbers and spoke to a man who sang Jamie's praises. When Debbie asked if the man had any other info, he admitted that he had lured Jamie away from a rival company. Although he didn't have a phone number, he did know the boss's name.

Debbie made the original five calls that Jamie had offered, and three more calls besides. The extra three calls proved interesting. She learned that Jamie was lured from his job for another twenty-five cents an hour. The boss had noticed building materials missing from the jobsite but couldn't prove where they were going. When Jamie left, the materials stopped going missing.

Another woman had mentioned that Jamie was only a laborer but acted like he was the boss. She spoke about how

Jamie liked to show up the actual boss all the time and that the two men were in constant disagreements. It got so bad that they finally laid Jamie off at the completion of that project. And the other man basically said the same thing. Jamie would get an idea of how something should go, and you couldn't change his mind with a stick of dynamite. He personally liked Jamie but found him a bit combative and a little arrogant.

She knew she'd have to tell Brad all this and that he'd be disappointed. Jamie wasn't really management material, at least not in her opinion. She felt defeated and sorry for Brad. He worked so hard, and she dreaded having to tell him what she had found out.

"Is anybody home?" Janice called out.

"Yep, I am in the dining room, slash office," Debbie answered.

"What are you up to? You have a strange look on your face like a kid caught with her hand in the cookie jar."

"I just finished calling some references for a new guy Brad hired."

"You know that if the guy provided you reference numbers, he is sure they are all going to give him a rave review, right?"

"Yes, I know that. That's why I asked them all for other contacts from companies he worked for. See, I made myself a note at the top of the page, to remember to ask."

"Ah, your famous notes everywhere. You have me doing the same thing now! When we have our staff meetings, it is me making notes of all the little things people mention to me throughout the day. You sure trained me well." Debbie smiled, knowing that she was a good teacher and that Janice had been like a sponge, learning how things run at the resort. No wonder she is now good at her job. She was well trained. Debbie took great pride in Janice's work ethic.

"Let's go into the kitchen. Are you up for a coffee or perhaps a glass of wine?" Debbie asked as Janice followed her and took a seat at the breakfast nook.

"I'd love a glass of wine. I am done for the day. Mark is taking me out to dinner with his parents tonight, and I'm a little nervous."

"Oh, Janice, don't be nervous. Just be yourself. If they do or don't like you, that's fine, as long as they are seeing the real you."

"I have tried on six different outfits and still haven't decided what to wear."

"Wear something comfortable. You would look gorgeous in a potato sack. I am sure whatever you choose will look marvelous." Debbie smiled knowing that Janice had the best fashion sense of them all. She could throw together an ensemble that Debbie would never think to put together, and then she'd accessorize it, and it would look fantastic.

"Oh, before I forget, the court-appointed supervisor made a report about me taking Zack and refusing to leave him with his drunken father. My lawyer got a copy, and he has requested another appearance before the judge regarding visitations."

"That sounds promising. Did you see a copy of her letter?" Debbie asked.

"No, but my lawyer read the highlights to me. It said that in the past six months, she had noticed other things as well. Like Tony driving Zack when she suspected he had been drinking, and Tony once leaving Zack alone with his mother for over an hour. I'm sure you remember me telling you that she is now permanently in a wheelchair, and part of the agreement was that Zack was not allowed to be alone with his grandma."

"Wow. Poor kid. No wonder he hates going to his father's house. Perhaps your lawyer should know these tidbits as well."

"He does. The thing that really gets to me is that Tony has zero interest in being a father. He is only going along with this charade because his mother is making him. If the judge does pull his visitation rights, he won't care. I know he wouldn't fight it."

"It would sure simplify your life if you didn't have to take him for visitation every other weekend. Do Zack and Mark get along?"

"Like two peas in a pod. Mark likes kids and has suggested that we should have a couple more. It's funny to watch them together. Zack will mimic Mark's actions, and Mark knows he's being watched, so he will do something stupid like the chicken dance or something, and Zack just follows along. Mark wanted to take Zack with us to dinner tonight, but I said no. Sometimes Mommy needs a break too."

"Well, that's a good thing at least. Zack needs a manly figure in his life. Are you seriously thinking about having more kids?"

"Not sure. Mark wants more kids, and if we are going to expand our family, we should be thinking about doing it sooner rather than later."

"Have you and Mark set a date for the wedding yet? I would like to suggest you get the wedding over before you start thinking about more babies."

"Mark and I have both been married before. He has suggested we just go to city hall and get it done."

"So, he is not a romantic then? Well, if you want my opinion, I think you should have a small wedding with family and close friends. I am sure you would get a good price from the resort if you wanted to hold the dinner and reception there."

"I'm sure I would. Maybe Mark and I will discuss it over dinner tonight."

"Maybe a Christmas wedding. We have had Christmas weddings at the resort before, and the photos were amazing. Just a suggestion." Debbie shrugged. "Do you want some more wine, sis?"

"No, I better not. I should get going. I sure do miss the good old days of working together in the lodge when I could just pop into the office and discuss things."

"I still miss it too. But I am glad that we are still close enough that you can just pop in here."

Janice had just left when the kids came bouncing through the door. After they removed their shoes and jackets, they came to Debbie for their hugs and kisses. "And how was school today?"

"Fine," Becky stated. "Ben and I both got gold stars on the pictures we colored."

"Congratulations to you both. I am right proud of you. Can I see your pictures?" Debbie asked.

"Nope! The teacher kept them to hang up in the classroom," Ben added. "What can we have for a snack, Mommy? I'm hungry."

"You can each have one cookie, and there is fresh fruit in the bowl on the counter."

"Yay," they both shouted in unison as they ran for the cookie jar.

The kids had taken their snacks into the living room and were engrossed with their cartoons when Brad came home a little earlier than usual. Debbie hadn't even started dinner yet, but she was planning spaghetti so she could have it ready in under half an hour. She was sitting at the counter having a tea, thinking about her ever-growing grocery list.

Brad wrapped her in his arms and kissed her. "How was your day, beautiful?"

"Oh, you know, just living the dream." Debbie headed to the fridge, and he followed. She started chopping the lettuce for the salad.

"Wine glasses!" Brad looked puzzled. "Is there anything you need to tell me, perhaps about your secret lover?"

Debbie knew he was teasing. "Oh geez, you caught me. Between doing laundry, making beds, and the vacuuming, I took an hour off to have a hot, steamy affair with my French lover, Pierre."

"Pierre, hum? I bet he's not near as good as me." Brad pulled her into his arms for a steamy kiss. "So, who else stopped by? I would guess one of your sisters, and, since the wine is white, I would bet it was Janice."

"If you ever change careers, you could be a detective. Yes, it was Janice. She just left before the kids arrived. She wanted to tell me that the court-appointed supervisor has reported Tony for several infractions to the custody agreement. Her lawyer has petitioned the judge to reevaluate the visitation ruling."

"That's good news for Janice. It still amazes me that Tony is playing the game since he has never shown one ounce of interest in that boy of his." Brad shrugged. "Did you get a chance to check out Jamie's references today?"

"Yes, I did. The notepad is still on the dining room table."

"Thanks. I am going to grab a cold beer, and I'll take a look at it." Brad stuck his head into the living room and said hi to the kids before heading to the office and his bar fridge.

Debbie cringed. She knew that when Brad read her notes, he was going to be so disappointed. Her heart went out to him. Brad only saw the best in people, and this would devastate him.

A few minutes later, Brad wandered back into the kitchen, a beer in one hand and the notepad in the other. "Seems to me that the extra calls were not that favorable. He is a good worker, from what I have seen so far, but if I am to believe any of this, I won't be trusting him as my assistant any time soon."

"I think that is a wise decision. He's already on the payroll so keep him on as a laborer and see how it goes," Debbie suggested. "I'm sorry, Brad. I know you had high hopes for him, but I think you need to keep an eye on Jamie. My biggest concern would be the stealing of materials."

"Yeah, I will certainly watch him closely. I think if any of my other guys saw him taking stuff from the site, they would tell me. I have two crews with a total of twelve men working full-time for me, and not one of them wants to be promoted to supervisor. Damn, I wish I could find another guy like Phil."

"If you want, I could put an ad in the newspaper and see if anyone applies," Debbie suggested.

"I'd rather not, but I might have to." Brad tore the top page off and tossed the notepad onto the counter. "Thanks for making the calls for me, hun."

"No problem. Always glad to help out when I can. You're home early. When would you like to eat?"

"The usual time will be fine. I have a couple of phone calls to make now and have a few estimates I need to work on after dinner."

Poor guy. I knew he would be disappointed. As Brad walked away, Debbie could tell by the look of the back of him that he was carrying the weight of the world on his shoulders.

Later that evening, after the dinner clean-up was done and the kids were bathed and in bed sleeping, Debbie sat down across the table where Brad was looking at blue-prints. "Hun, can we talk for a minute?" she asked.

"Sure, what's on your mind?" Brad rolled up the drawings.

Debbie hesitated, trying to find the right words. "I have been thinking about the B&B. I am wondering if this is the right time to start such a big project."

"I thought this was what you wanted. Have you changed your mind?"

"I, no, I just think that with the twins in school, another baby on the way, you always being so busy and everything else, I guess I am just wondering if perhaps we are taking on too much all at once. I guess I just want to know how you feel about it all."

Brad was quiet for a moment, then reached across the table and took her hand in his. "I think that you're just overwhelmed with it all right now. Everything will be fine. You'll see."

"How can you be so confident? Do you not worry about taking on too much work?"

"No, not at all. I have scheduled our new B&B into my plans. I have the manpower already in place and time carved out for our job. But if you're not sure, now would be the time to tell me."

Debbie looked deep into his eyes. "Maybe it's my baby hormones that are making me doubt myself. I guess if I am being honest, I'm just a little scared."

"There's nothing to be scared of. I think we should go ahead with the B&B, and once it's built, you can open it if and when you are ready to. There is no set time limit on when it opens. If you decide not to open it for another five years, that's fine too."

Debbie felt a wave of relief. "Thank you. I feel better now."

"Remember, you are not alone in this. I am right here beside you."

"Yes, I know you are, and I am so grateful. I'll let you get back to work."

"I'm done here." Brad stood and walked around the table. He slipped his arms around her and kissed her deeply. "What do you say we call it a night?"

EIGHT

"Morning, hun," Brad said as he passed her in the kitchen and helped himself to a coffee. "Are you baking cookies already or am I imagining things?"

"You have a good nose. I am making sugar cookies for the kids' lunches. I wanted to get a head start because I have the doctor's appointment this afternoon," Debbie reminded him. "Are you going to meet me there? The appointment is for two o'clock, and I have to come straight back home to be here when the kids get off the bus."

"I will try, but I might be late. I am meeting a client on-site, and sometimes they can have so many questions. But I will do my best. I am excited to be able to start telling people about the baby. We will have to have Mom and Dad over for dinner one day this week."

"Let's just confirm with the doctor first that I am pregnant. By my calculations, I think I'm about twelve weeks. And I am trying my best to hide my baby bump," Debbie said as she rubbed her belly.

Brad came over and put his hand over hers. "I think your baby bump is sexy."

Debbie laughed at him as she gently pushed him aside. "I need to get those cookies out of the oven. And you need to get to work."

"I will see you later." Brad gave her a quick kiss, grabbed his lunch box and thermos, and was gone.

As Debbie unconsciously rubbed her baby bump, she thought, *I wish I could be as excited as Brad is about this baby.* She knew she'd be the one doing feedings and changing poopy diapers. Brad loved being a father and was good with the kids, but he only spent time with them in the evenings and on Sundays.

A short time later, after the kids were dressed and had their breakfast, she bundled them up in jackets and went with them to the end of the driveway until they boarded their bus. There was definitely a nip in the air. Fall was officially here.

As she walked back to the house, she was thinking about what Brad had told her last night. The workers would be there Monday morning to start the digging for the pool and the addition to the house. Brad had told her that he hoped to have the foundation poured and the main framing up before the snow started. That only gave him a month, but he did know what he was doing.

She spent the rest of the morning tidying up the kitchen, starting dinner, making beds, and even throwing in a load of laundry on her way by. But she couldn't get past the nervous feeling in her gut.

Debbie noticed the time and scolded herself for letting it slip away. Now she would have to rush to get to her doctor's appointment on time. She ran upstairs, changed her shirt, and freshened her lipstick. Downstairs, she picked up her phone, threw it into her purse, dug out her car keys, and grabbed a sweater as she rushed out the door.

Half an hour later, Debbie pulled into the parking lot at the doctor's office. She saw Brad's truck and parked beside it. Brad was grinning ear to ear when he opened her door for her. “Hello, pretty momma. Can I be of assistance?” Brad took her hand, and when she stepped out, he leaned in for a kiss.

“You made it on time. I am glad you are here. Not sure why, but I am feeling a little nervous. Last time this happened, we ended up with twins. Are we ready for round two?” Debbie asked.

“Twins or not, we are going to be blessed with another baby. I love you so much,” Brad said as he gave her a reassuring hug.

“Well, let’s go find out.” Debbie headed for the office door and Brad followed.

Inside the examination room, they sat impatiently waiting for the nurse to come back with the test results. Debbie already knew she was pregnant, but the doctor did his own test.

“Congratulations. You are pregnant,” the nurse informed them. “Now let’s do an ultrasound and see what we can see.”

Debbie unconsciously held her breath.

“Just relax. This won’t hurt a bit,” the nurse reassured her.

She wished she could relax, but today, it seemed impossible.

“Looks like we have a healthy baby,” the nurse explained.

“Take a good look, will you please. Last time we had twins and didn’t know until six months in. One was hiding behind the other,” Brad blurted out.

“Well, all I can tell you is that right now, I only see one baby in there. You can get dressed and wait for Doctor

Barnes in the office across the hall. Good luck, and I'll see you back here in three months' time," the nurse said as she left the room.

Brad leaned over Debbie and kissed her. "Congrats, momma. We are going to have another baby."

"I am happy that there is just one this time. But I won't totally believe it until the next ultrasound." Debbie could see the strange look on Brad's face as he helped her down from the table.

"One or two, boy or girl, doesn't really matter. I am just excited that God has blessed us with another baby."

"I agree. But this has to be our last baby. While you are talking with the doctor, you best be discussing your options to make sure this is our last baby," Debbie said in her most serious tone. She and Brad had already discussed their options, and he knew what she was talking about.

"Yes, hun. I'll get that taken care of right away."

Doctor Barnes came into the office. "Mr. and Mrs. Mumford, good to see you. I understand you are pregnant again. Congratulations."

"Thanks, doc. Looks like just one baby this time," Brad stated. "But Debbie says she won't believe it until the six-month ultrasound. Remember last time with the twins and one was hiding?"

"Yes, I remember. I do need to caution you that there may be unexpected complications with this pregnancy," Doctor Barnes said, looking at the chart. "Debbie, sometimes with women your age, things don't always go according to plan. But don't be alarmed. We will be monitoring you and staying aware of any potential problems. I am sure you will deliver a happy, healthy baby. At this moment, I predict your due date will be the middle of May."

"May, that sounds like a good time to have a baby." Brad was smiling.

"Easy for you to say. You're not the one who can't drink coffee and is throwing up every morning," Debbie said in a shaky voice. She was on the verge of tears. Brad reached over and patted her hand.

"I'll see you back here in three months unless you run into any problems. If you do, you know where to find me." Doctor Barnes stood up to leave.

"Thanks, doc." Brad reached out and shook his hand.

On the drive home Debbie was quiet as she considered why she wasn't as excited as Brad. She almost felt sad and couldn't help but wonder what was wrong with her. Was it her age?

Debbie was home about fifteen minutes before the kids came running in the front door. After removing shoes and jackets, they found Debbie in the kitchen.

"Look, Mommy, we made Thanksgiving cards today at school." Becky handed her card to Debbie. "I made one for you, and Ben made one for Daddy."

"Let me see. Oh my, isn't that beautiful. I like how you drew a picture on the card first and then glued all the sparkles and things on top. Good job, Becky." Debbie gave her daughter a big hug. "Thank you for the beautiful card. I'll hang it here on the fridge where I will see it every day."

"Wanna see mine?" Benjamin asked. "My card is for Daddy."

"Do I want to see yours. We don't say wanna. Yes, I want to see your card. Oh, very nice. I see you didn't put any sparkles on yours, just macaroni, and what is this, pipe cleaners or rope?" Debbie asked.

"Some kind of rope. Do you think Daddy will like it?" Ben asked in all sincerity.

"Oh, I am sure he will. Why don't you put it at his place on the table and he will see it when he sits down for supper," Debbie suggested.

"What can we have for a snack? I'm hungry," Ben asked.

"How about a granola bar and a piece of fruit?"

The kids took their snacks and headed to the living room to watch their after-school cartoons.

Debbie called Brad's mother, Linda, before she forgot.

"Hello, my dear. How is everything? How're those precious grandkids of mine?" Linda asked.

"Good, thanks. The kids are good. They both made us cards today at school. I was just calling to see if you and Charles were free to come for dinner one night this week."

"Dinner, that would be lovely. Can't come tomorrow night; that's Charles's night to play darts at the legion. How about Thursday night then? Can I bring something? Perhaps I could bring dessert."

"Thursday night it is then. We will plan to eat about six o'clock, and yes, you can bring dessert if you want to. I know everyone loves your chocolate cake."

"Thanks, Debbie. Looking forward to it. Bye now."

She was lucky that she got along so well with Brad's parents, she thought to herself as she started supper.

When Brad got home, he hardly had his boots off when Ben was wanting to give him his card.

"What's this?" Brad took the card from Ben.

"It's a Thanksgiving card I made for you," Ben said proudly.

"That's so nice. Let me see here. Very cool. Did you make this just for me?" Brad asked.

"Yep, I did. Just for you. Becky made a card for Mommy, and I made one for you."

"Thank you, son. I really like it." Brad pulled Ben in for a big bear hug, and Ben squealed with delight all the way back into the living room.

"Hello, beautiful momma," Brad said as he pulled Debbie into his arms for a kiss.

"How was the rest of your day?" Debbie asked.

"Good, I guess. There was a mix-up with supplies at one site that I still haven't got sorted out yet but other than that, it was alright."

"Before I forget, I called your mom. They are coming for dinner on Thursday night. I thought maybe you could BBQ some steaks. By the nip in the air, we won't be able to do that much longer."

"Oh good, thanks for calling her. Yes, steaks sound good and burgers for the kids."

"I'll go do groceries tomorrow when the kids are at school."

"What are you cooking for dinner? It sure smells good. The aroma hit me as soon as I opened the front door."

"I threw a pot roast into the slow cooker before I left for town."

"The smell is sure making me hungry. I have a phone call to make. Call me when dinner is ready." Brad grabbed an apple from the fruit bowl and headed into the office.

As Debbie threw the biscuits into the oven and put the finishing touches on dinner, she couldn't help but think about the baby she was carrying. She was truly relieved that she was only carrying one baby but was dreading having to tell everyone that she was expecting. The twins were five years old, almost six, and here she was, pregnant again. Brad was so overjoyed that they had been blessed with another child, but Debbie was not. Regardless, they were going to have to start telling people, and Debbie wasn't happy about the idea, at all.

NINE

Thursday afternoon, Debbie was in the kitchen making preparations for dinner when Janice stopped in.

"Hey, sis, you busy?" Janice asked.

"In the kitchen. Come on in," Debbie answered.

"What's for dinner?" Janice helped herself to a coffee and then sat down on the other side of the counter.

"We are having BBQ steaks. Linda and Charles are coming over for dinner tonight."

"That's nice. I like them. They are good people."

"Yes, I like them too. Even as a teenager, I liked them both. I know how lucky I am to have good in-laws. So, what are you up to today?"

"Working. But I have a break and wanted to come talk to you." Janice was peeling a banana she had just taken from the fruit bowl.

"Is everything alright?"

"Yes, I just wanted to tell you I have a date for the judge to reevaluate the custody issue. It's next Tuesday at eleven o'clock. I was hoping that you could come with me, just for moral support."

"Yes, of course I will." Debbie went over to the fridge and made a note on the calendar. "I'll pick you up just after ten then."

"Thank you, sis. You are truly the best sister a girl could ever ask for." Janice threw her banana peel into the garbage and put her arm around Debbie's shoulders. "I can't tell you how much I appreciate all your love and support. When I lived in Ottawa, I always felt so alone and detached from my family, and now, here we are. I know I can always count on you to be in my corner."

"Of course. Janice, that is what family is for, and there's nothing more important than family." Debbie patted Janice's hand. "Speaking of family, I have some news. I am pregnant."

"What? Oh my. Congratulations." Janice squealed in delight.

"We are telling Brad's parents tonight. I am nervous about it."

"I thought you were putting on a few pounds the last time I was here, but I didn't say anything. Why are you nervous? You know Linda and Charles will be happy about having another grandbaby to spoil."

"I am nervous, not about telling his parents. I'm nervous about having the baby," Debbie said in a shaky voice. It was all she could do to hold back the tears.

"I don't understand. You are going to have another baby, and you are nervous about what exactly?" Janice turned Debbie around so she could look straight at her.

"I thought after the twins that I was done having babies. But now here I am, pregnant again. This baby is a total surprise. We were not planning on having any more. And, the doctor said because of my age, there could be complications. Oh, Janice, I am such a horrible person. I don't want any more babies." Debbie started to cry.

Janice pulled Debbie into her arms and let her cry it out. "It will be okay, sis. You are just overwhelmed right now, but you'll get used to the idea, and when the baby is born, you will fall in love with it, and everything will be fine. You are the best mom I know, and I am sure it will all work itself out."

Debbie wiped her tears away and composed herself. "Sorry about that. I know it will all work out. I just haven't come to terms with the fact that I will be spending the next few years changing poopy diapers, potty training, dealing with cutting teeth, and all the rest of it. I thought that when the twins started school, I was going to have more free time. I guess I am just being selfish. Please don't tell anyone that I am a nervous wreck. I will figure it out."

"I know you will. Have you told Susan yet?" Janice asked.

"No, we just had the doctor's appointment two days ago."

"Well, I still say congrats. You and Brad are good parents, and when you get over the shock of being pregnant, you'll see that everything will be alright."

"I know. I'm just a little overwhelmed at the moment. I will get it together, I promise." Debbie gave her sister a halfhearted smile.

"Of course you will. I have faith in you." Janice put her coffee cup in the sink. "I have to get back to work. You sure you're, alright?"

"Yes, I just needed to have a good cry. I feel better now," Debbie said in her most reassuring voice. "I will go with you to see the judge. No worries."

"Thanks, sis. Remember, you are the best mom in the whole world. You got this." Janice gave Debbie a hug and headed for the door.

"Thanks, Janice. See you soon."

After Janice left, Debbie took her tea over and sat in the

bay window, thinking about the breakdown she had just had in front of her. She needed to be happy about the news for everyone's sake.

Debbie scolded herself. *I have to pull it together. I have to put on a happy face and get on with the business of telling everyone how happy I am to be having yet another baby.*

Having worked so many years in the hospitality industry, Debbie was an old pro at putting on her happy face and dealing with the public. She could do that with ease, and she would do that now as she told everyone about having another baby. As her mom used to say, '*Fake it till you make it.*' Sometimes, she missed her mom so bad it hurt. Today was just one of those days.

It wasn't very long until the kids came through the door, and Ben immediately wanted to know what they could have for a snack. Debbie had made them Rice Krispie squares, and they both squealed with delight at the surprise. "You can each have one square and a piece of fruit," Debbie told them.

The kids were happily enjoying their treats in the living room when Brad came home.

"Hello, beautiful family," he shouted as he removed his work boots and jacket.

"Mommy made us Rice Krispies squares today. Maybe if you are good, she'll let you have one too," Ben shouted back.

"I'm always good," Brad called back as he came into the kitchen. "Hello, my beautiful wife. How was your day?"

"All good so far. You should run up and have your

shower. I told your folks dinner would be at six," Debbie told him as he kissed her.

"You could come wash my back," Brad said in a teasingly seductive way.

"I see you are feeling frisky. What's up with that, cowboy?"

"I'm just in a great mood. I am happy to be telling my folks our good news."

"Don't you think we should tell our kids first?" Debbie asked.

"Yeah, I guess we should. We'll do that as soon as I have my shower, or do you want to do that first?" Brad looked concerned.

"Let's do it now. That way they can have a chance to sit with it before we make the announcement at dinner."

"Now it is then. Kids, could you come into the dining room for a minute? We need to talk to you." Brad took Debbie's hand.

"What's up, Daddy? Am I in trouble?" Ben asked.

"No one's in trouble. Your mommy and I have some great news to tell you both," Brad started. "We are going to have another baby."

"What? When?" Becky asked.

"In the spring. In May. You will have a new baby sister or brother."

"How come we have to wait till spring? Why can't we have a baby now?" Ben asked.

"Well, the baby is growing in Mommy's belly, and it won't be ready to come out until spring."

"That means I am going to be a big brother then like Tommy is to my friend Jeremy," Ben stated.

"Yes, exactly. Just like that," Brad agreed.

"Cool. I like that idea. I will have a little brother to play with, and I'll be nicer than Tommy is." Ben nodded.

"We don't know yet if it will be a new baby brother. It might be a baby sister," Brad explained.

"I guess that would be alright too," Ben acknowledged.

"Becky, what do you think?" Debbie asked.

"I guess it's okay. It would be fun to have someone else to play with." She shrugged.

"Grandma and Grandpa are coming tonight for dinner, and we will all tell them together after dinner," Debbie suggested.

"Grandma's coming, yeah." Ben was happy.

As the kids ran off, Brad took Debbie's hand. "That went over better than I thought it would. Now I am going to go have my shower." He leaned in and gave Debbie a kiss. "You sure you can't come wash my back?"

"No, sorry, I have to finish getting ready for dinner." Debbie gently pushed his hands away. "Go on with you now. I have things to do."

About 5:30, Linda and Charles arrived. Brad and Charles went into the office to have a beer, and Linda sat at the counter talking with Debbie about flower beds and how to make pickles.

Brad fired up the BBQ and cooked the steaks and burgers, and they all sat down to dinner. Debbie had made both a Caesar and a tossed salad, as well as garlic bread to complete the meal. Linda had brought a banana dessert as well as a tray of watermelon for the kids.

"Dinner was excellent. I think I ate too much," Charles stated as he pushed his chair back from the table.

The kids had been excused and were busy, building a

mansion with the new set of blocks that Linda and Charles had brought them.

"Mom, Dad, we have invited you here tonight to share some good news with you," Brad stated.

"What is it son?" Charles asked.

"How would you feel about having another grandchild?"

"What? Are you expecting?" Linda asked excitedly.

Debbie nodded yes.

Linda got up and came over to hug Debbie. They all stood and hugs were happening all around the table.

"That is wonderful news. Congratulations to both of you," Linda stated. "Do you know your due date yet?"

"May the fifteenth," Debbie told her.

"Oh, there's nothing better than a spring baby to look forward to." Linda was all smiles. "I can't wait to meet my new grandson or granddaughter. Do you know yet if it's a boy or a girl?"

"No, not yet. We do know that there's only one baby, so far. Remember last time we didn't know it was twins until we were six months in," Brad explained.

"Twins are no problem, Debbie. You handled it like an old pro the last time, and I am sure you would again," Charles said.

"Twins or not, we are going to have a happy, healthy baby in May," Brad stated.

"This is just the best news. I am so happy for you both. Shucks, I am happy for all of us." Linda was still bubbling with excitement.

Brad was smiling from ear to ear. "We're pretty happy about it ourselves."

"How did the twins react to the news?" Linda asked.

"They seemed excited about the idea of having someone else to play with." Brad chuckled. "To tell you the truth, so am I."

"I have very fond memories of when you and your sister were young. You were always so full of questions. Ah, the good old days." Charles finished his coffee.

Debbie went to get the coffee pot. "Would anyone want another piece of this banana dessert?"

"I would," Charles agreed.

"Me too, please," Brad added.

"All I can say is that this new baby is getting the best parents any kid could ask for." Linda was still grinning.

"Thanks," Debbie said as she handed the guys their desserts.

"Well, May can't get here fast enough to suit me," Linda said as she stirred her coffee.

"Me too, Mom. Me too!" Brad was still grinning.

After Charles and Linda left, Debbie cleaned up the kitchen while Brad gave the kids their baths. By the time Debbie got upstairs, it was time for bedtime stories. Brad was reading to Ben, so Debbie went in to read to Becky.

When she closed the book, Becky asked. "Mommy, where is the baby in your tummy?"

Debbie lifted her bulky shirt and showed Becky her baby bump. "Here, the baby is growing here. Mommy's belly will get much bigger as the baby grows. Do you want to feel?"

Becky reached her little hand out and touched the bump. "You're getting fat, Mommy."

"No, sweetie, I'm pregnant. I'm not getting fat. It's the baby growing inside me. As the baby grows, the bump will get much bigger."

"Oh, I see. Like when Ben's friend Jeremy's dog had puppies. She was really big and then she had eight puppies. After that, she was small again."

"Yes, like that. I will get bigger until the baby is born, and then I'll get smaller too."

"That's alright then." Becky snuggled in and Debbie covered her up.

"Night angel. Sleep tight." Debbie kissed her forehead and turned out the light. Debbie chuckled. *Eight puppies, that poor dog. I'm worried about having one baby.*

TEN

Debbie woke up to Brad planting kisses all over her face. Her first thought was: *It's Sunday morning and I get to sleep in, so why is Brad waking me up?*

"Morning, sleepyhead. The kids and I have been up for over an hour. They are downstairs eating cereal and watching cartoons," Brad explained while he kept giving her little kisses.

"So, you decided you needed to wake me, why exactly?" Debbie asked, as she threw back the covers to make a mad dash to the washroom.

"I thought since the kids are currently occupied, we might have some alone time."

As Debbie climbed back under the covers, Brad pulled her into his arms and kissed her deeply. She returned his kiss with passion. When they finished making love, Debbie fell back asleep on Brad's chest. She was wakened this time by two kids giggling loudly.

"Guess it's time to get up," Debbie said as she threw the covers off of her, over the kids, and got up. "Brad, when you go down to the kitchen, would you please turn the kettle on for my tea?"

"Sure can. Come on, kids. Let's give Mommy a minute to wake up." Brad scooped a kid under each arm and carried them out of the room.

As Debbie stood in the shower, she couldn't help but think about the morning she had just had and the day before her. They were heading to Susan and Keith's for dinner so she knew she had the day off from cooking, and it was going to be a nice day.

Brad always cooked Sunday morning breakfast, and as she came down the stairs, she could smell bacon cooking. She hesitated at the bottom of the stairs to see if she was nauseated. The morning sickness was starting to slow down, although she still couldn't manage to drink coffee.

Debbie sat down at the counter, and Brad set her tea in front of her.

"Thanks, hun. Bacon smells good. Do you need any help? Perhaps I could set the table?" Debbie offered.

"That would be a big help." Brad pulled the plates down from the cupboard and handed them to her.

As soon as Debbie had the table set, Brad started passing her the food. "Kids, go wash your hands, please," Debbie said. "Breakfast is ready."

"Would you like eggs or pancakes this morning?" Brad asked.

"I think I'll try a pancake, please, and a couple of strips of bacon." Debbie poured the orange juice.

"I want both," Ben blurted out.

"You mean you would like both," Brad corrected him.

"Yes, please. I like both."

"Becky, how about you? What would you like this morning?" Brad asked.

"Same as Mommy, please," Becky answered. "I like pancakes better."

"Kids, don't forget we are going to Aunt Susan's for

dinner," Debbie reminded them. "Brad, what is on your agenda for today?"

"I have to go out for a bit. Probably no more than an hour or so. I have to go check on the jobsites."

"On a Sunday? You don't usually go to the sites on Sundays. Are there guys working today?" Debbie asked.

"No. I just want to check on things. I have been having trouble with the suppliers not delivering the orders, and I just want to see if I can figure it out." He shrugged.

"Daddy, can I come with you?" Ben asked.

"Sure, that would be nice. I would like that." Brad ruffled Ben's hair.

"Oh boy. I am going to work with Daddy today," Ben exclaimed in his mother's direction.

"You are sure one lucky little man. Do you know where your hard hat is?" Debbie asked.

"It's upstairs in my room. May I be excused?" Ben asked.

"No, you can finish your breakfast first, please, and then you can go get your hat," Debbie told him.

As Brad and Ben were leaving, Debbie snapped a picture of them. Ben was so proud of his little white hard hat. *These are the moments that make life worth living.* She couldn't help but wonder whether everything was alright though. Brad always made a point of having Sunday off for family time.

"Becky, how about you help Mommy clean up from breakfast? Then we can play dress-up while the boys are gone. How does that sound?"

"Sounds good," Becky said as she started carrying dirty dishes into the kitchen.

Debbie and Becky played dress-up. Debbie braided Becky's hair and put some makeup on her, and let her put on a pretty dress for going to Aunt Susan's for dinner. She complemented it with some beads from her jewelry box. Becky was quite impressed with how pretty she looked.

"I look so grown up, don't I, Mommy?" Becky asked as she watched herself twirl in the floor-length mirror.

"Yes, angel. You look like a big girl. Wait till Daddy sees you. He won't even recognize you." Debbie gave her a big hug. "Just don't grow up too fast."

"I won't, Mommy. I like being your little girl, even if I look all grown up."

"And I like being your mommy." Debbie pulled her in close for a hug.

A short time later, when Brad and Benjamin got back, Debbie was waiting to see Brad's reaction to his daughter. Brad stopped dead in his tracks. "Excuse me, young lady, but have you seen my little girl Rebecca anywhere?"

"Daddy, don't be silly. It's me," Becky told him.

"Oh, I guess it is. My, you look so grown up. You are so pretty, and I like your dress."

"You look yucky," Ben told her.

"I do not. Take that back."

"Ben, be nice to your sister. She looks beautiful, and if you don't agree, you should just keep that opinion to yourself, son," Brad told him.

"Girls are silly," Ben said. "So, what are we going to do now? Can we watch a movie?"

"It's such a nice day, let's go do something outside. Why don't we all go for a boat ride before we go to Susan and Keith's for dinner?" Brad asked.

Although there was a cool nip in the air, the sun was shining and they were all bundled up, so it was a nice afternoon.

Debbie always enjoyed being out on the water. The crispness in the air, the sound of the water slapping against the side of the boat, and the sound of the loons calling were all food for her soul. It always grounded her. As she looked around at the shoreline, she noticed the trees were starting to change color. She loved the peacefulness of the changing fall leaves and the crispness of the air.

"Look, kids, there at the end of the lake. I see a deer and her fawn. See them?" Debbie asked.

"Get a picture, Mommy," Becky suggested.

Brad slowed the boat so Debbie could take the picture, and a fish jumped out of the water right beside the boat.

"See, Daddy, I told you we should have brought our fishing poles," Ben said.

"Another time, big guy," Brad assured him. "It's getting late. I think we should head home."

Debbie enjoyed every minute of the ride, knowing it was the last boat ride of the year. On the way back to shore, she thought, *I am so glad we did this. I know Brad is planning on pulling the boat out of the water this week, so this is our last boat ride for the year.*

As they all walked home from the dock, Debbie said, "Thanks so much for taking us out on the boat. That was a good idea. I think we all enjoyed that."

"You're welcome. But now we all need to get ready, as it is time to go to Aunt Susan's. Ben, bet I can make it home before you." Brad took off running at a slow enough pace so that Ben could beat him home.

They got tidied up, and when they arrived at Susan's,

she told them that Keith and Josh were out in the woodshop, so Brad and Ben went to find them. Debbie and Becky went into the house to visit with Susan.

"Hello, Jefferson. So nice to see you. How have you been?" Debbie asked.

"I'm fine. Here, let me take your coats," he offered.

"Dad has been having some indigestion problems," Susan injected.

"I'm fine," he said in an annoyed voice. "Girl worries too much."

"Come on in, you two. My goodness, Becky, you look so pretty. I really like your dress. Katie isn't here, but there are toys in the box if you would like to find something to play with," Susan offered. The toy box was made out of wood with old-fashioned building blocks carved on the front. It matched the rest of the wooden furniture nicely.

"Where's Katie? I thought she would be home this weekend," Debbie asked as she sunk into a soft leather chair.

"She is, but she and Jeremy are visiting some friends. They will be back for dinner," Susan explained.

"Oh good. I am looking forward to seeing her."

"Sorry to interrupt. I was just wondering what you ladies would like to drink?" Jefferson asked.

"Two wines please, one red for me and one white for my sister," Susan stated.

"No, no wine for me thanks. Could I have a tea with milk, please?" Debbie asked.

"Tea, what's up with that? Are you pregnant or something?" Susan chuckled.

"Yes, I am." Debbie gave her a halfhearted smile.

"Say what now? Yes, you are what? You're not pregnant. You're just messing with me."

"Nope, turns out I am pregnant. Expecting this little one around the middle of May." Debbie pulled up her sweater and showed her sister her new baby bump.

"Wow, I'm stunned! I didn't realize you wanted any more kids. Well, congratulations. This is a big surprise." Susan gave Debbie a big hug. "I'm happy for you, sis. Surprised, but happy."

"It's a big surprise to us too. I told Janice a couple of days ago. I figured she would have already told you." Debbie fixed her sweater.

"I talked to her this morning, and she never mentioned it. Maybe she thought it wasn't her news to tell. She did tell me that you are taking her to her next court appearance. That is very nice of you," Susan offered.

Jefferson came into the living room with Susan's wine and Debbie's tea.

"Thanks, Jefferson. Whatever are you cooking? It sure smells good," Debbie asked as she set her tea on the coaster.

"I have a chicken roasting in the oven. Would you girls like some veggies and dip now, or do you want to wait until the guys come in?" he asked.

"We could have them now, Dad. The fellows can have our leftovers. That's what they get for choosing to be out in the shop," Susan stated. "I'm going to have another niece or nephew. Do you know yet if it's a boy or a girl?" Susan asked Debbie.

"No, not yet. The ultrasound only shows one baby, but the last time we didn't know we were having twins until the sixth month, remember."

"I remember. Are you hoping for twins again?"

"We weren't hoping for any, so it's all a big surprise."

"Thanks, Dad. This looks so nice," Susan said as Jefferson put a big tray of veggies and dip down on the table in front of them. "Did you hear that Debbie is expecting? I am going to be an aunt again. How cool is that?"

"Congratulations, Debbie," Jefferson said.

"Can I have some, Mommy?" Becky asked as she came over to see what the offerings were.

"Of course, just don't get too full and ruin your dinner."

Just then, the door opened, and Josh appeared, followed by Ben, Brad, and Keith.

"I told you they would be in here drinking and eating all the goodies," Keith said to Brad.

"You're all welcome to join us," Susan invited.

The kids were over in the corner of the living room playing and the adults were enjoying their drinks and snack. Jefferson was in the kitchen making dinner.

"Your dad is doing all the cooking? You are one lucky lady," Brad said to Susan.

"Don't I know it. I offer to help, but he just tells me to get out of his kitchen, out of his way," she explained. "He does let me do the dishes though."

"My mother is the same. She doesn't like anyone in the kitchen when she is cooking," Brad said. "Debbie will let me into her kitchen, but mainly because it is a big kitchen, and I can stay out of the way."

"I love your big kitchen. We thought about taking out the pantry and extending our kitchen, but we decided that we still need a place for all the pantry stuff so we might as well just leave it alone," Susan explained.

Katie and Jeremy arrived and had to get hugs from

Aunt Debbie and Uncle Brad. "Oh, my goodness. It is so nice to see you both. Katie, your hair is getting so long. It looks good. Jeremy, how're your folks?" Debbie said as she pulled him in for a hug.

"Good, thanks," Jeremy answered.

"Dinner is ready," Jefferson announced.

"We made it just in time to eat. Good job, Jeremy," Katie said as she headed to the kitchen.

"Kids, do you need to wash your hands?" Debbie asked.

Ben and Becky headed to the bathroom and the adults started making their way to the kitchen.

"I just love this big old table. I bet there have been many good meals served to a lot of folks over the years. I wonder how old it is. Keith, you did a great job refinishing it," Brad offered.

"There's a date written on the bottom of when it was bought. It's over a hundred years old and still in great shape," Keith said with pride.

"I agree. It's gorgeous. And in this old farmhouse, it fits in perfectly." Debbie smiled. "I was also noticing you have a new antique cabinet in the living room. I don't remember seeing that before."

"It came with the house. It has been out in the shop and Keith and Josh have just refinished it." Susan beamed.

"It had two damaged legs and looked like maybe a dog had chewed on them, so we had to make two new legs to match. I think it turned out well," Keith explained.

"Wait till you see the curio cabinet they are building right now. It's absolutely gorgeous," Brad said mainly to Debbie.

"You should go upstairs and see my new bookshelves that I just finished building," Josh suggested.

"When I retire, you two will have to teach me some of your tricks," Brad said as he pushed his chair back from the table. "Jefferson, thank you for dinner, and your pumpkin pie was delicious."

The men retired to the living room while Debbie, Susan, and Katie cleaned up the kitchen and loaded the dishwasher.

Debbie was elbow-deep in soapy dishwater, washing the pots and pans.

"So, Katie, how is school going? This is your last year, isn't it?"

"Good. Yes, hopefully this time next year, I will be teaching instead of learning."

"Did Aunt Debbie tell you her good news yet?" Susan asked as she took the pot that Katie had just dried.

"No, what good news?" Katie asked.

"I am pregnant, expecting another baby in May." Debbie handed her another pot.

"Pregnant. Wow, congratulations. I'm going to have another cousin. That's cool." Katie handed the dried pot to her mother.

"Am I finished? Any more pots?" Debbie asked.

"Nope, that's it. Pull the plug," Susan said as she refilled her wine glass. "Let's go see what the guys are yacking about."

The kids were busy exploring the toy box and the adults had a visit.

Brad stood and stretched. "Well, I hate to be the party pooper, but I have an early morning. You folks ready to head home?"

"Kids, can you put the toys back please?" Debbie took her empty tea cup into the kitchen. "Thanks for having us for dinner, and Jefferson, thanks for cooking us such a wonderful meal."

"Your pumpkin pie is the best," Brad acknowledged. "Looks like we are all ready. Thanks for having us. Night all."

ELEVEN

Before Debbie had her eyes open, she could hear a beep, beeping sound in her head. It took her a moment to realize the sound was real and coming from the outside. It was the first day of excavation. It must be some heavy equipment backing up. *Well, there's no turning back now.*

Debbie headed downstairs to the kitchen to turn her kettle on, and then she went to look out the back door. She was right. Two big machines were digging out a big hole behind her house. She didn't see Brad anywhere at the moment, but she expected he wouldn't be far away.

Benjamin came down the stairs, wiping the sleep out of his eyes. "Mommy, did you see the loader out there?" he asked her with excitement. "Isn't it just the greatest thing ever?"

"Yes, Ben. You can watch from the back door, but you have to stay inside."

"Oh, but Mommy."

If he had his way, he'd be outside helping the men digging in the dirt. Big machines were very attractive to a five-year-old boy.

Debbie gave him a few minutes to see what was going on and then joined him at the back door.

"Check it out, Mommy. Isn't this just the coolest thing you have ever seen?" Ben asked. "That guy running the backhoe is very good."

Debbie couldn't help but smile at him. "It's good to watch, but we have to stay out of the way. We can watch from in here. It's not safe to be out there unless your daddy is with you. Do you understand?"

"Yes, Mommy. I know," Ben said in a defeated voice.

"Where is everybody?" Brad asked as he joined them at the back door window.

"Watching the men work. This is so cool, Daddy. Can you take me out there?" Ben asked enthusiastically.

Brad lifted Ben up into his arms so he could get a better view. "Tell you what, when you get home from school today, we can go out and have a better look."

"I guess that would be alright." Ben hugged Brad tight around the neck.

Brad put Ben down and kissed Debbie. "Good morning, angel. Are you ready to build your new bed-and-breakfast, my dear?"

"Ready or not, it seems to be underway." Debbie leaned against him for a moment. "It's nice to see you home this early in the morning."

"You'll see more of me now that we are starting your job. You look like you're a little overwhelmed. Are you still on board with us building your B&B, even if you don't get around to opening it for business? This is just the building stage."

"Yes, I know. I'm ready as I can be. I am just worried about how we are going to keep Ben and Becky out of harm's way while we are under construction."

"We are both on duty, and I have warned my guys that there are two five-year-olds on-site."

"Thank you for that. I will like having my handsome husband home more."

"You'll get used to me popping in and out. Right now, I am looking for a coffee." Brad followed Debbie back to the kitchen.

"I'll have to put a new pot on for you," she told him.

"That's alright, hun. I'll get it. I know coffee is nauseating you right now."

"I'll let you. So, will you be home for lunch today? I could make you something hot, maybe soup or something?"

"That's very nice, but no, I have my lunch in the truck and have no idea where I will be at lunchtime. But thanks anyway." Brad made his coffee, filled up his large take-away cup, kissed her goodbye, and was gone again.

When she came back downstairs, Ben was standing with the back door open. "Benjamin Mumford, what do you think you are doing? Close that door."

"I was just looking, Mommy. I didn't go out. I just wanted to see."

"I want to see too." Becky went to see what all the fuss was about.

"Both of you, listen up. We need to set some ground rules here. This is a jobsite, and there will be big machines and workers here for the next little while. While this construction is going on, neither one of you is allowed in the backyard unless your daddy or I are with you. You are to stay in the house and this door is to remain closed. Do I make myself clear? Do you understand what I am telling you?"

"Yes, Mommy," they both said in unison.

Once Debbie had the kids on the bus, she headed back to the house. She had the morning tidy-up routine down to a science. She started upstairs by making the beds and picking up dirty laundry as she went.

She stopped in the laundry room and threw a load into the washing machine. As usual, there was a load in the dryer that she folded and set on the bottom of the stairs to be taken back up the next time she was going.

Then it was off to the kitchen. She had to get it tidied up and dinner started before Chef arrived at ten for her cooking lesson. She enjoyed having Chef visit and teach her some cooking techniques. He also loved to bake and would make some bread and other goodies before the cooking lesson.

Today she had roast beef to prepare. Chef was going to show her how he made his pot roast. She would have all the vegetables cleaned, and she'd be waiting for his instructions. She was also going to ask if he could teach her how he made tea biscuits. Hers always turned out like little hockey pucks and his were always light and fluffy.

Debbie changed a load of laundry and had just put on a new pot of coffee when she heard Chef at the front door.

"Morning. How's my favorite girl this morning?" Chef called out.

Debbie went to the door to meet him. As he walked through with his walker, Debbie shut the door behind him.

"Morning, Chef. I've been waiting for you. Come on in. I just put on a fresh pot of coffee for you."

"Thank you, child." Chef left his walker at the door. He didn't use it so much in the house as he had walls and furniture to hold on to. He followed Debbie into the kitchen and took his seat at the counter. "So, what's all that racket outside, and what are we cooking today?"

As Debbie handed him his coffee, she said, "That

racket is the excavation for the addition we are putting on the house for my new bed-and-breakfast. You promised to show me how you do your pot roast. I have the veggies already cleaned. I was also hoping you could show me how to make your tea biscuits and anything else you want to bake. The oven is already warming up."

"Sounds good. Just let me have my first coffee, and we will get started," Chef George said. "So, how have you been, girl? How're those sisters of yours doing?"

"I have some news to tell you. Brad and I are expecting a new baby in May."

"Oh my. That's wonderful news. Congratulations to you both. Is this because now that the twins are off to school, you need a new baby to keep you busy? Are you missing the pitter-patter of little feet?"

"No, it wasn't planned. It just happened."

"Oh, I see. Well, sometimes God has different plans for us than we have for ourselves."

I guess I'll have to trust that God wants me to have a new B&B and a new baby. I hope he knows what he is doing because I sure don't. "I guess so," Debbie responded. "Do you want the radio on or off? I am trying to drown out the beep-beeping from the big machines."

"I think on, but you may have to yell at me so I can hear you," Chef suggested.

Chef always made a couple of loaves of bread, and this morning, he also made a pan full of cinnamon buns. Debbie stood and watched in amazement as Chef rolled the dough out and then slathered it with butter, brown sugar, and cinnamon. Then he rolled it, cut it, and put it into the pan in about three minutes flat. Debbie was happy to clean up the mess he made.

They were just taking the pan out of the oven when Brad stopped in. "Well, hello, Chef George. So nice to see you," Brad said as he came around the corner of the kitchen. "Am I smelling cinnamon rolls?"

"Hello, Bradley, my boy. I understand congratulations are in order." Chef stuck out his hand and Brad shook it.

"Yes, we are having a new baby in the spring and a new B&B as well," Brad said proudly. "Any chance of me snagging one of those buns?"

Debbie put a cinnamon bun on a plate, and Brad took the seat next to Chef. As Brad and Chef chatted about the addition, Debbie tidied up the counter.

Brad explained the excavation process to Chef, which was of little interest to Debbie, so she left to go change the load of laundry. When she returned, Brad had refilled his coffee, gave her a quick kiss, thanked Chef for his cinnamon roll, and was gone again.

"He is a busy man. I don't know how he keeps up with all the projects he has going," Chef said.

"Yes, he just framed two houses and hopes to have the B&B framed before the snow flies. Then he will have three projects to keep his guys working over the winter. I just wish he could find a supervisor to work for him. He had Phil for a while, until he bought the resort, and now he can't find anyone to replace him."

"Speaking of Phil, I was at the resort the other night for dinner. They seem to be doing very well. He was telling me how good Trevor is doing. Phil cooks breakfast and Trevor is doing the lunch and dinners. I am so happy that Trevor is working out. He's a good cook."

"You trained him well. I am so glad they are all doing so well. The resort is a lot of work, but if you enjoy it, it's not that bad. I think Phil and Nancy and the girls will do well there. But Brad sure misses Phil on his jobsites."

"He'll find someone. Everything happens as it is supposed to. Even if it doesn't happen fast enough to suit us." Chef shrugged.

"Yes, you are right. But for Brad's sake, I hope it happens sooner rather than later. Now, about this pot roast."

Chef stayed for lunch, and before he left, he made cinnamon buns, three loaves of bread, tea biscuits, and a chocolate cake and showed Debbie some tricks for cooking the pot roast. He explained to her how he seasoned and started the meat in the oven first and told her to add the rest of the veggies at different times, as they all took different times to cook.

Once Chef was gone, Debbie had the kitchen almost back in order when Susan stopped by.

"Hello, Debbie. Are you busy?"

"No, I was expecting you," Debbie said with a silly grin.

"You were expecting me? Really?" Susan looked shocked.

"It's Monday, and you know Chef has been here."

"Oh yeah, I forgot it was Monday and Chef stops by for a visit." Susan mocked surprise.

Debbie smiled at her sister. She was also expecting Janice to show up at some point. Both her sisters made a habit of showing up on Monday afternoons.

Debbie shook her head at her sister. "Would you like a cinnamon bun?"

"Sure, why not. I guess I could eat a bun. Any chance you have a coffee to go with it?"

Debbie laughed at her sister's modesty.

"I see the big machines are digging in your backyard. How long does that go on for?" Susan asked. "Those beeping machines would get on my last nerve."

"I'm not sure. That's why I have the radio on, to drown out the beeping noise. As for how long they'll be, I think it depends on how much rock they hit. All I know is that Brad is hoping to have the framing done before the snow flies so the men will have work to do over the winter."

"Keith was telling me that Brad has some interior renovations lined up over the winter, and he has a big fireplace to reface or something like that."

"You know more about what my husband is doing than I do," Debbie stated. "He doesn't usually tell me any details unless I ask directly."

"Isn't that always the way?"

"I guess it is."

"What time is Janice's court appearance tomorrow? I thought I might meet you there."

"I think it's at eleven. She asked me only because I am home and available, but she wouldn't ask you because you are working. I'm just going for moral support," Debbie told her. "I really hope the judge sees how disruptive this is for her. Every other weekend, she takes Zack to see his father when Zack doesn't want to go and Janice doesn't want to take him. It's all just getting to be too much. And then when she gets there, Tony is passed out drunk at ten o'clock in the morning. I hope, for her sake, the judge finally puts an end to this craziness. I'm sure she'd be happy to have us both there for support."

"I could be available now that I know the time of the hearing. Don't mention it to her in case I can't make it, but my schedule can be flexible. Like today, I have a salesman watching the office so I could come get a cinnamon bun."

"Really. You are paying someone to watch the office so you could have a bun."

"Yes and no." Susan chuckled. "I am taking Dad to a doctor's appointment this afternoon. Stopping here for a treat is just a bonus."

"Is everything alright with your dad?" Debbie asked.

"I think so. But he has been having a lot of stomach issues, a lot of indigestion kind of stuff, and we just want to get him checked out."

"Hope he's alright. Since you are here, what do you want for your birthday? This is the big five-oh, right?"

"Yep, fifty. Can you believe it? I can't think of a single thing I need. You know me. I am just happy with a card. Do you remember when we were teenagers and we decided we'd all be happily married with kids of our own by the time we all reached fifty? Well, I'm turning fifty and we all have kids at least. And Janice is about to get married, for the third time."

"You're the only one turning fifty. Just saying. You have a beautiful family. But seriously, there must be something you want, something your little heart desires." Debbie already knew from experience that Susan would never tell her that she wanted anything. She expected that Debbie would know and give her something that she would either like or be able to return and exchange for something else. It was a sister thing.

"Not really. If I want something, I just go out and get it," Susan explained. "Guess I better get going. Thanks for the coffee and the bun."

"Keep me posted if you find out anything about your

dad." She handed Susan a goody bag and closed the door behind her.

Debbie was sitting at the counter thinking about the surprise party she was planning for Susan's birthday. She planned it for the Saturday before the actual day in an effort to keep it a surprise. Janice was going to do the cake and decorations. *I still can't believe my big sister is turning fifty.*

TWELVE

Debbie arrived early at the resort to pick Janice up. She had a tea and spoke with Nancy about reserving the banquet room for Susan's fiftieth birthday party. Janice sat down at her table.

"Morning, sis. You're early, aren't you?" Janice asked.

"Yes, I wanted to get the room reserved for Susan's party. I expect you will do the cake and decorations, right?"

"Of course. Are we still doing it the Saturday before? Is it still going to be a surprise?"

"That's the plan. But you know how hard it is to keep a secret from Susan."

"It is hard, but possible. Can you believe she's turning fifty?"

"Not really, but none of us are getting any younger."

Phil came over to the table. "Morning, Debbie. I understand congratulations are in order."

"Thanks, Phil. This little one is due to arrive in May," Debbie said as she rubbed her tummy.

By the strange look on Phil's face, Debbie realized that he didn't know about the baby. "Oh sorry, I thought you meant congrats about the baby."

"Umm, I was talking about the new bed-and-breakfast. But congrats on the new baby as well."

"Thanks, Phil. I guess you have been talking to Brad. He is very excited about building the B&B."

Janice was laughing at Phil's embarrassment. "It's

alright, boss. Debbie and Brad are both good at multi-tasking."

"Well, congrats on both. I best get back to the kitchen." Phil was blushing as he walked away.

"Are we ready to go then?" Debbie asked.

"Yes, I guess so. I am a bit nervous. I sure hope the judge is in a good mood this morning." Janice stood up and put her coat on. "I forgot my purse. I have to run back upstairs. Sorry, Deb. I'll be right back."

"Go get it. I'll wait right here for you." Debbie chuckled to herself about what an airhead her sister could be. Even if she did have a good reason to be flustered this morning. After all, her future was all in the judge's hands.

"Well, hello, stranger," Gail said as she walked into the dining room. "It's been a minute since I have seen you. What have you been up to, girl?"

Debbie stood and gave Gail a big hug. "Oh, you know, having more babies and building a bed-and-breakfast."

"Say what now? Having a baby? Are you pregnant? Well, congratulations. I am so happy for you. And a new B&B. How exciting!"

"Yes. A new baby in May and not sure when the new B&B will be ready, but yes, some big changes in my life. How about you? Anything new with you?"

"No, nothing as exciting as all that. I'm still here as the dining room manager, and Peter and the kids are all fine. You know us; we are just living the dream."

"Tell Peter I said hi." Debbie put her coat back on as Janice came back to the table. "I guess we're off to town. Wish us luck."

On the drive into Clifford, Debbie tried to distract Janice with the details about Susan's party.

"I was thinking that we need lots of balloons. Susan likes balloons. What do you think?" Debbie asked.

"What? Balloons, oh sure. Yes, there will have to be balloons."

"Are you planning on a color scheme, maybe fall colors, oranges and reds?"

"Sure, that sounds good."

"Have you thought of what you are giving her as a gift? I can't think of a thing."

"No, I haven't. I am working on crocheting a throw blanket for her couch, but I doubt I will have it finished in time." Janice shrugged. "I might have it finished for Christmas."

"I have no ideas. I was hoping you might have some." Debbie pulled into the court parking lot. "Let's go see what the judge has to say."

As they walked through the door, Janice grabbed Debbie's arm and pulled her over to the man standing off to the side. "There's my lawyer. I would like to speak with him before we go inside."

"Morning, Janice. Are you ready?" He handed her a folder.

"Yes, what's this?" Janice asked.

"I thought you would like a copy of the letter from the court-appointed supervisor. I understand that she will also be here, but I haven't seen her yet."

"Thank you. I will just take a moment to read it."

"I'll see you inside," he said as he turned and walked away.

"Morning, ladies," Susan said as she came through the door.

"Sue, I didn't know you were coming," Janice said with relief in her voice. "Thanks for coming."

"Thought you could use my support. Let the judge see that you have a great support system."

"Yes, thank you. I appreciate it." Janice motioned to a lady coming through the door. "Mary, good morning. I am not sure if you remember my sisters, Debbie and Susan. Ladies, this is Mary, the court-appointed supervisor who is overseeing Zack's visits with Tony. Mary, thank you so much for your report. My lawyer just gave me a copy, which I am supposed to read before we go in."

"Good morning. Yes, you should read it before we see the judge. There are some seats over there. Why don't you go do that, and we'll visit over here," Mary instructed.

"As I am sure you know, Tony isn't interested in having a relationship with his son. I still think it's the mother pushing him to do so," Susan offered.

"I suspect you are right. Hopefully the judge will see that as well. Tony is supposed to be here, but he didn't show up for his last scheduled appearance, so he probably won't show up today either."

Janice strolled back over to the group. "Thank you again, Mary. This is a good letter. Even I didn't realize that things were this bad. I know Zack hated going there, and now I see why."

"Ladies, you should come inside now. We are about to get started," Janice's lawyer said from the doorway. "Morning, Mary. Good to see you again."

As Debbie, Janice, and Susan took their seats, Mary said, "I'll sit up with your lawyer as I will be called upon to verify my opinions regarding the letter. Good luck, Janice. I hope this all works out in your favor."

The girls sat quietly and listened to three other custody cases before it was Janice's turn. As they sat there, Debbie couldn't help but wonder what was in that letter. What things did Janice not know about? How bad was it, exactly? The judge seemed to be on the ball, and hopefully he would realize that Tony was a deadbeat father at best and not doing Zack any favors by being part of his life. It was finally their turn. As they called Janice's case, Debbie squeezed her hand and whispered, "You got this, girl."

Janice's lawyer spoke first, and he introduced Mary and then the judge asked Mary some questions. He then asked Janice to stand. "I understand that you are providing the boy with a stable home life, and that it is your sole responsibility to see that your son, Zackery, is delivered and then picked up from seeing his father. Is that right?"

"Yes, your honor. Tony lost his license for drinking and driving, so I have to take Zack to his grandmother's house and then pick him up."

"Is it also true that you took Zackery to see his father, but his father was passed out at ten o'clock in the morning, and you refused to leave your son with the grandmother?" the judge asked.

"Yes, your honor. Tony's mother is in a wheelchair and not able to look after a busy child. I tried to wake Tony up but couldn't. I didn't feel it was safe to leave my son there," Janice answered in a shaky voice. "I took him home. But because I had to work, and since Zack was supposed to be at his dad's overnight, and my babysitter had the weekend off, my sister Debbie had to take care of Zack for the weekend."

"Is your ex-husband in court here today?" the judge asked her.

"No, your honor, I don't see him here. To be perfectly honest with you, I don't feel that Tony even wants to be a part of Zack's life," Janice blurted out.

"Could you elaborate on that statement, please?" the judge asked.

"From the first moment I told Tony that I was pregnant, he made it perfectly clear that he didn't want to be a father. Then when Zack arrived, Tony wanted nothing to do with him. It was like I was a single mother raising Zack alone. Tony never even tried to bond with Zack. When I caught him cheating and asked him to leave, he didn't even try to fix our marriage, and all through the divorce proceedings, he never asked about how Zack was doing, not even once. Then out of the blue, I got this letter in the mail saying that Tony wanted joint custody. I know that Tony isn't the least bit interested in his son, so I can only conclude that it is the grandma who is pushing to see her grandson. The problem is that the grandma is now in a wheelchair all the time, so she is not able to take care of a busy seven-year-old boy. Tony currently lives with his mother, and they both chain smoke," Janice explained.

"And how is Zackery handling the visits? Is he excited about seeing his father and grandmother?" the judge asked.

"No, sir, not at all," Janice stated. "Zack always cries when I have to leave him there. He is old enough now to know that Tony doesn't like him, but he doesn't understand why. I have to send snacks for Zack because, in that home, drinking is more important than eating."

"I see. So, as of right now, Zackery is going to see his father, who lives with his elderly mother, every other weekend and has a supervisor present all day Saturday and Sunday."

"Yes, your honor. I usually pick him up Sunday afternoon when I have a break from my job."

"Thank you, Janice. You may sit down," the judge instructed.

The judge paused for a few minutes before continuing. "After hearing from the court-appointed supervisor and speaking with Janice, the boy's mother, I am prepared to overturn the previous ruling and grant full custody to the mother. There will no longer be supervised visits. If the father wants visitation in the future, he will need to petition this court. Case closed."

"Thank you, your honor," Janice said as the three sisters stood up and left the courtroom.

Outside in the lobby, Janice cried tears of happiness. "It's finally over. No more forcing my son to visit his ungrateful drunken father," Janice said through her tears.

"That's wonderful. I think we should go somewhere and celebrate. My treat," Susan offered.

"Yes, let's go to the café and have some lunch. I, for one, am starving," Debbie added.

A few minutes later when they were seated in the café, Janice let out a big sigh. "I can't believe it's finally over. Tony never wanted to be a father and now he doesn't have to be. I wonder if his mom will be upset. I can't wait to tell Zack the good news. Did I tell you that Mark wants to adopt Zack?"

"Oh wow. That's big news. Have you and Mark decided on the wedding yet?" Debbie asked.

"We have discussed it and decided to do a small wedding at the resort. And before you ask, no, we don't have a date set yet. I have been so focused on this custody stuff that I haven't honestly given the wedding any thought," Janice admitted.

"When you get around to thinking about it again, let us know if we can do anything to help," Susan offered.

"I don't imagine there will be much to do especially since we are going to do it at the resort, although I am hesitant because that's where I married Tony, and look how that turned out," Janice said.

"If you don't want to have it there, perhaps you could do it at my house," Susan offered. "Keith could clear out his work shed for a day."

"Oh no, I couldn't put him through all that," Janice replied.

"Even if you hold it at the resort, it will be different than your last wedding. This one will be smaller for one thing. How many people are you thinking?" Debbie asked.

"I don't know, let me think. There's Debbie, Brad, Rebecca, and Benjamin. That's four. Then Susan, Keith, Joshua, Katie, and, of course, now Jeremy, so that's another five. I expect Mark's parents, so that makes eleven and maybe his sister and her husband. I would say eleven for sure," Janice explained.

"And Zack and the bride and groom. And what about my dad?" Susan suggested.

"Oh yeah, Jefferson. Now that's fifteen, and Sherry will be my maid of honor, and Mark's best friend Sam will be the best man. Either one of them could bring a date. So that's seventeen and possibly four more."

"So, you need to book for twenty-one then," Debbie said.

"I guess so. And this is a small wedding." Janice chuckled.

"And what about Chef? Will you have him walk you down the aisle?" Debbie asked.

"I don't know. He walks with his walker now. What do you think?" Janice asked.

"I think he could do it without his walker. He only uses it outside mainly," Debbie offered.

"So now, it's up to twenty-two, and I haven't even talked to Mark about who all he wants there. Before you know it, we'll be up to a hundred. The idea of eloping is getting more appealing by the minute," Janice stated.

"Don't you dare. I'd never forgive you if you got married without me," Susan told her.

Debbie inwardly chuckled. Susan wasn't afraid to wield her big sister club. She would never let either one of her siblings do anything that would displease her. She was the boss of them; she even said so. "Well, ladies, I hate to break this up, but I need to get home before the kids get off the bus." Debbie stood and put her jacket on.

"Susan, thanks for coming with us today. I wanted to ask you to come, but I know you are busy." Janice gave Susan a big hug. "You don't know how much it means to me to have my sisters' support."

"As Mom used to say, '*Being together is our superpower*,'" they all said in unison and laughed because they all had the same thought.

On the way home, Debbie tried to distract Janice with plans for her upcoming wedding.

"What kind of dress do you think you'll wear?"

"I'm not sure. This is my third wedding, so definitely not white. Hell, not even off-white. Maybe I should wear crimson red." Janice chuckled.

"Well, that would work, especially if you have a Christmas wedding."

"Maybe a soft pink or something. I don't know. I'll go to the city and see what's available for the three-time bride."

"You keep saying this is your third wedding. I don't think you should look at it that way. I think it would be better to forget your past and look to your future. This is your first wedding, to Mark. You are going to be Mark's bride, and you are going to have a wonderful future together. You are going to grow old together. Look ahead and not back. Leave the past where it belongs, behind you."

"You are right. I do look back too much. From this moment on, I am going to focus more on my future, on our future, Mark, Zackery, and me."

"Atta girl. That's much better. You are going to be a beautiful bride, regardless of which dress you choose."

"Thanks, Deb. You always know what to say to cheer me up. Although I am already cheery enough today. I can't tell you how relieved I am that this day is finally over. I wonder how long it will take Tony and Barb to hear the news?"

"Barb? Who's Barb?"

"Tony's mother."

"Oh, yeah. I forgot her name. Whenever they find out, I am sure Barb will be way more upset than Tony will be."

"You got that right. Tony couldn't care less. And it's a shame. Zackery is a great kid. Tony has no clue what all he's missing out on."

As they pulled into the driveway at the resort, Janice undid her seatbelt and reached over to give Debbie a hug.

"Thanks, sis. Thanks for everything. You are the best sister ever."

"You are most welcome. It was no big deal; it's just what sisters do for each other. See you soon."

Debbie headed home to prepare supper.

Brad arrived moments behind her.

"Hello, beautiful. How did Janice make out in court?" he asked as he kissed her with his hands behind his back.

"Good! She now has full custody. Zack won't have any more visitations with his drunken father."

"Fantastic. Look what I got for Benjamin today." Brad held up a tiny pair of work boots.

"Brad, they are so cute. Ben will be so excited. You are truly the best dad in the whole world. Did you get anything for Becky?"

Brad pulled another pair out from behind his back. "Yep, I got her a pair too."

"The bus is here. Remember you promised to take Ben out to the excavation, and Becky will probably want to go too."

"Why don't you put your jacket on and come with us?"

"I could do that."

When the kids came running in, they got hugs and kisses from their mom and today from their dad too.

"I got you both something today." Brad handed them their new work boots.

"Holy crap, would you look at these," Ben blurted out in his excitement.

"As soon as you two get your boots on, we are all going to go look at the big hole in our backyard," Brad told them.

Brad helped Ben and Debbie helped Becky get their

new little boots laced up, and the four of them went around the house and checked out the new hole being dug.

Brad explained to them that they would need to blow up the big rock in the middle of the hole with dynamite. Ben was quite excited about it all. Becky didn't show much interest, so Debbie and Becky went back into the house, and Brad and Ben stayed out watching the digging for quite a while.

Debbie had to go to the back door and call the boys in for supper. Ben could hardly contain his excitement about the big hole and wanting to be there to see the rock being blown up. Brad suggested that after dinner he would show Ben some explosions on his laptop since Ben would be in school when their rock would be blown.

It was a challenge to get Ben to sleep that night. All he could talk about was how cool it was to blow things up. Once Ben finally fell asleep, Brad and Debbie cuddled on the couch and talked about the day they had just had and what tomorrow would bring.

"The dynamite guy will be here tomorrow afternoon, and there will be some small explosions, so don't be alarmed. I will be here when it happens," Brad told her. "Ben is so excited. He wants to see it so badly. I am wondering if we could let him stay home from school tomorrow. It is kind of a big deal for him."

"Absolutely not. The kids can only miss school if it's for a medical appointment, which they have next Tuesday," Debbie stated.

Brad said with his best pouty face. "You're so mean."

"I guess you don't want to sleep with me then, if I'm so mean." Debbie stood up and stretched.

"I think I can overlook that one little flaw," Brad said as he pulled her back down for a kiss.

She snuggled up against him and they sat in silence, both knowing that despite whatever challenges lay ahead, they had each other for support, and for now, that was enough.

THIRTEEN

Thursday morning Debbie was just coming down the stairs with an arm full of dirty laundry when Brad and a police officer came through the front door.

"Hi, hun. Can you please put on a pot of coffee?" Brad asked.

"Sure, just let me throw this load into the washer."

As she entered the kitchen, Brad and the officer were looking at his laptop. She overheard Brad telling the officer, "I want him charged to the fullest extent of the law."

"What's going on? Who do you want arrested?" Debbie's heart sank.

"Jamie. I have caught him red-handed," Brad explained. "I put trail cams at the two jobsites where materials have been going missing, and I have him on tape, stealing from me."

"Wow. So, what happens now?" Debbie asked.

"We are waiting for another officer to arrive and then they are going to follow me to the jobsite and arrest the bugger," Brad stated.

"Oh, hun. I am so sorry. But we were warned that he could have sticky fingers. You are going to arrest him onsite? Isn't that kind of cruel?" Debbie asked as she poured them both coffees.

"CRUEL! Hell no! If it was up to me, I would beat the living daylights out of him." Brad was almost yelling.

"Calm down. Take a breath. He will be arrested and charged and that will have to be good enough." Debbie could see the frustration on Brad's face.

"Come in," Brad called out. When no one came through the door, Debbie went to see who it was.

"Is this the Mumford residence?" a police officer asked.

Brad stuck his head around the corner. "Yes, officer, we were expecting you. Please come in. Would you like a coffee?"

"No, I'm good. Thank you."

"So, what did you find out?" Brad asked the new officer.

"I went to his current residence, but there was no sign of any building materials, not outside at least," the officer explained.

"I wonder where he is taking them then? At this point, he has a substantial collection of materials." Brad offered the officer his laptop. "Do you want to watch the video?"

"Yes, please."

"I can't believe the nerve of this guy. I gave him a job and was even considering promoting him as my job supervisor. Well, he is done making a fool out of me. I want him arrested in front of all the other guys so they can all see that I mean business." Brad was pacing.

"Do you have a list of the materials that went missing?" the first officer asked.

"No, not yet. I will have to get back to you on that. At this point, I can only give you an estimate. I won't know for another week or so when I discover how short we are on the supplies to finish the current job that he was working on," Brad explained. "I do know the materials that I was short on the first house he worked on. But I can't complete the list until this current part of the cottage is done."

"That would be fine. Whenever you get your list completed, just drop it off at the station," the officer suggested.

"What kind of information will you want exactly?" Debbie asked.

"We will need a list of materials and the cost of each item, and then a total cost. You will also want to send this list to your insurance company if you are going to put in a claim," the second officer answered her.

"Thank you. I would have never even thought of that. We have never had anything like this happen before." Debbie smiled.

"Well, Mr. Mumford, are you ready to go do this?" the first officer asked.

"Please call me Brad, and yes, I am ready," Brad answered. "I will arrive first, and you fellows can come in a few minutes later."

"You don't plan on doing anything stupid, like punching the guy's lights out, or anything like that, right?" the officer asked.

"No, but I do want to be there. I want to see the look on Jamie's face when you arrest him," Brad stated. "My guys are going to have a million questions after you leave."

"We will also have to take the video of the theft for evidence," the officer said.

"Shouldn't we keep the original, or at least a copy of it for ourselves?" Debbie asked.

"Yes, make a copy, but we will need to take the original with us," the officer answered.

"Hun, can you do that please?" Brad asked as he handed her the laptop.

"Sure, let me see." Debbie made a copy to leave on Brad's laptop and sent a copy to herself in an email.

"Then I guess we are ready to go." Brad grabbed his jacket and both officers followed him out the door.

As Debbie watched them pull out of the driveway, she hoped Brad wouldn't lose his cool. She'd never seen him violent, but even someone as nice as Brad could get pushed beyond their limit.

An hour later, Debbie had just changed the load from the washer to the dryer and was standing looking out the back door window, watching the excavation going on in her backyard.

"Hun, where are you?" Brad called out.

"Are you alright?" Debbie asked as she leaned in for the kiss she knew was coming. "How did it go with Jamie?"

"Yes, I am fine. Jamie, not so much. They took him away in handcuffs. You should have seen the look on his face. At first, he was shocked, then he insisted he did nothing wrong, and then he finally acknowledged defeat as he realized he'd been caught."

"I'm so sorry you had to go through all that. When did you put the trail cameras up?" Debbie asked.

"Remember last Sunday, when Ben and I went to the jobsites? I put them up then. I had noticed materials were going missing, and I wanted proof of my suspicions. I knew someone was stealing, and since I have never had this problem before Jamie started working for me, I suspected it was him."

"Smart thinking. I'm surprised Ben didn't say anything."

"Ben was busy and didn't see me install them."

"I'm glad you caught him. Now we have to put together a list of materials and any equipment you are missing. I wonder where he was storing all the stuff he took?"

"The officer said they would try to get that out of him in the interrogation." Brad shrugged. "We may never know."

"Do you think we should try to put it through insurance?"

"I can't even think about that until I know the total amount. Off the top of my head, I don't even know what my insurance covers. The next time Sharon is here, I'll get her to look that up."

"Time will tell, I guess. I was just about to make a sandwich for lunch. Can I make you one?"

"Sure, that sounds good." He followed her into the kitchen.

"When you and the officer arrived, I thought perhaps you were in trouble." Debbie shrugged.

"Me, in trouble? Whatever for? I never do anything wrong."

"I thought it might be because we are going to blow up the backyard today."

Brad laughed as he wrapped his arms around her. "That's not doing anything wrong. I blow up rocks all the time. We do live on the Canadian Shield, and there's always a big rock in the way. Remember when you did the trails at the resort and that rock was so big? You made a hill out of it instead of trying to blow it up."

"Yes, I know that. I just naturally put two and two together. Today is the day we are going to blow up our rock, and it happens that you show up with the police. You can see how my mind jumped to that conclusion."

"It's all good. Would you like a pickle to go with your sandwich?"

"No thanks. Pickles don't agree with me at the moment." Debbie handed him his sandwich.

"Last time you craved pickles and ice cream if I remember correctly."

"This time, I am craving salty potato chips and ice cream."

"Whatever you need, little momma." Brad kissed her as she sat down next to him.

"So back to the Jamie thing. I bet the other guys were shocked."

"Yes. They also were aware that stuff was going missing, so they really weren't surprised. I think maybe they were even impressed that I caught him. One guy said that the camera was a personal invasion. I told him that he had nothing to worry about. I will take them down now that the thief has been caught."

"It's a good way to keep an eye on your jobsites."

"Yes, but my guys are good workers, and I don't care if they take an extra ten minutes on their coffee breaks. They are all hard workers, and they do good work. I don't want them to feel like I am spying on them. That was never my intention."

"I think someone's knocking on the back door," Debbie said.

"I'll get it," Brad answered.

Brad came back into the kitchen and explained that the dynamite guy had just arrived, so she should stay away from the back of the house for the next hour or so.

"I'll just go down to the resort for a break then."

"Perfect. I would be happier knowing you are well out of harm's way. Not that anything is going to go wrong. But better safe than sorry."

Debbie grabbed her phone, her purse, and a sweater on her way out the door.

Debbie always felt strange entering the lodge through the front door as a customer. As soon as she entered the dining room, Janice came over to greet her. "Hey, sis. Good to see you. Are you here for lunch or just a coffee break?"

"Tea with milk, please." Debbie sat down in the seat that Janice had pulled out for her. "Where's Gail today?"

"She's not coming in until five for the dinner rush."

Since Debbie was the only customer at the moment, Janice pulled out a chair and joined her. "I got a hostile call from Tony last night. He is pissed. Making all kinds of threats because he lost his visitation with Zack. Apparently, he was notified by registered mail. He was mad at me because he had to go to the post office to pick up the notification."

"Do you think he really cares? About Zack, I mean. Or is he just mad that he has lost his control over you?"

"He's never cared about Zack," Janice answered. "And I don't think he ever really cared about me either. Hell, he cheated on me before we were even married. Forsaking all others, that's a bit of a joke, isn't it?"

"At least now, you are finally done with him and his crazy mother. What did Zack say when you told him?"

"He was so happy, he danced. He even pulled me to my

feet, and I danced with him. We are both very happy to be done with all that nonsense."

"And now, you can focus on your wedding." Debbie smiled at her sister. "How are the plans going?"

A man entered the dining room from the kitchen and helped himself to a coffee from the waitress station.

"Who is that?" Debbie asked.

Janice said, "Don, come join us. I'd like you to meet my sister, Debbie. Deb, this is Don. Phil's brother."

"Hello, my dear. It's nice to meet you." Don sat down with them.

"Debbie used to run this resort. She has taught me everything I know about this business."

"You were taught well, from what I have seen so far," Don stated.

"So, are you visiting your brother then?" Debbie asked.

"Yes and no." Don shrugged. "My wife and I have just decided to call it quits, and I am currently in limbo. Phil has offered me a place to stay until I land back on my feet. I am currently looking for a job and a place to live. Basically, I am looking for a new life."

"That's tough. I am sure in time you will get things figured out," Debbie offered. "What kind of work do you do?"

"A little of this, and a little of that. My last official job I worked construction, but I haven't worked on a payroll for the past couple of years. I am a bit of a handyman and can also fix small engines, so I have basically been working cash jobs and doing very well. I'm quite handy at a lot of things, really," he explained.

"Don't be surprised if Phil has you doing handyman jobs around here," Janice suggested.

"He was just talking to me about painting some cabins," Don replied.

"Yep, that sounds like Phil." Janice chuckled. "Well, if you two will excuse me, I need to get the dining room set for dinner."

"Yes, I should be getting home too," Debbie stated. "They are blasting a big rock in my backyard, so I just came for a break while my husband blows things up."

"Why are they blowing up rocks in your yard?" Don asked.

"We are in the process of putting on a big addition to our house so I can have a bed-and-breakfast."

"Oh, I see. I think Phil mentioned that. Is your husband Brad Mumford?"

"Yes, he is. Why do you ask?"

"Phil mentioned that he worked for Brad for a while once when he and Nancy were having some troubles. He speaks very highly of Brad."

"Yes, Phil was a great help to Brad, and he was very sad to lose Phil when they bought this resort. Brad has yet to replace him."

"And today, he is blowing up rocks. Ah, that's just something any man could relate to. All us men like to watch things go boom."

"My five-year-old son is no exception. He was so upset that he had to go to school this morning. He wanted to stay home so he could watch the big boom."

"See, it's a male thing. Women like soft, fluffy things, and men like to watch things get blown up."

"Well, Don, it was very nice to meet you. I am sure you will get back on your feet, and if you are serious about staying in the area, you might want to talk to Brad about a job. I know he is always hiring good laborers."

"Thank you, I will give that some serious thought. I hope to see you again sometime."

As Debbie drove home, she decided she had to get Don and Brad together, especially if Don was half the worker Phil was.

FOURTEEN

Thursday morning, Debbie was getting the kids' jackets on when the phone rang.

"Is this Debbie Mumford?" the caller asked.

"Yes, it is."

"You are the emergency contact person for Henry Miller. I need to notify you that he is in the Clifford Hospital."

"Oh no, what happened?"

"Henry has had a heart attack."

"I'll be there within the hour. Thank you for the call."

"Mommy, what's wrong? Where are you going?" Becky asked as Debbie put her jacket on.

"I have to go to town. Henry is in the hospital."

"Is he sick?" Ben asked.

"He has had a heart attack. I am going to go see if I can help," Debbie assured him.

As soon as the kids were on the bus, Debbie called Brad.

"Hey, Brad, sorry to bother you. I just got a call and Henry is in the hospital. Seems he has had a heart attack. I am going into town to see what's going on."

"I am meeting a client in town for lunch. Keep me posted and call if there's anything I can do."

"I will. Talk to you later."

Debbie ran upstairs and changed her clothes. She had planned to spend the day around the house, but now that she was going to town, she best not wear her grubby clothes. As she dressed, she said a little prayer. "Please, God, look in on Henry."

At the hospital, the staff told her that Henry was in cubicle six. When she walked in, she had to take a step back. Henry was sleeping with tubes coming and going from his body, an oxygen mask covering his face, and beeping machines everywhere. "Henry, old friend. You don't look so good. I'm here now." Debbie needed some information, so she went out to the nurse's station.

"Can I help you?" a nurse asked.

"Yes, please. I am Debbie Mumford; I am the contact for Henry Miller. I was wondering if I could get any information about my friend's condition."

"Henry was brought in by ambulance at seven-thirty this morning. He has suffered a major heart attack," the nurse told her.

"Do you know if he was at home when it happened? Did he call the ambulance himself or did someone else call?"

"I believe he was at a golf course. Apparently, he fell off a ladder. He has a broken leg and three cracked ribs as well."

"Is it possible to speak with his doctor?" Debbie asked.

"The doctor on call is still in the building. I will see if he could come speak to you."

"Thank you. I would appreciate that." Debbie went back in to sit on a chair beside Henry's bedside.

As Debbie watched him sleep, she had a little cry and then pulled herself together. Her first call was to Brad to tell him what she knew so far. Her next call was to Thomas Townsend, the golf course owner. She felt bad because she was the one who suggested that Henry see Thomas about doing some painting and odd jobs at the golf course.

"Debbie, I am glad you called. Have you heard any news on Henry?" Thomas asked.

"Yes, I have just arrived at the hospital. They tell me he has a broken leg, three cracked ribs, and has had a major heart attack," Debbie explained. "Can you tell me what happened?"

"Henry has been doing some painting for me, and this morning, he was up on a ladder just starting to paint the clubhouse. I was just coming around the corner when I heard a crash. Henry had fallen off the ladder, and I could see he was in distress, so I called the ambulance. I didn't move him. I just put a blanket over him and tried to keep him warm until the paramedics arrived."

"That must have been scary."

"It was. He was having trouble breathing, but he never said a word."

"Thanks, Thomas. I will keep you posted."

"I'd appreciate that. I hope he is going to be alright."

"I hope so too. Bye for now." *He is going to be alright! He just has to be.*

A short while later, Brad came up beside Debbie and took her hand. "What have you learned so far?"

"I am so glad you are here." Through tears, Debbie relayed Henry's list of injuries to Brad.

"I don't understand why they called you," Brad said.

"Because I am his emergency contact."

"Oh, of course you are. I didn't think of that."

"I need to call his sons, but I am waiting to speak with the doctor first so I will know what to tell them."

Brad's phone rang, and he stepped out into the hallway to take the call. As Brad walked out, the doctor walked in.

"Good morning. I understand you wanted to see me," the doctor said.

"Yes, I was hoping you could give me more information before I call Henry's sons," Debbie said as Brad came back into the cubicle.

The doctor confirmed the injuries, with emphasis on Henry's cardiac arrest.

"Is he going to recover?" Brad asked.

"It is hard to say. His heart has been damaged, but we won't know how badly until we do some more tests. I am waiting on blood work results, and he is scheduled for an echocardiogram. Depending on what that tells us, if his heart can be repaired, he will be transported to a bigger hospital. We are not equipped to do open heart surgery here."

"The nurse said heart attack, but you're saying cardiac arrest. What's the difference?" Debbie asked.

"A heart attack is caused by blocked arteries which limit the blood flow into the heart. A cardiac arrest is when the heart stops beating. In other words, the heart's electrical system is not working properly."

"So did he have the cardiac arrest which caused the fall, or did he fall first and then have the cardiac arrest?" Brad asked.

"That we don't know. The next few hours will be critical. Henry has not regained consciousness since he arrived," the doctor explained as he made a note on Henry's chart. "Now, if you will excuse me, I have to go. I'll be back later when I have the latest blood work."

"I guess I better be calling Henry's sons," Debbie softly said.

"Let's go sit in the garden, and you can call them from there." Brad took her hand and led her from Henry's bedside.

"I don't want to leave him. What if he wakes up?"

"He's not going to wake up, and some fresh air will do you good. We can come back in after you have made your calls."

Brad led Debbie down a long hall and out the side door into the garden. Debbie was razor-focused on the calls she had to make. She called both of Henry's sons. She had to leave a message for Mike, but her second call was answered.

"Hello, is this John Miller?" Debbie asked.

"Yes, who's this?"

"Hi. My name is Debbie Mumford. I am a friend of your father's."

"Yes, hi. I know who you are. Dad talks about you all the time."

"John, I have to tell you some bad news. Your dad is in the hospital in Clifford. He fell off a ladder, broke his leg, cracked three ribs, and had a cardiac arrest. He's in bad shape."

"Oh no! Do you think I should come?"

"That is totally up to you. Since I arrived, he has not woken up."

"Alright, I am on my way. Did you call Mike?"

"I tried but had to leave a message asking him to call me."

"I have his new cell phone number. I'll try to call him. I

will be there as soon as I can. Probably about three hours or so."

"I'll stay with him until you arrive," Debbie assured him.

"Thank you so much for being there and for calling. I will see you soon."

Brad was off to the side and talking on his cell phone. Debbie could hear him talking about building materials that were late being delivered, so she headed back inside the hospital. The place was so gloomy with its battleship gray walls. It could do with a more cheerful color. Hell, even white would be better, Debbie decided.

As she came down the long hallway and turned the corner into the emergency department, she could see that there was a doctor and five nurses around Henry's bed. She recognized him as the doctor that she had spoken with earlier. As soon as a nurse saw her, she approached and asked Debbie to stay back. Then she pulled the curtain, obstructing Debbie's view of the cubicle.

"What's going on?" Brad asked as he came up behind her.

"I don't know. One of the nurses asked me to stay back before she pulled the curtain closed. I think Henry's in trouble."

The next few minutes felt like hours before the nurse pulled the curtain back and pushed a big machine out of the cubicle. The doctor stepped out and came over to Brad and Debbie. "I'm so sorry, but Henry didn't make it. He had another cardiac arrest. We did everything we could, but we couldn't save him."

"NO!" Debbie screamed. "Not Henry. Oh no!"

Brad pulled her into his arms and held her until she

stopped sobbing. By the time he had her calmed down, the nurses had removed all the machinery and tubes from Henry. The last nurse to leave the cubicle came over, touched Debbie's arm, and said, "I'm so sorry for your loss. If you want, you can go in and say your goodbyes."

"Thank you," Brad answered for Debbie.

"I have to call John back and tell him not to bother coming," Debbie stated.

"Alright, but first, let's go say goodbye to Henry." Brad took her hand and they went to Henry's bedside. "Godspeed, Henry. We're sure gonna miss you." Brad stepped back and let Debbie have a moment.

"Henry, I'm so sorry you never got over for that lasagna dinner we talked about. I am sad to lose you, old friend. It has been my privilege to have known you these past twenty years. I hope you can now rest in peace," Debbie said through her tears.

Brad took Debbie's hand, and they walked together to the parking lot.

"I still need to call John," Debbie said.

"Are you going to be okay, or do you want me to stay with you?" Brad asked.

"I'm good. Thank you so much for being here for me. I really appreciate that." Debbie gave him a big hug. "You are always here for me."

"Of course. You're my wife and I love you. You are always my top priority. But if you're alright, then I am going to have to get back to work. I'm meeting a client in twenty minutes, and I have to stop at the lumberyard before I leave town."

"Thanks, hun. You can go back to work. I'll see you at home later." Debbie leaned in for her kiss.

As soon as she got into the van, she called John back.

"John, it's Debbie again. I have some more bad news. Your dad had another cardiac arrest, and he didn't survive it. John, your dad is gone."

"Oh no. My poor dad. He never even woke up then?"

"No, they tried to revive him, but they couldn't. I'm so sorry to have to be the one to tell you. If you need anything, if there's anything I can do, please call me. You have my number."

"Thank you. I will."

On the drive home, Debbie thought about Henry. She had known him for such a long time. *I still can't believe he's gone. Just like that.* She thought about the last time he was in the hospital when he was worried that she'd forget to pick him up. She was sure going to miss Henry popping in for a visit.

As soon as she got home, she called Thomas at the golf course to tell him that Henry had passed away. Everyone else would just have to be told later. Right now, she had things she needed to do.

Debbie had every intention of tidying up the kids' rooms and making her own bed, but she got sidetracked in Becky's room. She picked up the teddy bear that was on Becky's bed and wandered around aimlessly. At some point, she sat down in the rocking chair with the bear in her arms and had a good cry. She was remembering things about her friend Henry. She remembered the first time she had met him and how he had become such a big part of her life. They had been through a lot together, and even now, if she had a problem and Brad wasn't around, Henry was the first person she'd call. She remembered that when Brad was first dating her, he used to tease her that Henry was his competition because she spent so much time with Henry. She decided that, yes, she was going to miss him, no doubt about that.

When Brad came home a couple of hours later, he found Debbie upstairs in Becky's room, sitting in the rocking chair with a teddy bear in her arms. Brad knelt in front of her. "You alright, babe? You've been crying."

"This is Becky's favorite teddy bear; Henry bought it for her. Out of all these toys she has, this is the bear that she loves the best. This is the bear that she sleeps with," Debbie said as she started to cry again. "Oh, my goodness, what time is it?" She jumped up out of the chair. "I haven't even taken anything out for dinner. I'm so sorry." Debbie looked as defeated as she felt.

"No worries. Maybe we could go to the lodge for dinner tonight," Brad suggested.

"Let's do that," Debbie gratefully agreed. "I'll call and make a reservation. What time should I say?"

"I have three estimates to work on after, so we could eat earlier. Let's say five o'clock." Brad followed her downstairs.

"Sounds good to me." Debbie reached for the phone off the kitchen counter.

"First, could a tired husband get a hug and maybe even a kiss from his beautiful wife?"

"Yes, he sure can." Debbie gladly fell into his arms.

FIFTEEN

When the kids came barreling into the house, they kicked off their boots and jackets and came looking for Debbie for their hugs and kisses.

"Hey, Daddy. You're home early. What can we have for a snack, Mommy?" Ben asked in a flurry.

"Hello, son. Did you eat all your lunch?" Brad asked.

"I sure did. I love Mommy's jelly sandwiches, and everyone loves her cookies," Ben stated proudly.

"What do you mean everyone?" Debbie asked.

"Sometimes he trades his with other kids," Becky told her.

"Ben, if you don't like my cookies, I can give you store-bought ones instead," Debbie suggested.

"That's a good idea, and you can save the good ones for me," Brad said.

"Daddy, Mommy bakes those cookies for us for our lunches," Ben told him. "You stay out of our cookie jar."

"Well, if you are just going to give them away or trade them, I don't see why I can't have some too."

"I guess you can have one, but just one. That's all we are ever allowed to have," Ben explained.

"You can both have one piece of fruit for a snack. Your daddy is taking us all out to the resort for dinner," Debbie said.

"Cool. Can I have chicken fingers?" Becky asked.

"I don't see why not." Brad lifted her up so she could choose which fruit she wanted out of the bowl. She chose an apple and headed in to watch cartoons.

Brad was pretending that he didn't see Ben standing beside him. "Daddy, are you going to lift me up, or what?" Ben asked.

"Oh, sorry, big guy. I didn't see you there." Brad picked Benjamin up and twirled him around in circles until Ben begged him to stop. "Daddy, I would like a banana, please." Brad handed it to him, and he went to join his sister in the living room.

"We have such great kids, even if they do trade their cookies." Brad pulled Debbie into his arms for a hug.

"How did your lunch meeting go today?" Debbie asked.

"Good, I think. This new client is friends with the guy whose house we are currently building. He has been to the jobsite, and likes what he sees. He has some different ideas about the layout, but it will be basically the same square footage when it's all said and done."

"Clients are getting you more clients. How cool is that?"

"Exactly. I really don't even advertise much anymore. My phone never stops ringing. I do have some work to do after dinner. Sharon will be here tomorrow morning, and she will type the quotes up for me."

"Don't forget to ask her to look up your insurance policy for the theft."

"Yes, it's on my list. We also have to make a list of materials that were stolen. That's going to be hard. How can you guess you are missing half a box of nails or a hammer that could have been stolen or just misplaced?"

"Have you heard back from the police whether Jamie told them where all the missing materials are?"

"No, only that they have his phone and are tracking down numbers that he has called."

"That might lead them to someone. How are the other guys responding to all this?"

"I only had one guy complain about the cameras being on-site. The other guys didn't seem to care."

"Did you take the cameras down then?"

"No, not yet, but I will. I think I have decided to leave them up until the project is finished."

"They won't be any good once the work moves inside."

"That's when I will take them down. I guess I should go grab my shower before we head out for dinner."

"Yes, we need to leave in fifteen minutes."

When they all arrived at the lodge, Gail met them at the front door. "Hey guys, come on in. I have a table saved for you right here. Is there a special occasion we are celebrating tonight?"

"No, just a real hard day," Brad answered as they were seated.

Janice came over to say hello.

"Janice, I will tell you and Gail at the same time. Henry passed away today from a cardiac arrest," Debbie said.

"Henry, oh no! That's horrible. What happened?" Janice asked.

Debbie looked at Brad, and he understood that she wanted him to explain it. "Apparently, he was painting for Thomas at the golf course, and we're not sure if he had the cardiac arrest and fell off the ladder and broke his leg and cracked three ribs, or if he fell off the ladder and then went into the cardiac arrest. Thomas didn't see him fall. He heard it, but didn't see it happen."

"Poor Henry. I assume Thomas called the ambulance then. Did they take him to Clifford?" Gail asked.

"Yes. Debbie and I went to the hospital, but he never regained consciousness. He had another arrest while we were there. The doctors tried to revive him, but they couldn't," Brad explained. "Needless to say, it's been a long, trying day, and we decided to let you do the cooking tonight."

"We'll take good care of you. What would you like to drink?" Gail asked.

Brad ordered them all a pop, and when Gail brought their drinks, she told them the dinner specials.

Brad chose a steak, Debbie chose a chicken Caesar salad, Becky had her chicken fingers, and Ben chose spaghetti. They were all hungry, so the dinner conversation was limited. The meal was good and when they finished, the kids both had ice cream for dessert.

Nancy stopped by their table just as they were finishing. "How's everyone tonight? How was dinner?" she asked.

"We're much better now that we all have our tummies full, aren't we kids?" Brad asked. "Phil does charbroil a good steak." He pushed back from the table and said, "If he's not too busy, tell him we are here if he wants to pop out and say hi."

"I'm sure he will. Let me go see what he's doing," Nancy said as she walked away.

"I haven't had the chance to tell you that Phil's brother Don is staying here at the resort for a while."

"Daddy, we are done. Can we have some quarters for the video game, please?" Becky asked.

"Alright, but no fighting. You have to take turns." Brad fished two dollars' worth of quarters from his pocket and gave four quarters to each kid.

"I didn't know Phil even had a brother. How did you find that out?" Brad asked.

"I met him the day you fired Jamie and blew up the rock in our backyard. I came down here for a coffee and Janice introduced us. He seemed like a good guy."

"Bradley, so nice to see you. Hi, Debbie. How was dinner?" Phil asked.

"Have a seat if you have a minute," Brad said. "The kids are playing video games."

Phil pulled out a chair and sat down. "I have been meaning to call you. I wanted to introduce you to my brother Don. He's very much like me. A bit of a handyman, jack of many trades, master of none. He's upstairs. I just asked Nancy to go give him a poke. I think you should meet him. His marriage has just broken up so he's here looking for a new start. Kind of like I was when we first met."

"Sure, I would like to meet him. I just fired a guy when I caught him stealing from me."

"Oh no, how did you manage to catch the thief?" Phil asked.

"On a trail cam."

"Nothing worse than a thief. I'm glad you caught him. Did you teach him a lesson, at least?"

"I called the cops, and they arrested the bugger. Still don't have my materials back, but at least he's been caught."

Don walked up to the table and Phil did the introductions. "This guy is my brother Don. Don, this is my old boss, Brad Mumford, and I believe you have already met his wife, Debbie."

"Please join us," Debbie offered.

"Thank you, I will. Brad, it is nice to meet you." Don extended his hand and Brad shook it.

"Phil tells me you have just moved here and might be looking for work. Have you ever done any building before?" Brad asked.

"Honestly, not in the last ten years, at least. But I did some building when I was a much younger man. I am more of a handyman kind of guy. I can do a bit of carpentry, a bit of electrical, a bit of plumbing, a little bit of everything."

"Don quit his full-time job about ten years ago and has been doing lawn care and small engine repairs as of late," Phil offered. "You'll have to excuse me; I see Gail just put another order into the kitchen, and I am the only cook on tonight. It was great to see you both. Have a good night."

"Thanks, Phil. The steak was perfect," Brad said as Phil nodded and headed into the kitchen.

"So, I suppose you have never seen a set of blueprints before?" Brad asked.

"I am familiar with them, but I wouldn't stake my reputation on my knowledge. I spent one summer as a teenager working for an architect where I learned the basic principles of them."

"That's half the battle right there." Brad nodded. "I just had to fire a guy for stealing from me. I guess you could say I'm a little gun shy, a little cautious about hiring new people."

"That's understandable. But let me assure you, you won't have that problem with me. You can ask Phil. Our dad raised us better than that. He taught us our work ethic. I personally believe in doing a day's work for a day's pay. I show up on time and follow orders. I am grateful to have a job I like doing. I also like to learn new things, which, at my age, gets harder and harder to do." Don shrugged.

"If Phil vouches for you, that means a lot. I liked Phil's work ethic just fine. Hell, he'd still be working for me if he hadn't bought this damn resort." Brad chuckled at the look on Debbie's face.

"How many properties are you building right now, if I may ask?"

"Three. One house, one cottage, and one bed-and-breakfast addition to our house."

"Are they all framed yet?" Don asked. "It won't be long and the snow will be here."

"We are pouring the concrete tubes for the B&B tomorrow, and the other two jobs are almost finished with the outside framing and siding done," Brad answered. "Would you be interested in working as a laborer for the winter then?"

"Yes, absolutely. Like I said, I am looking for any full-time work. Anything I don't know how to do, I will learn quickly." Don's answer was enthusiastic.

"I don't know if I can use you full-time, at least not all winter. Do you have your own vehicle to get to work?" Brad asked.

"Yes, I have my old truck that gets me where I need to go."

"Alright, I'll put you to work, on a two-week trial basis. Be ready Monday morning at seven, and I'll stop by so you can follow me to the jobsite. That would be easier than trying to give you directions. Some of the cottage roads don't have any signs. Most people get lost."

"Sounds good to me. Monday at seven. I'll be ready. Do I need to bring my own tool belt, or do you supply tools?"

"My guys all have their own tool belts with hammers and measuring tapes, that kind of thing, but I supply all the power tools. Do you have a tool belt?"

"Yes, I think I do. It's in one of those boxes in the back of the truck."

"Whatever you don't have, I am sure one of the other fellows would help you out."

Ben and Becky came back to the table, and Brad introduced them to Don, who had stood to offer Becky her chair back.

"Would you be available tomorrow morning to come up to the house to fill out some paperwork? My secretary, Sharon, will be there, and she will need your credentials to get you on the payroll. She is there from nine till around two."

"I'll do that. Thanks so much for giving me a chance. I really appreciate it, and I am looking forward to learning all there is to know about building homes and cottages." Don shook Brad's hand again and excused himself. "Night all."

"He seems like a nice enough guy. Kind of reminds me of Phil," Debbie suggested.

"If he's half the worker Phil is, I'll be happy. You kids spend all my quarters?" Brad asked.

"Yes. And guess what? I even got high score on the one game," Ben said.

"Should I go beat your score or leave it there for now?" Brad asked.

"Well, I guess you could try," Ben said with a smirk.

"Maybe next time. I think we should be heading home.

I still have a pile of work to do before I can call it a night." Brad picked up his receipt and left Gail a tip. They all said goodnight to Aunt Janice and Gail.

When they got home, Debbie and the kids watched a movie while Brad worked away at the dining room table. By the time the kids were bathed and into bed, Debbie was exhausted. She put on her pajamas before she came back downstairs.

"I'm going to make a tea; would you like one?" she asked Brad.

"Sounds good. I should be done here in a few minutes. Meet you on the couch."

Debbie made the tea and a snack of cheese and crackers for them and was sitting on the couch reading a book when Brad joined her.

"I'm curious why you never mentioned Don to me. You know I am looking for more help."

"Well, it's like this. That was the day you had fired Jamie, and you were a bit overstimulated. That was also the same day you were blowing things up in the backyard. I had planned to tell you about Don, but I decided that it could wait a day or two, and then, it just slipped my mind."

"I see. Well, all is forgiven. I know you have a lot on your mind these days. How have you been doing with the morning sickness?"

"Seems to be alright, as long as I don't try to drink coffee." Debbie shrugged as she took a sip of her hot tea.

"And no strange cravings so far, besides potato chips and ice cream, of course?"

"You know it. Nothing new, not yet anyway."

"You told Don to come up to the house to see Sharon, but you never gave him directions."

"I did that on purpose. Let's see if he's a problem solver or not. Just kidding. I am sure Phil or Nancy will give him directions. Wouldn't it be wonderful if Don turns out to be as good as Phil? He was at rock bottom when I met him. I remember Phil didn't have much experience either, but he was a quick learner and quickly became invaluable to me."

"Yes, that would be nice. But remember, Don isn't Phil. He said he had a basic understanding of blueprints, so that should be helpful at least. Do the rest of your guys understand blueprints?"

"A couple of them do. But that's my job anyway. I tell them to build this room whatever size the blueprint tells me, and they build it."

"So, you're like the interpreter then?"

"Yes, I guess you could say that." Brad shifted her under his arm. "My guys are builders; they don't need to be able to read blueprints. They just build whatever I ask them to."

"So, if Don is good enough to become your assistant, it would be good if he could read them too?"

"Yes, it would. If I wasn't on-site, and there were any questions, he could look at the blueprints and confirm what is required to meet the specifications."

"Are they ever wrong? Are there ever mistakes?"

"Rarely. Everyone makes mistakes, but the architect that I work with most of the time never makes mistakes. He has an eye for detail, and nothing gets by him."

"Well, here's hoping that Don works out for you. I've met him twice now, and he seems to be a good guy. I get a good feeling from him." Debbie smiled up at Brad.

"That's good to know. I trust your instincts about people."

"As you should. You liked Jamie, but I got a bad vibe from him. He bragged about his big accomplishments so much that I thought he was arrogant. And turns out I was right."

"Yes, hun, you were right. That's why I trust your instincts." Brad finished his tea, stood up, and stretched. "Well, I, for one, am pooped. Are you coming to bed?"

"Right behind you, cowboy."

SIXTEEN

Debbie was upstairs tidying up the kids' rooms when she heard Sharon call out, "Morning, Debbie."

"Morning, I'll be down in a few minutes."

"Take your time, I'll be in the office."

Debbie finished making Ben's bed and picked up an armful of dirty clothes on her way downstairs. She passed the office on her way to the laundry room, where she moved a load from the washer to the dryer and put in a new load. She stopped in the office and dropped into the chair in front of the big desks. "Another crisp fall morning."

"Yes, it's getting to be that time of year. I noticed some of the trees are starting to turn color already," Sharon responded.

"I expect Brad will be in and out all day today. But, before you get buried in your work, I wanted to ask if you could babysit for me next Saturday night. We are having a surprise birthday party for Susan down at the lodge."

"Sure, I could do that. What time do you want me here?"

"I think perhaps by six. The party doesn't start till seven, but I will go down early and make sure everything is set up."

"I have it marked on my calendar. How are you doing with the morning sickness?"

"I think the worst of it is over. But I still can't drink

coffee. When I make a pot, I stand over it and enjoy the aroma of it while it's dripping."

"Guess a smell is almost as good as a taste."

"Almost. I'd better get myself moving and let you get back to work." Debbie stood to leave.

"Before you go, I am looking at Brad's to-do list, and I don't understand this note about the insurance policy he wants me to look up. Do you know what he is asking for?"

"He caught Jamie, the new guy, stealing and wants to know what his business insurance covers regarding missing materials."

"Stealing, no kidding. I'll pull the file and see what it says."

As she folded a basket of laundry, Debbie's thoughts were scattered. She thought about how much she liked Sharon and how much Brad did too. Maybe a little too much. He almost idolized her. He respected Sharon's business sense, and Debbie wondered if some of his ideas were actually hers. Debbie had set the clean basket of clothes on the stairs when Brad came in.

"Good morning, beautiful. How's your day going so far?" Brad asked as he gave her a quick kiss.

"Living the dream," she answered. "Sharon's here, but you probably know that because her car is in the driveway."

"Yes, I did. And the guys are already pouring cement for the foundation pillars," Brad said with excitement. "Next, they'll start putting up the framework. The lumberyard truck will be making a delivery this afternoon."

"Guess you best be getting back to work then."

"Yes, I need to talk to Sharon. And Don is supposed to stop by at some point as well.

As if on cue, she heard a knock on the front door. "Come in," Brad shouted.

"Is this the right place?"

"It sure is, Don. Come on in," Brad invited. "My office is back here if you want to come this way."

"Hi, Debbie. Nice to see you," Don said as he followed Brad out.

Debbie had just seasoned and seared the roast, just like Chef had taught her, and had placed it in the oven when she heard another knock on the door. She was drying her hands on a towel as she opened it.

"Hi, Debbie, right? You probably don't remember us. I'm John, and this is my brother Mike Miller."

"Come on in. It's been a minute since I last saw either of you. But I do remember your dad brought you both into the resort for dinner a few years back." Debbie motioned them to follow her. "Can I get either of you a coffee or something?"

Both of them looked like their dad. Nice, clean-cut men. Debbie felt an instant liking to both of them. They were both dressed casually but still very stylish.

"No, don't go to any trouble for us. We just wanted to ask you a few questions if we could," Mike stated.

"It's no bother. My husband, Brad, is in the back office. I'll introduce you when he comes in for a coffee. Please have a seat." Debbie pointed to the breakfast nook counter. "I'm so sorry for your loss. I thought very highly of Henry. As you know, he worked for me at the resort for over ten years until we sold it."

"Yes, and he talked about you all the time, even after he wasn't working for you anymore," John said.

"Do you know the plans for your dad's service yet?" Debbie asked.

"He's being cremated. Since we don't live here, we don't know any of his friends here. We were hoping to have a celebration of life for him but don't know where to start. Would you help us with that?" Mike asked.

"Of course. Henry had many friends here. I know he was also involved with the local legion and, I think, also with the Shriners. I don't know any of them, but I could make a few phone calls and see what I can find out," Debbie offered.

"That would be a huge help. I think we will have his service at the lodge, perhaps this Saturday afternoon," John stated.

"What time were you thinking?" Debbie asked.

"I don't know, say two o'clock. Does that sound alright?" John asked.

"Why don't I call Nancy at the resort and see if that time slot is available? I'd guess for around fifty people. And you'll want the standard cold buffet served about four o'clock then?"

"Yes, that all sounds good. I told John you would know what we needed to do to make this happen," Mike said.

Debbie called Nancy and confirmed that Saturday at two o'clock would work fine. Nancy said the banquet room, which could hold fifty people, was available and that they could serve a cold buffet.

Debbie hung up the phone. "There, that's taken care of."

"Thank you so much," Mike said. "Now, what do we need to do?"

"I would think you will want Henry's ashes in an urn with a nice big picture of him, and you'll want some flowers. I would suggest you go in to talk to my sister Janice at the resort. She can give you guidance on the flowers you will need."

"I don't know where we'll find a nice picture of Dad. I may have something on my phone from the last time I was up, but that was over a year ago," Mike said.

"You can also do a picture board of your dad if you have enough pictures. I may also have some pictures on my phone," Debbie suggested, and they all sat scrolling through their phones.

"Here's a nice one. This was about seven years ago at Janice's wedding." Debbie showed them both.

"That's a very nice picture of Dad. Could you send it to me?" Mike asked.

"Yes, of course. I'll send you any that I have on my phone. If you are thinking about making a collage of pics, I may also have some older pictures in my photo albums. I will take a look, and if I find any, I'll snap a picture of them with my phone's camera and send them to you as well," Debbie offered.

"That would be greatly appreciated," Mike replied.

It wasn't long before Brad strolled in for his coffee. "Brad, these two gentlemen are Henry's sons, Mike and John. This is my husband, Brad."

"Nice to meet you." Mike stood up and shook Brad's hand. John did the same.

"I understand that you and Debbie were with Dad when he passed away. Thank you both so much for caring enough to be with him," John stated.

"That's just what friends do, and we have both been friends of Henry's for a long time," Brad offered. "I know he was proud of you both, and we are all going to miss him."

"Thank you. That was very kind of you to say," Mike replied.

Brad had gone over to refill his coffee cup when he noticed that the guys didn't have any cups in front of them. "Would you guys like a coffee? Debbie has just made a fresh pot."

"No, thanks. We need to get going. We just wanted to ask for Debbie's help arranging the celebration of life."

"Wise decision. Debbie is the best at organizing things like that. Well, I have to get back to work. It was nice meeting you both."

After Brad left, Debbie showed them another picture of Henry from her camera. "This was taken about three years ago, I would guess. Henry had just helped Brad rake the front lawn, and the kids were jumping into a pile of leaves. I don't know who was having more fun, the kids playing in the leaves or your dad watching them."

"That is a great picture. Very natural. I think that should be the picture we get framed. The other picture is nice but very formal. We are not used to seeing Dad in a suit, but in this one, he is relaxed, in his normal clothes. He looks very happy in this one. Don't you think so?" Mike showed the picture to John.

"I like it, but aren't funeral pictures supposed to be somber?" John asked.

"It can be whatever you choose. If you're asking me, I like the natural one better. After all, it is a celebration of his life."

Debbie let them know where they could get the photos

printed and framed. She also suggested they visit the flower shop in town.

"Thank you so much for all your help. Neither one of us has any experience with funerals, and you have made this all look so easy. Guess it helps when you know what you are supposed to be doing," Mike said.

"I would do anything for Henry. I loved that man. We had a very special bond. He was like a father figure to me. I have a lot of good memories of your dad. He has left a big hole in the middle of my world, and I am glad that I can help you both to say your goodbyes."

"We were also wondering if you wanted to come up to Dad's house and pick a keepsake or anything," John asked.

"Thank you. That is very kind of you to offer. Actually, I have something of his that one of you may like to have. I have his pipe. The day he decided to quit smoking, he gave it to me for safekeeping. I still have it somewhere," Debbie offered.

"You keep that. He obviously wanted you to have it. And if you want to come up to the house, you can choose any other mementos you would like to have," Mike suggested.

"I'm not much for keepsakes, but thank you. I have lots of good memories, and that's all I need." Debbie smiled at them.

"Well, we'll get out of your hair. Thanks again for all your help. We will see you on Saturday if we don't see you before."

"Good luck. And I will look through my photo albums and see what other pictures I have of your dad. Don't hesitate to ask if there's anything else I can help you with."

"Thanks again," Mike said, then surprised Debbie with a hug.

"Let me know if there's anything else you need," Debbie said as John also gave her a hug.

"Oh, I almost forgot. We are going to put Dad's house for sale, and I remember him saying that one of you girls was an agent."

"Yes, you need to talk to my other sister Susan. She has an office in town. Be sure to tell her I sent you. I'm sure she would be glad to help sell your dad's house."

After the boys were gone, Debbie went back to peeling her veggies for dinner. John and Mike seemed like such nice guys, but she wasn't surprised. Henry was a nice man too. She remembered he had told her that his wife had died when the boys were still teenagers. That must have been hard for them, and now they'd lost their dad too. It had been seven years since she had lost her mom, and she still thought about her every day.

SEVENTEEN

It was Saturday morning, and the kids were busy watching cartoons. Debbie had some small birdhouses and decorations that the kids could paint covering the dining room table.

She was planning on spaghetti for dinner for Sharon and the kids and was busy chopping the lettuce for a Ceasar salad when Brad stopped in for a coffee refill.

"How are you doing, hun?" Brad asked as he leaned in for a kiss.

"I guess so. I have kept myself busy trying not to think about Henry's celebration of life this afternoon. You know, when something like this happens, you can't help but take stalk of your own life." Debbie handed him a bowl to put into the fridge.

"You been taking stock then? That sounds pretty serious. Anything I need to know?"

"No, just makes you stop and think. Henry's gone and here we are, bringing another life into the world."

Brad took her into his arms. "Henry lived a happy, colorful life, and now he is at peace. Now, you better run up and get changed. Sharon will be here before you know it."

True to her word, Sharon arrived around one o'clock, and Brad and Debbie headed to the resort. Before I forget to tell you, you look very pretty today," Brad said as he took her hand and helped her out of the van.

"Thanks, hun." Debbie gave him a kiss for his efforts.

As soon as they stepped into the lodge, Debbie could smell the flowers. There were two big vases filled with an assortment of fall colors on both sides of the doorway. The fragrance from the lilies was very poignant and lovely. Debbie decided she liked it. The sunlight was shining through the front windows, with reds and golds reflected everywhere around the main dining room.

Mike came over to them right away. "Hi guys, please come into the banquet room. We are all set up in there."

"Are you ready for today?" Debbie asked and gave Mike's arm a little squeeze. Debbie was impressed. Mike looked so handsome in his suit. She felt a sense of pride as she stood there talking to him.

"I guess so. John and I had a few beers last night and have come up with a couple of funny stories to tell about Dad," John explained as they walked into the banquet room.

Debbie complimented him on how nice the room looked and how beautiful the flowers were. Debbie and Brad then wandered up to the front table where the urn sat alongside a big picture of Henry and the picture boards covered with photos of Henry throughout his life.

Janice came up and joined them. "Wasn't that picture taken at my wedding?"

"Yes, it was. I had it on my camera," Debbie explained. "I went through some photo albums and sent the boys any pictures I had. They came up with quite a collection." Janice quickly excused herself, and Brad and Debbie went to find John.

"What do you think?" John asked. "Did we do it right?"

"Yes! It looks like a celebration of life. You boys did right by your dad."

"Thank you. I was wondering if you wanted to say anything about Dad. You don't have to if you don't want to, but you are welcome to, if you do want to. You know what I mean." Debbie could see how flustered John was.

"Yes, I know what you mean. I'll have to think about it." Debbie touched John's arm. "Relax. This is a celebration."

"I know, right? I am a bundle of nerves." John was starting to sweat.

"At the end of the hall, there is a door that goes outside. You may want to take a moment and get a breath of fresh air."

"That sounds like a great idea. I'll talk to you later."

Debbie saw that Janice had opened the room divider to accommodate the overflowing crowd of people. Debbie had taken a guess at fifty, but looking around the room, she should have guessed a hundred. There were more chairs already set up in the adjoining room. She wasn't sure if her sadness was about losing Henry or about losing the resort. It was probably a bit of both. She felt the loss every time she came here.

She recognized most of the people there but only knew about twenty by name. She made the rounds and spoke with the people that she knew.

Just before two o'clock, she spotted Brad, and when their eyes met, Brad joined her, and they took their seats. Brad reached over, took her hand in his, and pulled it into his lap.

"First of all, thank you, everyone, for coming out today. For those of you who don't know me, I am John Miller, and this is Mike, my brother. We are both overwhelmed to realize that our dad, Henry Miller, had so many friends."

Mike and John both shared stories of growing up with their dad. A few people from the community also said a few words, and before she knew it, Debbie was called upon to say something.

She momentarily froze. She hadn't agreed to speak, but Mike obviously hadn't got that message. She stood, took a look around, and stepped forward. *I can do this. I need to do this for Henry and for the boys' sake.*

"Oh, Henry. What can I say about my dear old friend?" Debbie took a deep breath. "When I first met him, he pulled up in front of my lodge with a beat-up old truck and a head full of dreams. He was looking to buy a house somewhere in the area and had stopped in for lunch. That had to be about fifteen years ago.

"He did buy a house, just up the road, actually, but being retired was too boring for him. Turned out that he liked Chef George's cooking better than his own, so we struck up a deal. Over the course of ten or so years, Henry did odd jobs around the resort in exchange for a small salary and some of Chef's good cooking. It was a win-win situation.

"Henry had his whole life rattling around in boxes in the back of his old truck. I used to tease him that I should see if his old truck could pass our annual inspection. He assured me that I best not be doing that. I would get lost in there and never be seen again.

"There are new owners here at the resort and when we sold it, Henry had finally retired. After I moved up to the house, Henry found excuses to pop in for a coffee. Just a couple of weeks ago, he pulled into my driveway to borrow something, and, although I don't have near the cooking abilities as Chef George, he stayed for lunch anyway. We both had a shared fondness for tomato soup and grilled cheese sandwiches."

Debbie put her hand on the picture of Henry on the front table. "Henry, it has been my privilege to have known your friendship for all these years. I am going to miss you, old friend."

When Debbie sat back down, John asked, "Does anyone else want to say something about Dad?"

There was no response. "Well then, before we go, on behalf of my brother and I, we would like to say a huge thank you to you all for coming out and a special thanks to Debbie and Janice for all your help in putting this celebration together. I understand there are snacks and drinks available at the back of the room. Please help yourselves."

As folks started to make their way to the back of the room, Debbie noticed John and Mike standing off to the side, watching the migration. She took Brad's hand and went over and spoke to them. "That was a lovely service. You boys did your dad proud."

"Thank you for speaking. What you said was lovely," John told her.

"Yes, it was a nice service. You never really know how many lives one person can touch, and your dad was such an outgoing person that people were naturally drawn to him," Brad added.

"Thank you. That is very kind of you to say," Mike offered.

Debbie asked, "Did you get in touch with Susan about selling your dad's house?"

"Yes, she has already come and taken pictures, and I believe the listing starts on Monday," John said.

"That's good. Henry loved his house almost as much as his truck. I remember him saying that it might not be a mansion, but it was home to him. Knowing Susan, she probably has potential buyers lined up," Debbie said.

"We hope so. We listed at a low selling price, as we just want to get it sold and be done with things," John replied.

"It's difficult to take care of all this stuff when we are not physically here, and we both have jobs we need to get back to," Mike offered.

"If you would like, I can check in on the house on a daily basis until it gets sold," Brad said.

"Thank you. That would be great. I'll make sure to get you a key," John replied.

"No need. I already have a key for Henry's house." Debbie smiled. "Unless he has changed the locks in the past few years."

"No, still the same key it's been from the start," Mike said.

"Henry loved that old house. I just hope the new owners realize how special it is," Debbie said quietly.

Someone Debbie didn't recognize was standing waiting to speak with the guys, so she took Brad's hand, and they wandered back to the snack table.

"That was so nice of you to offer to look after Henry's place. Brad, you are just the nicest guy I know."

"Golly gee, thanks. You are going to make me blush. Are we still planning to stick around for dinner? Did you make our reservations?"

"No, not yet. I will, but I'll see if Janice might be able to join us. Is that alright?"

"Of course, I don't mind." Brad took the empty plate she was offering and chose a few snacks. He eyed up the beautiful desserts, but he limited himself to the egg salad sandwiches he loved.

"Hi, guys," Susan said as she joined them at the snack table. "Sorry I am late, but I just got away now. How was the service?"

"Very nice. The boys did a good job," Debbie said. "I am going to go over there and sit down. Grab a plate and join us. Actually, we are going to stay for dinner. Would you and Keith like to join us?"

Susan thought for a moment. "Yes, I think we could. Keith is probably on his way home as we speak. I'll give him a call in a few minutes and ask him."

Debbie scanned the crowd, and Brad asked her who she was looking for.

"I'm trying to catch Janice's attention. She is behind the food table," Debbie explained as Susan joined them.

"I understand you are listing the Miller house for sale. Just so you know, I have offered to cut the grass and check on the house daily," Brad told her.

"That's good. That's very nice of you. I don't expect it to be on the market for very long. It is definitely priced to sell," Susan said.

"Janice will be over in a minute." Debbie nodded in Janice's direction. "I'm going to see if she can join us for dinner too."

"Probably not. This is Saturday, after all, and they are likely busy for dinner," Susan stated.

"Yes, but I thought I should ask, just in case." Debbie shrugged.

Thomas from the golf course walked over and

commented on Debbie's tribute to Henry. "That was very nice, what you said about our Henry. I still can't believe he's gone."

"Thanks, Thomas. Guess you'll have to find another handyman now. I was the one who suggested he stop in to see if you needed any help," Debbie said.

"Henry has done odd jobs for me in the past. I still chuckle when I remember the time I commented that he moved slower than molasses in January and he told me that at his age, he was amazed that he was still moving at all."

"That sounds like Henry." Brad chuckled. "He was slow and steady, but if he was doing any kind of a job, you knew it would be done right."

"Between the lodge, the ski hill, and the golf course, he was as busy as he wanted to be," Debbie said.

Susan added, "Don't forget that he came and helped me paint the new house before we moved in."

"I had forgotten about that. And, before today, I did not realize all the volunteer work he was doing for the Shriners and the legion." Debbie nodded.

"I also learned things about Henry today. I guess you never truly know everything about people, and you don't realize how many lives one person has touched," Brad commented.

"Hey guys, how's the lunch?" Janice asked as she joined them.

"Good. We are thinking about making a reservation for dinner and wondered if you were working or if you could join us," Debbie asked.

"Sorry, guys. I am working, but thanks for asking," Janice said. "But I can make the reservation for you if you'd like."

"We're in," Susan said as she dumped her phone back into her purse. "I just spoke with Keith, and he'll be here in half an hour."

"So, a table for four then?" Janice asked.

"Thanks, sis. That would be good," Debbie replied.

"Should we have invited John and Mike for dinner?" Brad asked.

"I imagine that they will probably just want to go home and crash when this is all over. But you could ask them if you like," Debbie added.

"You're probably right. If it were me, I'd get takeout and go home and get into my pajama bottoms," Brad said.

"I know they are both heading back to the city tomorrow," Susan offered. "I have both of their contact information, and we will stay in touch by phone and email."

"Do you have anyone in mind that you want to show the house to?" Debbie asked.

"A couple of buyers, yes, and if neither of them is interested, I will do an open house in a few weeks' time."

"The crowd is thinning out. What do you say we go into the lounge until our table is ready?" Brad suggested.

Debbie took his hand and followed him. "You are good at lightening the mood," she said as she squeezed his hand.

As they were seated in the bar and had drinks delivered, Janice told Susan about the service she had missed.

"It was a nice celebration of Henry's life. The boys really did a good job. Don't you think so?" Debbie asked Brad.

"They sure did. Thanks to you. You do know how to put on a good show, regardless of whether it's a funeral or a party. You are great at organizing events, and the guys knew you were the right person to help them."

"Debbie has always been good at organizing things. Even as a kid, she was always hosting little tea parties and things," Susan said.

"Oh shush, the both of you. It just comes naturally to me. I like to plan things out and see them come to fruition. I love nothing better than when a good plan comes together."

"Here you guys are. How was the service for poor old Henry?" Keith asked as he took the last seat.

Susan brushed some sawdust out of his hair. "You were out in the woodshop, weren't you?"

He chuckled. "How could you tell?"

"It was very nice. Sad, but nice. I am sure going to miss Henry. He was so easygoing, so laid back, that you couldn't help but like him," Debbie said as she took a drink.

"He worked at such a slow pace, it's a wonder he ever got anything finished," Keith suggested.

"Slow but steady. He took his time sure, but you knew when he did finish that it was done right," Brad stated. "I think we should do a cheer to Henry. To a life well lived and the friends left behind. Cheers to you, Henry Miller. May you rest in peace."

EIGHTEEN

Sunday morning, Debbie woke up to total silence. She rubbed the sleep from her eyes, straining to hear something, anything. It took her a moment to realize the house was dead quiet.

She headed downstairs to see where everyone was. Usually Sunday morning, her bed was full of her husband and kids, but this morning, the house was eerily silent.

She went into the kitchen and turned the kettle on and then looked in the driveway. Brad's truck was still there, so they must be home. Debbie headed to look out the back door.

The three of them were there, knee-deep, digging in the mud. By the looks of the castle they were making, they had been at it for a while. Debbie went back to retrieve her camera. She quietly opened the back door and took a few snapshots of her family. The sound of giggles and laughter filled the backyard up as much as the morning sun.

Brad looked up and saw her in the doorway. He gave her a knowing smile and went back to his digging.

The kettle was whistling in the kitchen, and as Debbie was headed to turn it off, the phone rang.

Debbie looked at the caller ID. "Good morning, Val. How are you this fine morning?"

"Just peachy. How about you?" Val asked.

"I'm literally just up. The house is in complete silence. Brad and the kids are in the backyard making mud castles."

"My house is quiet too. James has taken Timmy fishing. So, what do you guys have planned for today?"

"Not sure yet. I imagine Brad will be cutting grass at some point today."

"James suggested I call and invite you all for dinner at the resort tonight."

"Thanks, that is very nice, but we were just there last night."

"Oh, what was the occasion?"

"Yesterday was Henry's celebration of life, and Susan and Keith joined us for dinner."

"I heard about poor old Henry. He's in a much better place now, I bet."

"I would think so. Anyway, let's plan dinner for another time. Or better yet, I'll ask Brad if he wants to BBQ steaks for dinner, and you guys could just come over here. But I'd better ask him about his plans before I make the invitation official."

"That would be alright, I guess. As long as I don't have to cook, I'm happy," Val agreed. "Talk to Brad and call me back. Later."

Debbie made her tea and was sitting at the counter when her troops came charging in.

"Stop. Not one step further," Brad firmly stated. "For just one second, stop and think about the mud you are both about to track into a clean house. Don't you think we should remove our dirty clothes before we go any further?"

Debbie came around the corner and took one look at her family. All three of them were covered in mud.

"Morning all. Could I make a suggestion? You all strip down to your undies and let Daddy take you both upstairs for a quick bath. That includes washing the mud out of Ben's hair."

"Yes, Mommy. You need to go see the castle we made in the backyard. It's so cool. The workers are sure going to be surprised in the morning," Ben told her.

"I surely will. Now, out of all those muddy clothes, please. You too, Daddy. Your jeans are filthy."

"Sorry, hun. We might be muddy, but we had fun, didn't we kids?"

"We sure did." Ben could hardly contain his excitement.

"How about you, Becky? Was it fun building your castle?" Debbie asked.

"I got to be the fireman," she answered.

"You mean foreman, sweetie. That's the boss on the project," Brad said.

The kids raced up the stairs, but before Brad left, he reached over and kissed his wife. "Morning, beautiful. I'll be down to cook breakfast shortly."

Once the baths were all done and her family was back to normal, Brad made them all a big breakfast.

"Val called and invited us out to the lodge for dinner. I suggested perhaps we could have BBQ steaks over here instead. What do you think? What are our plans for today?" Debbie asked while she set the table for breakfast.

"Why don't we go there and let James BBQ? I'm already cooking brunch," Brad commented.

"Val never suggested that."

"Well, I guess if you want me to, I can cook. But I'll suggest to James that he also has a BBQ. Just saying."

"Sounds good, but one of us will need to run into town for some groceries."

"You are hoping I will volunteer, aren't you?"

"You know me too well. If we are having steaks and burgers, I have a lot of things to do beforehand. I'll make you a list."

"When do you think I will find time to cut the grass?"

"I'm sure you will have time this afternoon." She winked at him.

They had just finished brunch and Debbie was clearing the dishes when there was a knock on the door. She glanced at Brad, who was up to his elbows in dishwater. "You expecting anyone?" she asked.

Brad shrugged and shook his head. Debbie opened the door.

"Good morning. Hope we are not too early," John said. "These are for you." He handed her a very large bouquet of flowers from the celebration of life.

"They are so beautiful. Thanks so much. Come on in. Brad, look at the flowers the guys brought me."

"Very nice. Do you guys have time for a coffee?" Brad asked.

"No, thanks. We are just heading home to the city but wanted to drop these flowers off and thank you for all your kindness," Mike offered.

"That's what friends are for. It's no trouble," Brad said.

"Here is our contact info in case you need to reach either of us with anything regarding the house. You are probably better off trying me first as I sit at my desk all day, while Mike is usually on the road," John suggested.

"Good to know. I am sure there won't be any issues. I'll keep the grass cut and make sure the place is presentable for Susan to show it." Brad took the cards John offered.

"Alright then, we are off. Thanks again to you both for

everything. Your kindness is so very appreciated." Mike stepped forward, shook Brad's hand, and hugged Debbie. John did the same.

As soon as the guys left, Brad took her list and got ready to head into town. He asked the kids if they wanted to go with him, but they chose to watch cartoons, so he went alone.

Debbie had to call Val. She had thought about what Brad said, and he was right. They did have a BBQ at their house. But they never put forward the invitation. Any time Val and James invited them, it was always to the resort. Maybe James didn't like to cook either. According to Val, he didn't do anything around the house. Debbie picked up her cell phone and hit the speed dial for Val's number. "Hey, what are you up to?"

"Doing a week's worth of laundry, changing beds, vacuuming, just the usual weekend housework," Val explained.

"I talked to Brad, and he is going to BBQ for dinner. I just sent him to town to pick up steaks and a few other things."

"Sounds great. What time should we come over?"

"Well, he has to cut the grass, so I would think any time after five."

"I'll bring the wine."

"Just for you. I'm on the wagon, remember."

"Oh yeah, sorry. I forgot you're knocked up again."

"Oh, Val. You do have a way with words. I'll see you later then."

Val sounded as if she wasn't enjoying being a wife and mother, and Debbie found herself wondering why, but she couldn't take responsibility for that. Val's happiness was up to Val. Although Debbie felt a bit sorry for her, it wasn't her problem. Val made her own choices, and now she had to live with the consequences. Debbie also felt bad for James. He was such a laid back, easygoing guy that he probably had a hard time living with Val. Debbie loved her dearly, but sometimes she had to wonder about her friend.

Later that afternoon, Brad was just putting the lawn mower away when James, Val, and Timmy arrived. Val headed straight to the house, but the guys went to the backyard.

"Hello, we're here," Val called from the doorway.

"Come on in here, girl." Debbie was drying her hands as Val came around the corner.

Val dropped the bottle of wine on the counter and gave Debbie a big hug. "It's so nice to see you, little momma. You are definitely starting to show."

"Thanks, I think." Debbie brought Val a wine glass. "Did you get all your chores done?"

"Yes, I swear, I work like a dog all week at my job and like a slave all weekend at my house."

Val was sure wound up. She was always a bit sarcastic, but she was taking it to a whole other level. "Doesn't James help with any of the household chores?" Debbie asked.

"Only if I get mad and yell at him, and now Timmy is following in his father's footsteps. I swear, the laundry hamper is sitting right there, but neither one of them can hit it."

"I guess I am lucky. Brad will help without me even asking."

"You have no idea how lucky you are. I bet Brad cooked you brunch today, didn't he?"

"Yes, he cooks every Sunday morning. He likes cooking, and we like eating, so it's all good."

"James thinks cooking is a woman's job. It's beneath him. He cuts grass, shovels snow, and watches TV. Oh yeah, and he drinks beer. That's his job."

Val sounded like she needed a vacation. "Have you tried to talk to him about it?" Debbie asked. "Maybe suggest he help out or take a little more interest in his home life?"

"Like I said, he only helps if I get mad and yell at him. And Timmy is getting to be just as bad."

A while later, Brad cooked the steaks and burgers, and everyone enjoyed their meal. Debbie made a mental note to watch Val and James interact with each other during the dinner. She felt that Val was trying, but James seemed oblivious to everything going on. Val softened when she focused on Timmy but was more businesslike around James.

After James and Val had gone home and the kids were bathed and tucked in for the night, Brad and Debbie enjoyed a tea together on the couch.

"I get the feeling that Val isn't that happy. She says that James does absolutely nothing to help around the house. Hell, he can't even throw dirty clothes into a hamper. I'm so glad you are not like that."

"James is an only child, and he was never made to do any of that stuff for himself. My parents taught me that we all work together for a common goal."

"I must remember to thank your mother for raising such a good son."

NINETEEN

Tea in hand, Debbie stood looking out the back door. The cement pillars were poured, and the guys had already started the framing. Now that the framing was up on the ground level, Debbie could see just how big the addition would be. Even from the inside of the door, she could hear the sound of skill saws, drills, and hammers. Things were starting to take shape.

The place looked like it was big enough for six rooms and two washrooms. It reminded her of the resort's upper level. If she was being honest with herself, she was starting to get a bit excited but still doubtful. She blamed her pregnancy hormones for her changing thoughts.

It was after lunch before Brad popped in. "Hi, babe. How's your day going?"

"Good. Hey, before I forget, what are you planning to do with all the big rocks you dug out?"

"When we are done excavating, I will take them to the guy where I buy all my gravel and stone. He will give me a credit on future material. Why do you ask?"

"I was wondering if you could make me a small waterfall at the top end of the pool. Here, come look at these pictures." Debbie turned her laptop for him to see. "I really like this one. See how the water cascades down over the rocks and into the pool? Not only is it beautiful, but it will help aerate the pool."

"I like it. That's a very good idea, hun. I really like this one here. It looks very natural. We can build a little hill up above the pool, insert a liner and a big pump, and voila, you have a small waterfall. Yes, I think we can do that easily enough."

"Great. I like it too. I think it will make our pool different from any other pools around." Debbie leaned over and kissed him. "If you are digging the hole for the pool now, are you planning to pour the foundation right away?"

"Yes, I think so. But we won't be putting water in until spring. This way, the cement will have lots of time to dry."

"Sounds good. How did your lunch meeting go?"

"Great. I have a new cottage to build in the spring on the back side of the lake. I have been thinking about buying a barge and using my own lake access road to shuttle the supplies over. Or I could see if Phil has a spot on his dock for me. I just don't like having deliveries made to the dock when he has guests there."

"Could you not have all the supplies delivered before he gets busy?"

"Yes and no. I could try, but it's a big two-story cottage, and even when you order all the materials in advance, if the client decides he wants a hardwood floor rather than pine, then I would need to take back the pine and bring in the new hardwood. There are always deliveries over the course of the build."

"So, if you had your own barge, you could get the materials as you need them and not disturb anyone but the neighbors."

"Exactly. I think I am going to go over and talk to Jerry and Sheila. Why don't you come with me? We can go for a walk and just stop in."

"You want to do that now?"

"Sure, there's no time like the present," Brad suggested.

Debbie and Brad walked down to the lake on their access road. The neighbors' homes weren't visible because of the row of cedar trees Brad had planted there years before.

Brad handed her a measuring tape. "Here, hun, could you stand right here and hold this. I want to see how wide this road actually is." The tape unrolled as he walked across the roadway.

"If you're going to put me to work, you'll need my personal info to put me on your payroll," Debbie said with a chuckle. "Or, perhaps we could just take the payment out in trade."

Brad didn't reply to her silly comment. "I will need to widen out the road for the delivery trucks, but I have lots of room on this side."

"Once you widen the road, then what else do you need?"

"I'd still need a barge. I know I am not allowed to put in a dock because it is only an access road, but the barge could be tethered to the shore."

"Will you rent a barge or make your own?"

"Going forward, it would probably be cheaper to just build one of my own. I haven't had a chance to cost it out yet. But common sense tells me that if you borrow or rent something more than three times, you should get one of your own."

They walked hand in hand back up the roadway and saw that Jerry was in his garage. "Let's go say hi to Jerry," Brad suggested.

"Well, hello, stranger." Brad shook Jerry's hand. "How's everything?"

"Hello to you both. Let me go tell Sheila you are here."

Debbie looked around the garage and was glad they didn't have one. It was just another place to collect junk, and the mess would get on her nerves.

"Hello, this is a nice surprise," Sheila said.

"We were just out for a walk. Hope we didn't catch you at a bad time," Debbie said.

"No, not at all."

"Is it alright if I look at your flower beds," Debbie asked. "They are all so beautiful."

"Sure, let me show you around." Sheila led the way out into the yard.

After Sheila showed Debbie around, she invited her into the house for a coffee. "I'd have a tea if it's not too much trouble. Brad will always have a coffee."

The men joined them and the four of them sat around the kitchen table, where Brad told Jerry about their new addition.

"We are hoping to get the pool poured this fall. Probably in the next couple of days," Brad explained. "I hope the incessant beeping from the equipment isn't driving you crazy over here."

"No, not really. We didn't even hear it until yesterday," Jerry stated.

"Until then, they were working behind the house, and now they are digging the pool beside the house."

"I wish we had a pool," Sheila said wishfully. "I have always enjoyed a cool swim on a hot day."

"So have you got any new homes to build for next year?" Jerry asked.

"Just starting to take bookings. I just had lunch with a guy who is building a huge two-story cottage on the back side of our lake," Brad answered. "You know, I was thinking, I have two choices for getting material across the lake. I can rent a barge and dock space from the lodge like I have done in the past, or I could buy my own barge and use my access road. I was just over there and would need to widen it about three feet, on the other side, for the big trucks. I am wondering if it would bother you folks any if there were deliveries to the shoreline from the access road?"

"I don't see a problem with that. Those cedars block the view, so the only disturbance to us would be the beeping of the truck backing up," Jerry stated.

"And we are going to be away most of the summer anyway," Sheila reminded him. "We just bought that big RV parked in the backyard and are planning some trips this summer."

"Yes, I saw it. Looks like a very nice one," Debbie said.

"Now that the kids are gone, we have decided to do some exploring while we still have our health. By the way, that was a beautiful service for Henry. Debbie, your speech was very nice, very heartfelt," Sheila said.

"Thank you. It was directly from my heart. I, for one, am going to miss him popping in for a coffee or lunch," Debbie said. "Hun, as soon as you finish your coffee, we should get going. The bus will be here any minute."

"Thanks for the coffee. Anytime you want to pop over and see the new addition, just come on by. If my truck is in the driveway, I am there somewhere," Brad suggested as she stood to go. "And if you need someone to water plants or cut grass while you are away, I could do that. Just let me know if I can be of any help."

"Thanks, but we already have someone lined up to take care of things around here. But we would definitely like to come see your new addition. We have both been curious about what's going on over there," Jerry admitted.

"Stop by anytime."

As they made their way back to the house, Debbie saw the school bus leaving their road. "The kids have never come home and not found me there. It will be interesting to see their reactions."

"There you are. Mommy, you scared us. Where have you been?" Ben demanded.

"We just went for a walk. We're here now. Can a mom not get any loving around here?" Debbie stood, looking neglected.

Both kids gave her the usual hugs and kisses, and this time, Brad got in on the hugs and kisses too.

"I have to go check on my jobsites. Do you kids want to go with Daddy or would you rather watch your cartoons?" Brad asked.

The cartoons won out. "See you all later." Brad gave Debbie a kiss and was gone again.

The kids both took a snack and headed to the living room. Debbie went to the kitchen to finish prepping dinner. She was thinking about Jerry and Sheila. She was happy for them but, at the same time, a bit envious. They had raised their kids and were now going to enjoy their retirement years. She wondered if Brad and she would be able to do something like that when their kids were all grown up and moved out. Ugh, it was good to dream, but that was still twenty years down the road. Right now, she had dinner to prepare.

Brad was gone for over an hour before he came rushing

in. "Hun, you are never going to believe this. The police just called; they found all my materials that Jamie stole."

"That's fantastic. How did they find them?"

"They called all the numbers in Jamie's phone and pretended they were Jamie and had more materials to hide. One guy said he'd meet him at the barn in an hour. They had his phone number, so they tracked down his address. An hour later, they went to the barn, arrested the guy, and found all my missing materials."

"Wow, I figured you'd never see them again. The police did a good job and arrested another felon in the process. That's amazing. So how do you get your stuff back?"

"The officer didn't say. I'll call him back tomorrow and find out. I am guessing they will probably have to hold it as evidence for a while, but sooner or later, I will be able to get it back."

"You, sir, are one lucky man. Three good things have happened to you today!"

"Three things? What three things?"

"You got a new cottage to build in the spring, Jerry and Sheila don't care if you use the access road for your deliveries, and the police found the stolen materials. Good things happen in threes. That's your three for today."

Brad gave her a crooked smile. "I still see three more good things. My amazing wife is going to cook me a nice dinner that I will share with my great kids, I am going to get this estimate done for Sharon to type up, and later, I am going to make love to my beautiful wife."

"If you don't fall asleep before she gets there." Debbie laughed at the surprised expression on his face. "Dinner in ten minutes."

After dinner, Brad worked on his latest estimate and the

kids watched a movie in the living room. When the movie finished, Ben asked for another movie. Debbie suggested they instead color or play with their toys.

"Oh, Mommy, we have played with all these toys. We have them all played out," Becky stated.

"So, I can give all these toys away to some other kids who might like them?" Debbie asked.

"No, don't do that. We still play with them," Becky said.

"Tell you what. I am about to make some cookies and could use some help with the measuring and the stirring. Why don't you two go wash your hands and come help me for a while?"

"Yay," they yelled as they raced to the bathroom to wash up.

Debbie got all the ingredients down from the cupboards and pulled two stools up to the counter. The kids were quite interested in what she was doing. She showed them how to measure things out and let them stir it all together. Debbie tasted the dough. "Chocolate chip is one of my favorites."

"Can I taste it, Mommy?" Ben asked.

"You sure can. Just stick your finger in and scoop a little bit of dough like this." Debbie showed him. "Becky, would you like to try some?"

"No, that's yucky. There are raw eggs in there." Becky gave her mother a gagging look.

Becky was still talking, so Debbie took a bit of dough on her finger and inserted it into Becky's mouth.

"Umm, that's not bad," Becky admitted.

"We have to make sure they taste good before we waste the power to cook them," Debbie stated. "I think they are good enough to bake. Don't you?"

"Yes," they both said in unison.

She showed them how to spoon the dough onto the trays. Ben sat in front of the oven door for the ten minutes it took the batch of cookies to bake. As soon as they came out of the oven, Ben wanted one.

"You will have to wait till they cool off a bit. If you were to eat it now, it would burn your mouth. I am going to put them onto this rack to cool while another pan bakes."

"But I'll be careful, Mommy," Ben stated.

"You can have one in a minute, but first, they need to cool down. Now, do you want to make some sugar cookies?"

"Yes," Becky answered. "They are my favorite."

Again, Debbie showed them how to measure and then mix all the ingredients together. "Now, with sugar cookies, you need to roll them into little balls like this, and then we will flatten them and put sprinkles on them before we bake them."

"What's going on in here? I smell chocolate chip cookies," Brad said.

"We are just waiting for them to cool. And now we are making sugar cookies with sprinkles," Ben informed him.

"Well, I am going to sit right here and wait for my cookie."

Debbie took the second tray of cookies from the oven and transferred them to the cooling racks.

Once the sugar cookies were baked, Brad poured four glasses of milk, and they sat around the dining room table and enjoyed their cookies.

"These cookies are the best cookies in the whole world. And we made them ourselves," Ben stated proudly.

"And imagine you take them to school and trade them for other cookies instead," Brad pointed out.

"Not these ones, Daddy. These are the best."

"Let's go up and do our baths and get into jammies. It's getting late," Debbie said.

"Why don't I do baths while you tidy up the kitchen?" Brad offered.

"Thank you. That would be nice." Debbie gave him her best smile. *I bet James would never do that with Timmy.*

Once the kids were in bed and had each had a bedtime story read to them, Brad came downstairs and joined Debbie.

"Thanks for the tea." Brad pulled Debbie up beside him on the couch.

"Thanks for bathing the kids. I was just thinking that James and Timmy are missing out on a lot of good stuff like that."

"It was fun watching the kids help you with the cookies. I think they are getting old enough to start wanting to learn new things, don't you?"

"Yes, I do. I wouldn't let them run the stove, but they could learn to use the microwave. And I think we need some new toys, perhaps for more older kids. All the toys they have are quite juvenile."

"Whatever you think they need is fine with me." Brad kissed her. "I was also thinking that they need a dog."

"A dog, please no. We will have a new baby in the house in a few months, and I will not have time to house-train a puppy."

"Maybe we could get one that is already trained."

"No, thanks. Ask me again in five years."

"What about a hamster or a cat?"

"Where is this idea about pets coming from?"

"I had pets growing up. I had this one dog called Lucky, and he was my best friend for ten years or so. I was so sad when he died. Dad had a burial for him in the backyard and everything. It taught me a lot about responsibility. It was up to me to feed him, bathe him, brush him, and just take care of him. I just think the kids are missing out, and if we were going to get a dog, now would be the time to do so. Then the puppy would grow up with the kids."

"I was raised at the resort, so I couldn't have pets. I see what you are saying. I just don't know if I can handle the twins, a new baby, and a new puppy too."

"Hun, you don't have to do it all alone. I can help too."

"Yes, I know you can. I just don't know if I am ready for potty training a puppy and a toddler too."

"It only takes about two weeks of strict discipline to house-train a puppy. If we got a puppy now, it would be trained before this baby is even born. Just think about it, please? Just think of how much it would add to the kids' lives, to all our lives for that matter. If not, perhaps maybe a kitten. They come already housebroken. Give them a litter box and they are trained."

"I can see you are serious about this. But this is all new to me. Let me think on it for a couple of years, I mean days." Debbie chuckled.

"I hope you do. The kids are old enough now that they could help take care of a cat or a dog."

"I understand what you are saying. I just don't know if now is the right time to get a pet."

"That's only because you have never had one. A dog becomes part of the family. All they require is food and water, and in return, they bring joy and an endless supply of unconditional love. I believe that a dog would help teach the kids about responsibilities and be a good protector when they are outside playing."

"You don't need to sell me. I said I would think about it, and I will," Debbie said with a touch of annoyance.

"It was just a thought. Just so you know, my vote is yes."

TWENTY

Debbie had just finished tidying the kitchen when Sharon arrived. She was babysitting the kids for the evening as Debbie and Brad were going to the lodge for Susan's surprise birthday party.

"Come on in," Debbie said as she dried her hands and hung the tea towel over the oven door to dry.

"So, what are the kids and I going to be doing tonight?" Sharon asked.

"I have some new coloring books and a new movie for them before bedtime. They will both need a bath, and there are bedtime stories to read."

"Sounds good. Is your party for your sister still a surprise?"

"I think so. She called last night and wanted to make plans for us all tonight. I had to tell her a fib that we were going out with friends and would get together with her Thursday night for her birthday. She told me that Keith is taking her out on Thursday, so we made plans to get together next weekend. So, I think she will be surprised. At least I hope she is."

"Nice to see you, Sharon," Brad said as he came through the back door.

"How's the new addition coming along?" Sharon asked.

"Good. The framing is almost finished. I think it's going to be done this week."

"Brad, are you going to change your shirt? I still have

to get changed, and we should leave here in about ten minutes," Debbie interrupted.

"Yes, I will. I'll race you upstairs," he said as he gave her a gentle slap on her bum.

"He's in a silly mood tonight," Sharon stated.

"He's been in a good mood ever since he found out that the police have recovered all his stolen materials."

"That's amazing. Well, you go get ready. I am going to make myself a tea."

When Debbie entered the bedroom upstairs, Brad was standing bare-chested in the closet doorway, trying to decide which shirt he wanted to wear. Brad pulled her into his arms. "We could be fashionably late if you want to fool around a bit."

As he kissed her playfully, Debbie gently pushed him away. "Not now, cowboy. We need to get going."

"Ugh, can't a guy have any fun around here? Good thing you're so cute."

"If you are a good boy, maybe we can have some fun when we get home." Debbie gave him her best smile.

Brad gave her his pouty lip look and went back to choosing a shirt.

"Could you help me with this zipper?" Debbie asked as she turned her back to him.

Brad planted little kisses down the side of her neck. "You sure I can't talk you into some lovin' before we leave?"

"As tempting as that is, we have to get going. Now zip me up, please."

"Well alright, if I have to. But I will be glad to help you unzip this dress later."

"Sure, cowboy. That's a deal."

Brad and Debbie walked down the stairs, hand in hand. They said their goodbyes to the kids and Sharon and headed out.

At the resort, Brad helped Debbie out of the van and pulled her close for a quick kiss. "You look beautiful tonight."

"Thanks. You're quite handsome yourself."

They walked hand in hand into the lodge.

"There you are. I was wondering when you would get here," Janice said. "Wait till you see all the decorations."

As they followed her into the banquet room, Brad asked, "Is this still a surprise for Susan?"

"As far as I know, it is," Janice replied.

Debbie stood in the doorway for a moment, taking it all in, the beautiful decorations, the beautiful flowers, the sound of soft jazz playing in the background, and all the colorful balloons. "Oh, Janice, the room looks amazing. I love all the fall colors. You are so gifted at decorating. Susan is going to love all the balloons. Where did you ever find orange and yellow ones?" Debbie asked. Janice was so talented. She could take anything mundane and turn it into a beautiful masterpiece. Debbie wished she had some of that talent, but no, she had none. But she was glad that she "had a guy," or in this case, she had a sister who was creatively talented.

"I have a supplier that can find me almost anything." Janice smiled.

"Of course you do. As usual, you have done an amazing job," Debbie said. "So, what can I do to help?"

"You can sit and relax, that's all," Janice told her sister. "Brad, if you want anything from the bar, help yourself. Ted, the bartender, won't come in till seven o'clock."

"Can I get you ladies anything while I'm here?" Brad asked.

"I'll have a white wine, and what about you, sis?" Janice asked Debbie.

"A sparkling ginger ale please."

"Janice, the room looks amazing," Nancy said as she walked into the room.

"Thanks. Susan likes balloons, if you're wondering why there are so many," Janice explained.

"I just wanted to come in and say hi to Brad and Debbie before the party gets started." Nancy sat down at the table. "How's everything going? Are you over your morning sickness yet?"

"As long as I stay away from coffee, I seem to be alright. This being pregnant is not for the faint of heart. I can't have coffee, I can't have wine, I can't see to tie my own shoes, and I always have to pee," Debbie stated.

"But you are going to be rewarded in just a few months," Brad said and kissed her forehead.

"There you are. I wondered where you got to," Phil said to his wife.

"Here I am," Nancy answered. "I wanted to see Janice's decorations and Brad and Debbie."

"Hey, buddy, how's it going?" Phil asked Brad. "How's that brother of mine working out for you?"

"He's doing fine. Kind of reminds me of you."

"I know he's a hard worker, but is he getting the hang of the building business?"

"Seems to be. I only have to show him something once, and he's got it," Brad said.

"That's good. I'm sure he will do a good job for you.

Guess I better get back to the kitchen. Just wanted to pop in to say hi."

"You'll come join us when the kitchen closes, won't you?" Debbie asked.

"Yes, we will," Nancy said as she took Phil's hand, and they left together.

"So, what else do we have to do to be ready for this party?" Brad asked.

"The only thing left is to bring the food and the cake from the cold room. I could use your help with that, but not until about ten o'clock. Other than that, I think we are ready."

Katie and Jeremy came through the door. "Hello, everyone," Katie said. "Aunt Debbie, you are absolutely glowing. And Aunt Janice, you are beautiful as always."

"What about me? Doesn't your Uncle Brad deserve a hello?"

"Hello, Uncle Brad. You are as handsome as ever," Katie said as she gave him a hug.

"That's better," Brad responded. "You look beautiful yourself, young lady. How are you, Jeremy?"

"Fine, thanks." Jeremy helped Katie with her jacket.

Nancy and Robert Martin from the ski hill had arrived moments before Thomas Townsend from the golf course. "Hello, everyone," Nancy said. "Where are you putting the gifts?"

For the next half an hour, a steady flow of friends arrived, and by seven o'clock, over fifty people mingled around the banquet room.

"Brad, I don't think you have met my fiancé, Mark, yet. Mark, this is Debbie's husband, Brad Mumford." Janice made the introductions.

Brad extended his hand. "Nice to meet you."

"Come sit here with us," Debbie invited. "Janice is sitting over there, but you know she doesn't sit down much."

"Thanks." Mark sat down beside Janice's empty chair. "I see the bar is open. Does anyone need anything while I'm up there?" Mark asked.

The music was playing, the wine was flowing, and everyone was having a great time. Gail came over to Janice and informed her that Susan and Keith had just arrived.

Janice turned the music off and asked for everyone's attention. "Susan and Keith are sitting in the bar. Gail is going to bring her in, and if we are quiet until she gets here, we can all yell 'Surprise.' Are we ready? Alright, Gail, bring her in."

"SURPRISE," everyone yelled in unison. Susan just stood in the doorway, looking around at all the decorations. It wasn't until she saw the happy birthday banner and the big five and big zero balloons that it registered that this surprise was for her.

"Oh, my goodness, is this all for me? I am shocked. I had no idea. I wondered why Keith insisted that he wanted to come here for a drink tonight," Susan said.

"Did we actually manage to surprise you?" Janice hugged her sister.

"Yes, you certainly did. I had no idea." Susan hugged Debbie. "I thought you had plans with Val and James tonight."

"We do. They're here." Debbie chuckled.

Brad handed Susan a glass of red wine and Keith a beer. "Happy birthday, Sue." Brad kissed her cheek.

"Thanks, Brad. I love the decorations. Janice, where did you get all the balloons? They are beautiful."

"I have my sources. We have seats for you here at our table whenever you are ready." Janice indicated where they could sit.

"I'll set my purse down, but I want to mingle with everyone first," Susan said.

"That's what I figured," Janice replied.

They spent the rest of the night dancing and having fun. At ten o'clock, trays of food were served: sandwiches, cheese and crackers, an assortment of pickles, veggies and dip, fancy desserts, and a huge birthday cake.

Janice lowered the music to make the announcement about the buffet being ready. "Please come help yourselves. We'll give you all time to eat, and then in about fifteen minutes or so, Susan can blow out the candles on her cake, and we can all have some."

As they were all sitting, eating, and chatting, Debbie turned to Janice. "I notice the music has changed to smooth jazz. Nice touch."

"I learned from the best," Janice responded.

"Learned what?" Susan asked.

"Debbie taught me that when people are eating, you put on quieter music so they will stop dancing and actually sit still long enough to eat," Janice explained.

"Oh, I never even noticed. It always amazes me all the little things you two know about the hospitality business."

"I don't know about the rest of you, but I am ready for some cake." Janice stood. "Brad and Keith, can you boys help me, please?"

Mark also stood up. "Can I help, hun?"

"Thanks, but I think we've got it," Janice answered.

Brad and Keith carried the cake over and set it in front of Susan. Everyone sang "Happy Birthday" while Susan blushed.

Janice had done a nice job decorating it, and Debbie made sure to get some pictures of it before Susan cut it up.

While they were eating their cake, Jeremy led Katie to the middle of the empty dance floor.

"Ladies and gentlemen. If I could interrupt this evening's festivities, there is a very important question I need to ask this beautiful young lady," Jeremy loudly stated to the crowd.

Everyone quieted down and looked at the couple on the dance floor. As Jeremy got down on one knee, Katie stood with the same surprised look that her mother had earlier.

"Katie, love of my life. From the first time I saw you, here in this very lodge, I knew you were my future. Over these past few years, I am only stronger in my convictions. I look forward to every day we can spend together, and I know I want to spend every day for the rest of my life with you by my side. Katie, make me the happiest man on earth and say yes. Will you marry me?"

"YES! Yes, I will marry you," Katie answered before he kissed her. The crowd whistled and cheered.

"Did you guys know he was going to propose?" Debbie asked.

Susan answered, "I knew he would get around to it sooner or later, but I didn't know he was going to ask tonight. Hell, I didn't even know there was a party tonight."

"He asked my permission to marry my little girl about a month ago, so I knew he was going to ask her, but I didn't know it would be tonight," Keith said.

The sweet gesture reminded Debbie of how Brad had

proposed to her in this very room, at Janice's wedding. "Well, I, for one, think they are the cutest couple. I think it's so sweet that they finish each other's sentences. Brad, let's go offer our congratulations to the happy couple."

"We'll all join you," Janice said as the whole table stood up and followed her onto the dance floor to where Jeremy and Katie were standing.

The party continued until Ted announced that it was last call for alcohol. Brad ordered a round for the table. Everyone was in such a festive mood, and no one wanted to leave, but Debbie was tired.

Brad helped Debbie with her coat as they said their goodbyes to everyone. They left hand in hand, and Debbie drove the short ride home while Brad prattled on about how much fun he had at the party.

When they got to the house, the kids were in bed sleeping and Sharon was sitting and knitting. Sharon said goodnight, and Debbie took Brad's hand and led him upstairs.

After they made love, Debbie curled up on his chest. As she was falling asleep, the thought crossed her mind, *We don't need big fancy parties; we just need each other.*

TWENTY-ONE

The following morning, after the kids left for school and Brad stopped at the house to top up his morning coffee, Debbie saw an opportunity to talk with him about the whole Val and James situation. "You know, I was watching Val and James at Susan's party. They seemed to be happy, seemed to be having a good time. But I know how unhappy Val really is. She is not enjoying the domestic part of her marriage. I wish there was something I could say or do to help her."

"I think it's sweet that you are worried about your friend, but the only one who can help Val be happy is Val. I sometimes think that she is one of those people who would rather have something to bitch about than try to fix it," Brad said as he unrolled a set of blueprints.

"I know what you mean. I told her that she should have Sunday family days like we do. She didn't seem interested in that idea. I love our Sundays and look forward to them. We spend quality time with our kids doing something that we all love to do. I will gladly do the cooking and the cleaning knowing that Sunday is a family fun day. I do love you so very much for carving time out for us."

"My family is my number one priority, now and for always." Brad helped himself to coffee and went back to the dining room table to study his blueprints. "I actually stopped by to let you know that the framing is almost done. Would you like to have a walk-through?"

"What do you mean by a walk-through? If you mean we can go see it, then yes, I would love to. Can we go now?"

Brad took her hand and led her down the hallway to the back door. "This door will eventually be gone. Out here, the office and the laundry room will both be extended, each by another six feet, with a door on each side. These two rooms are storage. I figured you would use the big one for your linens, sheets, towels and whatever, and the smaller one for storage or a pantry, whatever you need. There will be a set of stairs here, leading upstairs. Back here, this will be a solid wall. On your right will be one apartment. This room will be the living room with the windows looking out onto the pool area. The apartment on the other side is the same layout, but that window will look out to the lawn and the bush. And the kitchen will go here."

Debbie was happy that Brad explained the plans to her. Otherwise, she couldn't visualize it.

Brad was still holding her hand, leading her through the tour. "In here is the bedroom. You may think it's huge, and it is. But if we ever needed to, we could put a wall here and make it into two bedrooms. Then this room will be the bathroom, which will have a bathtub over there, the sink on this wall, and the toilet beside it, over there."

"I don't understand the framing here between the bedroom and the bathroom," Debbie said.

"That will be closet space. This area will be a bedroom closet accessible from the bedroom, and this smaller one will be a linen closet accessible from the bathroom side."

"Very clever. That's going to be a nice apartment. I think I would like to move in."

"Yes, they will be nice, but I'd rather you stay in the

house with me and the kids. There will be a door here that leads out to the lobby area. And now, up the stairs to the top bedrooms."

"So, there will be stairs on both ends then?" Debbie asked.

"Yes, exactly. These steps can be accessed from outside, and at the other end, they are in the hall which will lead to our kitchen. This small area will be a two-piece bathroom. On the other side will be a small storage closet. Next is a bedroom. All six rooms are basically the same. A bedroom and a small sitting area."

Don and another worker she didn't know were working. "Good morning, guys. I am getting the five-cent tour this morning. I'm Debbie, Brad's wife."

"This is Greg, and you already know Don," Brad said.

"Nice to meet you, Greg." Debbie stepped over a toolbox and extended her hand.

"Yes, ma'am. Nice to meet you too." Greg wiped his hand on his jeans before he took Debbie's.

"How are you, Don?" Debbie asked.

"Fine, thanks. What do you think so far?" Don asked.

"I can see the potential. I think it's going to be very nice," Debbie said. "I'll let you boys get back to work."

Brad continued on with his tour. "As I was saying, all six rooms are the same. At this end, there is a full bathroom with a shower, sink, and toilet. And this hole will be where the stairs will go down to the hallway off of our kitchen."

"Shouldn't that hole be covered for safety until the stairs are put in?" Debbie asked.

"No need. The only people up here are my guys, and they are aware. Besides, the steps are outside and will be installed in the next couple of days. So, that concludes the tour. What's your first impression?"

"Honestly, I don't really understand a lot of it. I will see it all better when the walls are up. I can see the basic layout, but I'll get a better impression later on." They headed to the other end of the hallway so they could take the stairs down to the ground-floor kitchen.

Back in the kitchen, Brad's phone rang while he refreshed his coffee. "I have to take this," he said as he kissed her and headed out the door. The kettle had just boiled, but Debbie was tempted to try a coffee. She lifted the coffee pot and inhaled the aroma. She wanted coffee so badly but didn't want to be sick. Reluctantly, she threw a teabag into her cup and added the hot water.

She took her tea over to her favorite spot at the bay window. She needed a moment to herself. As she sat looking out past the lawn, to the tree line brilliant with an array of colors, and the lake rippling from the wind, she never really noticed the beauty before her. She had too much weighing on her mind for her to simply enjoy the splendor of it all.

She wondered what was wrong with her. She should be excited about her new B&B and her new baby, but she wasn't. She couldn't muster up excitement for either. She knew she had to pull herself out of the funk she was in, but she didn't know how. She thought about asking Janice or Susan, but she didn't want to worry either of them.

Debbie blew the steam off the top of her tea and took a sip, considering who she could talk to. Janice was so in love that she had stars in her eyes. Debbie was happy for her and Mark, but with Janice's predictable track record, she had her doubts. And Susan was always hyper-focused on her real estate business. It even took priority over her beautiful family and her solid marriage. Susan loved selling homes and cottages. She was fond of saying that she sold dreams. She made people's dreams come true.

Debbie tried another sip of tea. She definitely didn't want to discuss this with Val, as she was busy playing with fire with her own troubles. She didn't seem interested in fixing her home life; she was too busy flirting with Steve. Debbie couldn't imagine how James had convinced Val to settle down. She didn't even know if money could fix all of Val's troubles. If Val could afford to hire nannies, maids, and butlers, would that solve her problems? Probably not. Brad was right: Val did prefer to have something to bitch about.

Self-doubt crept in, and Debbie began to wonder if others thought of her the same way. She regretted telling anyone about her thoughts on the new B&B and new baby.

Brad came in to refresh his coffee. "Deb, are you alright?" he asked. He had to repeat it to get her attention.

"I'm fine. Guess I was daydreaming?"

"What is my beautiful wife daydreaming about?"

"Nothing really, just thinking about the B&B and the new pool."

"Speaking of the new pool, could you print off that picture you showed me of the waterfall you want? I want to show it to the guy running the backhoe. We have the hill in place, and it would help him place the rocks if he could see a visual of what we want."

"I'll see if I can find it again." Debbie went to the kitchen counter and opened her laptop. After a few minutes, she found it. "Here it is. This is the one I liked. Is this the one you were thinking of?"

"I think so. There was another one with lights that looked similar. Keep looking, will you."

"This one?"

"Yes, that's the one. See the lights under the rocks. I like that look, I think, better than yours, which is almost the same but with lights."

"Do we really need lights? Do you plan on swimming in the dark?" Debbie gave him a puzzled look.

"Yes, wouldn't it be nice to be able to go for a swim after the kids are all asleep?"

"I guess so. I just never thought of that. Isn't that going to be expensive?"

"Not really. We have to run the water and electricity up to the pump, and we have lights around the pool, so it really wouldn't be much of an added expense."

"Alright then. Lights it is. But I still like the way these rocks are placed better in this picture." Debbie shrunk each picture small enough so that she could show both pictures side by side. "See here how the rocks go from biggest to smallest. I like that."

"I see what you're saying. We can have the best of both. Your rock pattern and my lights under the rocks."

"So, you'll place the rock now then?"

"Yes, might as well, while we have the backhoe here. And besides, the rocks will need time to settle a bit."

"Thanks for indulging my wishes." Debbie gave him a big smile. "It is good to have friends in the right places."

"Most clients do change their minds about things or add things to the project. It's just part of the building process. I expect clients to do things like that. I have learned to take it all in stride." Brad smiled back. "But I should warn you that when a client asks for changes, the price always goes up."

"Oh, I see. So, I guess I should be asking how much extra the waterfall is going to add to the cost of my project."

"Oh, I don't know. You already have the materials; the rocks are already available. It would just be the cost of the backhoe and the labor for the guy driving it, and the cost of the lights. Probably between five hundred and a thousand dollars."

"That's alright, then. When you look at the total cost for the complete project, a thousand is just a drop in the bucket. The picture is done. It's on your printer in the office."

"Thanks. I'll go get it and show it to the guy." Brad kissed her forehead. "We do make a great team, don't we?"

"We truly do."

TWENTY-TWO

"Morning, hun," Brad said as he leaned in for his kiss. "How are you feeling this morning?"

"Good, as long as I stay away from coffee." Debbie shrugged. "Someday, I will be able to have it again, but apparently, not yet."

Brad refilled his takeaway cup. "I'll have to drink your share for you then."

"You're too kind." Debbie noticed that Brad was very somber and looked defeated. "Everything alright? You look like you just lost your best friend."

"I have some bad news. The pool guy was just here, and he suggested we wait to pour the pool foundation till the spring. He thinks we can't take the chance of it drying this late in the year. We are expecting frost within the week."

"That's alright, isn't it? Either way, we will be enjoying our pool next summer."

"I know. I'm just disappointed. I thought we could at least get the foundation poured. But at least the excavation is done, and I know there aren't any giant rocks in the way." Brad shrugged.

"And the rocks are all in place for the waterfall. They will have time to settle in place."

"Yes, I really like the waterfall. It looks so natural."

"I agree. In the meantime, the guys can work on finishing our B&B," Debbie suggested.

"My guys have three projects to work on over the winter, as well as several indoor projects. We are going to reface a fireplace in a big cottage over on the next lake. I just had all the stonework delivered last week."

"Sounds interesting. I've been meaning to ask you how Don is working out."

"Good! He catches on quickly. I like him well enough."

"Do you plan on making him your assistant?"

"Not sure yet. I don't really need an assistant in the wintertime. All my jobs are lined up, and my guys know what they are doing. I need a supervisor in the summertime when I am busy meeting with clients and can't be available on the sites. I may promote him then, if he's still around."

"Do you think he may move on?" Debbie asked.

"Who knows? His life just exploded, and he is footloose and fancy-free at the moment. I think he'll stick around, but who knows. Time will tell."

Brad's phone rang, and he checked it but didn't answer. "Just a supplier. I'll call him back. You got any more of Chef's cinnamon buns left?"

"Check the cookie tin on the counter. I think there are still a couple left."

"Perfect. I love these things." Brad took a big bite for emphasis.

"Val called and invited us to the lodge for dinner on Friday night."

"Sounds good to me. What did you tell her?"

"I told her I would ask you and call her back, of course."

"I'm in, if you are. Is it adults only, or are we taking kids?"

"Don't know, she didn't say. I'll have to confirm with

her. You know, if there is ever a Sunday that you want to go fishing with James, you could. Then we could do something with the kids when you get home."

"I'm really not that big on fishing. I'd much rather spend the morning with you and the kids."

"That's so nice of you. We love spending the morning with you too. But if you did want to spend some time with your best friend, we'd understand."

"Thanks, but I am good. Sunday is the only day I get to lounge around and spend time with my family."

"It was just a thought. I sure hope those two can figure their crap out. I know for a fact that Val is not happy with her home life, and I don't see James doing anything about it. I wonder if he even knows there's a problem."

"I don't know. He's never mentioned anything to me about it." Brad shrugged.

"Perhaps as his best friend, you could bring it up to him?" Debbie turned the stove on for tea.

"No thank you, ma'am! I am smart enough to stay out of his marriage. I wish him all the best of luck, and if he ever wants to talk about it, that's fine, but I will never bring it up to him."

"Val brings it up to me almost every time we talk these days."

Brad's phone rang again. "I do need to answer this. See you later." He leaned over, kissed her forehead, and was gone again.

Debbie sat at the counter drinking her tea. She couldn't blame Brad for not wanting to get involved in James and Val's marriage. She didn't want to either, but Val kept bringing it up. If she spent half as much time and effort on her husband as she did on Steve, Val would be better off. She was impossible to please.

"Anybody home?" Janice called out.

"Morning, sis. Come on in."

"Look at you sitting here drinking tea, doing nothing. Usually, you would be running around making beds or vacuuming or doing something domestic."

"Brad just left. We were talking about having to postpone the pool's foundation till the spring."

"I can't wait to try out your pool. But I understand putting it off till spring. Probably a wise decision. The maple trees are almost done dropping their leaves, so you know snow is just around the corner," Janice said as she helped herself to a coffee. "What have you got for a snack?"

"Cinnamon buns in the cookie tin." Debbie pointed.

"Great, thanks. I just dug out our winter coats and boots yesterday."

"I have already done that. Not sure if the kids' stuff will still fit. I have been meaning to get them to try them on."

"You best be getting that figured out. Before you know it, they'll be needing winter coats."

"Don't you wish sometimes that we lived somewhere in a warmer climate and didn't have to have all this extra stuff just for a season?"

"Besides all the extra clothes, there are also all the winter toys, like toboggans, skates, and sleds," Janice reminded her.

"Exactly. So, how is Mark? Have you set a wedding date yet?"

"He's fine. Susan is helping him look for a house somewhere between here and Clifford so we will be between both our jobs. We have decided on a December wedding at the lodge. Here's your official invitation."

"Oh wow!" Debbie opened the envelope. "December the fifteenth. Gosh, that's right around the corner. What can I do to help?"

"Just show up. We are keeping it very simple. We are only inviting family and a few friends. Less than thirty people." Janice smiled.

"Sounds wonderful. Have you decided whether you are going to ask Chef George to walk you down the aisle again?"

"No, I am going to ask Zackery to do it instead."

"That's nice. I'm sure he'll be excited."

"Yes, he really likes Mark. They spend a lot of time together."

"Can I ask you the tough questions?"

"Sure, what?" Janice frowned.

"For starters, is Mark prepared to sign a prenup?"

"Already done. I learned my lesson when I married Tony."

"That's good. You won't have that to worry about. Are you still thinking of letting Mark adopt Zack?"

"I haven't decided on that. At this point, it would just be a formality. Mark already treats him as his son."

"I have given that some thought, and if you want my opinion, I think you should just keep that on the back burner for now. Maybe do it for Zack's sixteenth birthday or some other special occasion in his life."

"That's just your nice way of saying you think I shouldn't do that."

"No, I just think there's nothing to lose by putting it off

for a while. You will already be a family, with or without the official adoption."

"You're not wrong. I know that Mark wants to adopt Zack, but I have yet to discuss it with Zack. He is smart for his age, but I decided to put it off for a while."

"I think that is wise. So, December the fifteenth. A Christmas wedding. How exciting."

"Everything will be held in the banquet room at the lodge. Of course, I will do the decorations and the cake as well."

"Will you do a tiered cake or a flat cake?"

"I don't know. I haven't decided. But I do know the color scheme will be red and gold, for Christmas."

"Any ideas on what I can get you for a wedding gift?"

"Nothing. If you read the invitation, it says best wishes only."

"Yes, I read that. But you are my sister, and I would like to get you and Mark something, even if it's only some ugly glass bowl to put on your coffee table." Debbie laughed at the strange look on Janice's face. "Well, if you won't tell me what you want, then you have to accept whatever I choose for you."

"Why can't best wishes just be enough?"

"You already know you have my best wishes."

"Yes, I do know that. But both Mark and I have been married before, and there's nothing either of us needs. Perhaps when we move into a new house, then you could get us something we need for the house."

"We'll see. I am sure I can think of something."

"Guess I should get going. I just wanted to pop in and give you your invitation. I dropped Susan's off last night after the dinner rush."

"How is everyone out there? I haven't seen Sue in a couple of weeks."

"Susan and Keith are fine. I'm not so sure about Jefferson."

"Oh, is he still having indigestion problems?" Debbie asked.

"They have decided now that it is his heart. Susan insists that he slow down, but he's not having any part of that. He is a stubborn man."

"Aren't all men stubborn? I know Brad was totally annoyed and out of sorts when he had to tell me that he has to postpone building his pool until spring." Debbie shrugged.

"They are worse than babies when they can't get their own way, aren't they?"

"Exactly. Thanks for the invitation. I will have to get a new dress for the wedding. Nothing I own fits me in this condition," Debbie said as she automatically rubbed her belly. "Oh, my goodness, I think I just felt the first kick. Here, feel this." Debbie took Janice's hand and placed it on her belly.

"Oh my, yes. I felt that. How exciting. You should soon be having your six-month checkup, shouldn't you?"

"No, not for another month yet. I am looking forward to finding out how many babies are in there. I pray that it's only one."

"Are you hoping for a boy or a girl?"

"Either would be fine, but I am hoping for just one baby this time. I love the twins, but they are a lot of work."

"Mark wants us to have another baby. I can't make up my mind."

"Sometimes, God makes your mind up for you. Like

with this little one in here. Wait till I tell Brad that I felt the first kick. He'll be disappointed that he missed it."

"So don't tell him until you two are together so that he can feel the first kick."

"That's a little deceitful, but I like that idea. I'll do that. But then you will need to keep it to yourself." *It will make him so happy. What's the harm in telling him a little white lie?*

TWENTY-THREE

Walking the twins to the school bus on the first day it snowed was a challenge. Of course, they wanted to have a snowball fight before the bus arrived, and when it did, she had to remind the kids to rescue their lunches from the snow before they boarded the bus. She only had on a light jacket and hurried back to the house to get warmed up.

As she entered the kitchen, she noticed the answering machine for the private line was flashing. She turned on the kettle to make her tea and then listened to the message.

"Deb, it's Susan. They just took Dad to the hospital by ambulance. I think he is having a stroke. Call me as soon as you can."

Deb called Susan right back, and Susan advised that she was on the way to the hospital, following the ambulance.

"Oh, Sue, I'm so sorry. Is Keith with you?"

"No, he already left for work."

"I'll be there as soon as I can." Debbie turned off the now-screaming kettle, called Brad and left him a message, then raced upstairs to get ready. In less than five minutes, she was on her way to town.

When she entered the hospital, she was overcome with the sterile smell, the sounds of beeping monitors, and the coldness of it all. She shivered as the memories of her last visit with Henry came rushing back. She went over to

Susan, who was pacing the hallway. Debbie gently wrapped her arms around her sister.

"Deb, I am so glad you are here. They won't let me see Dad. They are all in there with him."

"What happened?"

"I was to meet a client not far from the house, so I hadn't left yet. Normally I would have been gone just after Keith left, but today I was still at home. When I came downstairs, Dad was half in and half out of the recliner. I asked him if he was alright, and he couldn't answer me. He couldn't speak. Anything he tried to say was just jibber-jabber. And his face was distorted. I called the ambulance right away and helped him get into the chair. I was so scared. And now, I'm here, and they still haven't let me see him."

"They'll have to check him out and do some testing. You just need to be patient." Debbie tried to comfort her sister.

"I know, but it feels like it's been an hour. I am so scared that he's had a stroke. God only knows what the permanent damage from it will be."

"Let's sit down over here until they say you can go in." Debbie took Susan's arm and led her over to some chairs in the waiting area.

Susan sat down for a minute and then jumped back up when the doctor finally approached her.

"I understand you are Jefferson's daughter?" the doctor asked.

"Yes, I am Susan, and this is my sister Debbie."

"Well, your father has had a bad stroke. We will be sending him for some testing to try to determine how severe it was. From all preliminary tests, it appears he has lost mobility on his left side. As a precaution, we are also monitoring his heart. You may go in and see him now, but be aware that he still can't speak."

"Thank you, doctor," she said through her tears. She took Debbie's hand and asked, "Come with me, please."

Debbie followed Susan into the cubicle. Jefferson's eyes were closed. Debbie noticed the heart monitor hooked up to his chest and the intravenous bag dripping into his body, but her mind wasn't really registering what she was seeing. She hated being in this place. It may even be the same damn cubicle where they had lost Henry.

"Dad, it's Susan. Can you hear me? Can you open your eyes?"

Slowly, Jefferson opened his eyes and looked at her with a blank expression. The left side of his face had fallen which made him look very distorted.

"Hi there," Susan said to him. "Glad to see you are awake. You are in the hospital. The ambulance brought you in. Do you remember that?" Jefferson stared at her but said nothing. Susan took his hand in hers. "I'm here for you, Dad. The doctors are going to do everything they can to help you."

A nurse came into the cubicle and explained that they were taking him down for an MRI and would be gone about half an hour.

"Let's go to the cafeteria and get a coffee," Debbie suggested.

Susan followed her but said nothing until they were seated.

"What are we going to do if Dad can't function anymore?" Susan asked.

"You are going to figure it out as you go. Just like you

do with any crisis. Sue, you will get through this. Do you want to call Keith now or wait till you get more information?"

"He's teaching classes until noon, so all I can do is leave a message. I might as well wait until I know more. We better get back up there; he should be done his test by now."

"They said it would be half an hour, and that was only ten minutes ago. Why don't you finish your coffee?" They sat in silence for a few minutes. Debbie sure hoped Jefferson would pull through. She needed to be there to support her sister, but she'd rather be anywhere else. It felt like only yesterday that Henry had passed away.

They were just rolling Jefferson's bed back into the cubicle when the girls arrived. Susan went directly to his side. "Glad to see you back. How was the ride?"

Jefferson tried to speak, but it didn't make any sense. It all sounded garbled.

"It's alright, Dad. Don't try to talk. I'll just sit here quietly with you until the doctor comes and tells us the results of your tests." Susan sat down and took his hand in hers.

Debbie was sitting quietly on the other side of his bed when she noticed Brad coming in.

"Hi, hun. How's Jefferson doing?" he asked as he came to stand beside Debbie. "Susan, how are you holding up? I brought you ladies a coffee and a tea. Thought you might need it."

"Thanks, Brad. That was very nice of you." Susan took the coffee. "Dad has had a stroke. He has just come back from having an MRI, and we are waiting to see what the doctor says."

Debbie stood and left the cubicle with Brad, then explained what had happened.

"Geez, I hope he's going to be alright. I had to come to town, so I thought I would come early and check on you girls. I won't stay, but I am only a phone call away if you need me."

"Thanks, Brad. You are the best husband in the whole world," Debbie said into his chest as he hugged her.

"Should I come back and check on you after lunch?"

"I don't know. I'll call you with any updates. If you turn your phone off for lunch, I'll just leave you a message."

"Sounds good. I'll talk to you soon." Brad gave her a quick kiss and left.

As soon as Debbie sat down, Susan turned to her and said, "You are so lucky to have such a kind, caring husband. That man loves you more than words can say."

"I know he does. I am lucky, but I work at it too. Luck only comes to those who work for it."

"Alright then. I have some test results," the doctor said as he entered and flipped through papers on Jefferson's chart. "Your father has had an ischemic stroke. That's a fancy word that means there is a blood clot in his neck stopping the blood from flowing to his brain. We are giving him medication to dissolve the clot, and we'll have to wait for another couple of hours to see if it works. If not, we will do a minor surgery to insert a catheter into the artery and pull the clot out."

"That sounds serious," Susan stated. "Why are you waiting? Why not just do the surgery and get that damn clot out of his neck?"

"If the medication works, it is obviously less invasive. The medication works most of the time, but in the event that it doesn't, we will be ready to go in and pull the clot out," the doctor explained.

"So, it's a hurry up and wait deal," Susan said sarcastically.

"Basically, yes. We'll give the medication time to work first and then go from there." The doctor made a note in Jefferson's chart. "Your dad will be going for another MRI in two hours and then we will decide if he needs the surgery."

When the doctor left, Debbie could see that Susan was crying. She handed her a tissue and just stood quietly behind her with her hand gently on her sister's back.

Jefferson lay motionless on the bed. His eyes were closed, but his mouth was hanging open and drooping on the left side. Susan spoke quietly to him. "I'll be right back, Dad. You just rest. I need to get out of here and make some phone calls." Susan stood and left the cubicle.

"Put your coat on. Let's get some fresh air," Debbie suggested.

Debbie led Susan out to the garden. Even with the first snow blanketing the patio, she could see all the shrubs she hadn't noticed the last time she was there. While Susan was on the phone, Debbie took the opportunity to call Brad. He didn't answer, so she left him a message.

After a brief time outside, they went back in to check on Jefferson, who was still sleeping. They still had the better part of two hours to kill. "Let's go back to the cafeteria. It will help us pass the time," Debbie suggested.

Susan silently followed her sister.

"I am going to go check out the salad bar. Why don't you come see if there's anything you want?" Debbie said.

While they sat eating their salads, Susan was unusually quiet. Debbie was doing her best to try to distract her.

"How is the sale on Henry's house going?" Debbie asked.

"I have had three people look at it, but only one really low-ball offer," Susan informed her. "It never ceases to amaze me how pathetic some people are. The house is already listed about as low as the boys want to go. One couple offered half of that and stated that it was their final offer. The guys saw it for the insult it was."

"Well, that's too bad. So, what do you do now?"

"I was planning an open house this weekend. But that may need to be put on hold. We'll have to see how Dad makes out. What am I going to do if he needs around-the-clock care?"

"You are worrying about things that haven't even happened yet. I know you can't help but think about it, but let's just wait and see what happens. I know you can hire caregivers to be with him during the day, when you are both at work. You'll figure it out as you go."

Susan's phone rang. It was Keith; he told Susan that he would finish his last class at three o'clock and would stop at the hospital then.

As Debbie looked around at the décor, she could feel the coldness of it all. She sat and watched the staff coming and going in a constant flow. The chatter in the room was almost deafening. After sitting there for two long hours, they finally headed back upstairs. Jefferson was still sleeping. The nurse stepped in to tell them that he had just come back from the MRI and that the doctor would be in shortly.

It was only a few minutes, but it felt like hours before the doctor came in. "Seems that the blood clot has not dissolved so we are taking him into the operating room shortly. We will be inserting a catheter into his neck and removing the blood clot. With any surgery, there are risks, but this is very straightforward. We have no choice but to do the surgery. We can't leave the clot there, or part of his brain will die," the doctor explained.

Two nurses came in to prep Jefferson for the surgery. "How long should the surgery take?" Susan asked.

"I would think about an hour," the doctor answered. "The procedure itself will only take me about ten minutes, but then there is recovery time. I am going now to scrub up, and I'll come and talk to you when the surgery is finished."

Susan clutched Debbie's arm as they wheeled Jefferson away. "I'm terrified," she whispered.

When Debbie spoke with Brad, he agreed to be home before the kids got off the bus. Debbie would stay with Susan at least until three, when Keith could come and be with her. By then, the surgery would be over.

After waiting an hour, they still hadn't seen anyone or heard anything about Jefferson. Finally, the doctor came in.

"The surgery is done. We managed to remove the blood clot. Now it's just a waiting game to see how much damage has been done. We will be keeping Jefferson here overnight and will do another MRI in the morning," the doctor advised.

"Thank you, doctor," Susan said.

The nurse came in to tell them that Jefferson was upstairs in a room, and they could go see him. When they arrived, Jefferson was sleeping peacefully.

"Dad, are you awake? Can you hear me?" Susan was rubbing his hand.

Jefferson opened his eyes but didn't say anything. He looked at her as if he was trying to focus on her face.

"Dad, can you say hi to Debbie?" Susan pointed in her direction.

Jefferson did nothing. He just stared at Susan. Debbie's heart broke for her sister.

Time passed slowly as Susan sat holding Jefferson's hand. Debbie sat quietly, looking out the window. True to his word, Keith was there just after three.

"Dad, Keith is here to see you. Can you say hi?"

Jefferson tried to speak, but the words coming out of his mouth didn't make any sense.

They all stepped out into the hall to discuss their plans. Debbie would head home, and Susan and Keith would stay with Jefferson for a while longer. Susan would return first thing in the morning.

On the drive home, Debbie thought about how things were going to change for Susan and Keith. Susan wouldn't let any setback slow her down. *Strange how life keeps throwing us curve balls. All we can do is catch them and deal with them, one by one.*

TWENTY-FOUR

The next morning, after the kids left on the bus, Debbie zipped around and got her chores done. She quickly made the beds, straightened up the kids' rooms, dusted, and ran the vacuum upstairs. She was just headed down the stairs with an arm full of dirty laundry when Brad stopped in.

"Morning, hun. I see you've been busy."

"Yes, I am getting caught up from yesterday. And I want to have things done in case Susan needs me today."

"I thought Keith was going to the hospital with her today?"

"He is. I'm just being proactive in case she needs me."

"You are such a good sister. They are both lucky to have you."

"That's what sisters are for. What are you up to this morning?"

"Just stopping in to check on my guys here. I have already been to my other two jobsites, and everything is going fine there."

"Have time to take me on another tour of my B&B then?"

"Sure, just let me refill my coffee, and I'll take you through."

The B&B's walls were up now, and things were making more sense to her.

"First door on your left is the washroom," Brad explained.

"It's bigger than I thought it would be."

"There will be room for a chair, so that if a couple were to use it, there's someplace to sit if need be."

"I see. Maybe a wicker chair for here then. I think I should be making notes." Debbie smiled.

"There will be lots of time for that."

"When do you estimate it being finished?"

"I was really hoping you weren't going to ask me that question. Out of the three big jobs we are doing right now, the other two have timelines to be finished. I was hoping this job could be the buffer."

"I see. The wife's job always comes last."

"Well, I know with the baby coming that you are not planning on opening it right away, so there is no big hurry to finish it. Am I wrong?"

"No, you're not wrong, but I am looking forward to the day when it is finished and I can start showing it off."

"This will be one of the rooms." Brad stood back to let her enter.

As she entered, the smell of fresh paint overwhelmed her senses. "Nice and big. Lots of room. I think it is going to be very nice."

"All six bedrooms look the same," Brad said. "At this end of the hall is the small storage closet and the small bathroom."

Debbie followed Brad down the stairs at the back side of the addition. With the walls up, she could get a sense of where things would be.

"Now I will show you the two apartments. This one will overlook the pool."

"This bedroom is huge. You told me that it could be made into two bedrooms if need be. Could I suggest that one of them be a two-bedroom and the other a one-bedroom? I don't want to have this newly built unit being remodeled before someone even moves in."

"Yes, we could do that easily enough. Which one do you want to be the two-bedroom apartment?"

"I think the other one facing the woods. If it were someone like Janice, the kid would prefer to see the woods, I would think."

"Done. Anything else?" Brad asked.

"Lots of electrical plug-ins. I would like at least one plug-in on each wall, like in the bedroom. And in the living room, a plug-in at least every six feet. I hate extension cords."

"Well, now is the time to say so. The electrician will be here to start wiring tomorrow."

"I also think there should be motion-censored lights inside and outside the lobby area here. We don't want guests stumbling around in the dark."

"I was thinking motion-censored lights in both the upstairs bathrooms so that when there is no one in there, the lights will go out."

"Yes, I agree," Debbie said. "Thanks for the tour. It is starting to make sense to me now."

Brad followed her back to the kitchen. "I guess I should get going. I am expecting an inspector on-site at the cottage, and I like to be there for that. Keep me posted when you hear anything about Jefferson." He kissed her forehead and was gone again.

Debbie sat finishing her cold tea, wondering why Susan

hadn't called yet. She was texting when her phone rang, and she jumped.

"Hi, Deb. I just thought I should check in," Susan stated. "Keith and I are here at the hospital, but there is no change in Dad. He's still in the same condition he was in when you saw him last."

Debbie could hear the quiver in her sister's voice.

"Is there anything I can do?"

"No, not really. The doctor just told us that because Dad is showing no signs of improvement, he suspects that Dad will remain in this state permanently."

"Oh, hun, I am so sorry. Will you be bringing him home? Or perhaps he needs a nursing home where he will have around-the-clock care."

"Keith and I are trying to decide what is best for him."

"Is there a bed available for him in the nursing home?"

"We don't even know that yet. I am waiting to hear back from them. I guess that will be the deciding factor. If they have a bed here in Clifford, that's one thing, but if not, I am not putting him anywhere out of town. He might as well be at home with us, and we will hire nurses."

Debbie could hear how scared Susan was, just from the sound of her voice. "Well, keep me posted. I am here if you need me for anything, even just moral support."

"Yes, I know, and I thank you for that. Talk soon," Susan said before the line disconnected.

Debbie's heart sank. Susan had such a tough decision to face. Debbie knew how much Susan loved and respected her father. And rightly so. Jefferson was a very caring, thoughtful person. He made a point of being useful and was always helping out, which could be helping with house-work, cooking dinner, or helping the kids with their homework when they still lived at home. He had been basically a total stranger to Susan when he had moved in with them, but his generosity had won them all over. She decided that Susan would be lost without him.

Debbie finished the laundry and was in the kitchen preparing a pot roast for dinner when Janice came in.

"Morning, sis. I am on a break and wanted to come to find out if you have heard from Susan."

"Come on in."

Janice helped herself to a coffee. "I just finished the pot. Should I put another one on?"

"I will set it up but won't start it until Brad comes in. I just talked to Susan. There is no improvement in Jefferson. She is talking about putting him in a nursing home if there is a bed in Clifford."

"Oh my, that's got to be a tough decision. Is there anything I can do to help?" Janice helped herself to a cookie, took her coffee, and sat at the counter.

"Nothing we can do except be moral support for her. This is going to break her heart. Jefferson can't even speak to her. When he tries to talk, it's just jibber-jabber, like a child."

"Can he still walk?" Janice asked.

"I don't know. From what I saw yesterday, I don't think so. The blood clot was in his neck, and it was blocking blood flow into his brain. When the brain is damaged, sometimes the damage is permanent. Yesterday, he wasn't showing any signs of body movement."

"Geez, that's terrible. I wish there was something I could do to help."

"Me too. But unfortunately, there is nothing either of us can do. Other than support Susan's decisions."

"I am off this afternoon and thought I might go to the hospital. Do you think I should?"

"I don't know what to tell you. Maybe wait and see if he is going to be moved, and if so, where he will go. Susan said if he can't get into the home in Clifford, he'll go to her house, and she'll hire nurses for home care."

Debbie put the roast in the oven and came to sit beside Janice. "So, how're the wedding plans coming? You must be getting excited."

"Fine. Because we are having it at the resort, it's mostly being taken care of. Sherry is coming up on the Friday before, to help with the last-minute things."

"That's good. It will be nice to see her again. She seems like a level-headed kind of lady. You two have been friends for a long time, since what, high school?"

"Yes, and we went to the same college and have remained friends all this time."

"And how goes the guest list? Is it still going to be a small, family-only kind of deal?"

"Yes, we are keeping it as small as we can. Neither of us wants a big splashy wedding. Just something small and intimate."

"I like small weddings. I like all weddings, but small is always nicer. So, you've already gotten your dress, you'll do the cake, and the flowers and the decorations will already be done for Christmas. Are you planning a honeymoon?"

"No, we decided not to bother with that. We may take a trip next fall before Zack goes back to school, but right now, I am too busy doing Christmas parties to even think about going away."

"Yes, I have at least two parties to go to this month and one wedding."

"You will be as busy as I am then. I can't believe it's December already. We have banquets and parties booked every weekend from now into the new year."

"And to think, when I started managing the resort, we didn't have any winter business at all."

"Crazy how time changes things. With the ski hill business, we are running about sixty percent occupancy for weekends through to the spring."

"I am so happy that Phil and Nancy are doing so well. At least all the hard work we put into the resort is paying off for them."

"Do you still miss it? The day-to-day grind?" Janice asked as she took her empty cup to the sink.

"Yes and no. I think a part of me will always miss it, but now I have other things to occupy my time."

"Well, I need to get back to get ready for the lunch rush. Keep me posted if you hear anything from Susan."

"I will." Debbie shut the door behind her sister.

The private phone rang, and Debbie picked it up.

"Hi, Deb. Just wanted to let you know that we are transferring Dad to the nursing home later this afternoon," Susan stated.

"That's good they have a bed for him. How do you feel about it all?"

"I'm not sure. I know if we brought him home, there would be a lot of traffic in and out. If he's at the nursing home, I will know that he is well taken care of, with around-the-clock care."

"Yes, I can see that. And because he is in Clifford, you can stop in to see him whenever you want to. I think you have made the right decision, even if it is breaking your heart."

"Thanks. I needed to hear that."

"Can your dad move his arms or legs?"

Debbie could hear Susan's voice quiver. "Very limited arm movement and nothing from his legs. And he still can't talk. It sounds like baby talk when he even tries. The lady from the nursing home says they will do therapy with him. Deb, he might never recover from this."

"So, he is being transferred sometime this afternoon then? Will you stay there with him until then?"

"Yes, Keith and I will stay and go with him to see that he is settled into his new room at the nursing home."

"So, there's nothing I can do to help?" Debbie asked.

"No, not really. I'll call you later when the move has been done."

"Alright. Talk soon." Debbie hung up the phone and sent a text message to Janice.

As she stood at the sink peeling vegetables for the pot roast, she was thinking about Susan and how busy December was going to be. They still needed to get a Christmas tree, and she had shopping to do. She needed party dresses, and she had her six-month doctor's appointment coming up. She decided that December was definitely going to be busy.

TWENTY-FIVE

Debbie could not believe how nervous she was on the drive to the doctor's office. She desperately wanted only one baby. She loved the twins, but she'd prefer to only have to care for one baby.

Brad was already there, waiting in his truck. "There's my pretty little momma," he said as he opened the van door to help her out.

"Hi, hun. Been waiting long?" Debbie asked as he kissed her.

"Nope, just got here a couple of minutes ago. Are we ready? I can't wait to see the ultrasound and find out if we are having a boy or a girl."

"You'll find out soon enough." Brad held the door and Debbie walked through.

As soon as they checked in, a new nurse that they had never seen before escorted them into the room for the ultrasound. Brad helped Debbie up onto the table, and the nurse covered Debbie's stomach with the cold gel. "Are you folks wanting to know the sex of your baby?" she asked as she passed the wand over Debbie's stomach.

"Yes, please," Debbie answered.

After a few moments, the nurse turned the screen for them to see. "I would say you have a millionaire's family in there. Looks like one boy and one girl."

Debbie instantly started to cry. She felt her chest tighten, and she was struggling for air. She couldn't do this.

She couldn't take care of the kids at home and also have two more babies to feed and burp and change poopy diapers. *God, please, I know I can't do this.*

"It's alright, hun," Brad tried to reassure her. "I know it's overwhelming, but let me remind you, you're not alone. We're in this together."

Debbie knew she had to pull it together. "Twins, again. Aren't we blessed!" she said with all the happiness she could muster.

"I take it that you already have twins then?" the nurse asked.

Brad was grinning like a fool. "Yes, ma'am. We have a set of five-year-old twins at home."

"Well, congratulations. You are going to have another set in about three months." The nurse wiped the gel off of Debbie's stomach. "When you are ready, Doctor Barnes will see you in his office. You can just wait for him in the room across the hall."

"Thank you." Brad couldn't stop smiling, and Debbie couldn't stop crying. "Honey, please don't cry. This is great news. We can do this. The last time, you handled it all like a pro, and I am sure you will again."

"Brad, just give me a moment, please." Debbie couldn't breathe. She felt like she was having a panic attack.

Debbie finally got her crying under control, and they went next door to wait for the doctor.

"Well, congratulations, you two. I see you are having another set of twins." Doctor Barnes smiled.

"We sure are." Brad stood and shook the doctor's hand. "And you will get to deliver these babies as well."

"Yes, I am looking forward to that. Debbie, how are you feeling?"

"Happy and sad all at the same time." Debbie swiped annoyingly at the tears rolling down her cheeks.

"Hormones can do that to a person," Doctor Barnes said. "We'll keep a close eye on you, monitor you closely. I think you should come back in a month just for a checkup."

"We'll be here," Brad assured him.

Brad helped Debbie with her coat and walked her out to the van. "I can't believe we are having twins. I love you so much. I feel like the luckiest man in the whole world," Brad said before he kissed her.

"Yes, Brad. You are lucky." Debbie climbed into the van. "I'll see you at home later. Right now, I am going grocery shopping."

Debbie needed to get away from Brad for a minute, so she started the van and somehow managed to drive to the store. She sat there for a while. *Damn, damn, double damn.* She couldn't believe her luck. Twins again. How could she raise these babies, open a bed-and-breakfast, and continue cooking and cleaning for her soon-to-be family of six? She wasn't Wonder Woman, after all. Debbie wiped the tears from her face, took some deep breaths, and got out of the van.

Feeling like she was on automatic pilot, she managed to get through the store, picking up the few groceries she had on the list, and managed to get herself back home.

That night at supper, Debbie told Ben and Becky that she was going to have another set of twins.

"Like us, another boy and girl?" Ben asked.

"Yes, just like you two," Brad answered.

"That's cool. I'll have a little brother to play with," Ben stated.

"And another little sister too," Brad reminded him.

"Mommy, how come you always have two babies and Aunt Janice and Aunt Susan only had one baby at a time?" Becky asked.

"Not sure why exactly. I guess we are just blessed."

"Maybe it's because you are such a good mommy. That's probably why," Ben stated.

Debbie's heart melted. "Well, thank you, son. Maybe you're right." Debbie smiled. "Now eat your dinner. I bought a raspberry pie for dessert."

When the dinner dishes were done, and the kids were bathed and finally in bed, Debbie and Brad cuddled on the couch.

"Hun, are you alright? You don't seem very happy about the prospect of us having twins again."

"I'm just a little shell-shocked. Like the doctor said, it's probably the hormones." Debbie gave him her best smile.

"You don't have to pretend you're alright for my benefit. I know you have some uneasy feelings about all of this. Let me reassure you that you are not alone. I will help out too."

"I know you will. I think I am just overwhelmed. I am not hiding anything; I just don't understand why I am so sad about it all. I wish I was as happy as you, but I am just tired. Tired of thinking about it all."

"It will be alright, you'll see. I'll help out, and you know my mom would love to help out again, like she did before."

"Yes, I know. I think I just need a little time to process. Where are we going to put all these kids? Becky is already in the nursery. Where are we going to put her?"

"I've been thinking about that. We will eventually need another two bedrooms. I think the best way to handle that is to build them onto the side of the addition. I am sure the architect could simply add them to the drawings."

"Well, I guess now would be a good time to do it since we are adding the bed-and-breakfast already."

"Exactly, I think we could simply attach to the existing structure. I'll talk to my architect and see what has to happen. I can't see any problems, and you are right. Now would be the time to add the rooms."

"Can you remember back to when your house was just a nice little house? And now, we keep adding on to it."

"I am quite happy with all the additions to it. It's for my family, and you know there's nothing more important than family."

"So, if the additional rooms could be added on, Ben and Becky would both be excited about having new rooms, and that would allow me to turn Becky's room back into a nursery. The kids will be happy about it all, I am sure." Debbie smiled.

"I would imagine. Maybe they could even pick out the colors they want their new rooms painted. I imagine Becky will choose either pink or purple, and Ben, well, who knows."

"So, that would solve our bedroom problems, at least. I am also wondering about storage. Bed and Becky are getting some new toys for Christmas, and I don't want to get rid of the toys they have now, as the new twins will need them. I also still have most of the clothes from when Ben and Becky were babies. They are all in totes stacked in the closets. Could we build a storage unit outside, out of sight, where we could put some of this stuff?"

"Aren't you going to be needing the clothes in totes for the new babies real soon?"

"Yes, but I have several totes that I wouldn't need for a while. If I had a storage shed, a lot of it could be moved out there."

"We could do that. But for now, you are going to have one empty bedroom for the next couple of years. You could store stuff in Ben's old room for a while at least."

"I guess you're right. And this time, when the new twins are done with things, I can give them away since we will never need them again. Right?" Debbie asked.

"Yes, right. I have a doctor's appointment in the new year, and I will guarantee that these little ones are the final addition to our family." Brad rubbed her belly for emphasis.

"Good, I'm glad to hear that. This baby-making machine is getting too old and needs to be put to rest."

Brad brushed the hair back from her face and shifted the topic. "Did you hear from Susan today?"

"Yes, she called this morning. Jefferson is all settled into the nursing home. She stopped in to see him this morning before she went into the office."

"How's he doing?"

"Not good, from what Susan says. She told me that he can't speak and has no use of his legs. He does have some slight movement in his arms, but very limited."

"Poor guy. I think we should plan on going to see him, maybe tomorrow. I can take you out to lunch afterward. How does that sound?"

"Sounds good to me. I also have a parcel at the post office that I need to pick up. I think it's a dress I ordered."

"For the wedding?"

"I have had to get three new dresses. Two for your parties and one for the wedding. Is the party this Saturday for the workers or is this one for the Cedar Grove Sledders?"

"The first one is for the workers and clients. The club party isn't for another two weeks."

"And we have the wedding next weekend. Our social calendar is full."

"This party for my guys is the whole thing, dinner, then drinks and dancing. How are we doing with the RSVPs?"

"Last time I spoke with Sharon, all of the workers were coming, and out of the possible thirty-six clients, only twenty-four have replied so far. So, at that point, there could be between fifty and sixty-two, plus us, of course."

"Sounds good. Can you keep an eye on that for me? I have to confirm the final head count with Janice on Friday," Brad said.

"I will. And did we remember to invite Sharon? Your mom and dad have agreed to watch the kids that night."

"I know. I stopped in there for a minute yesterday and Mom was all excited about it. She even bought a new movie for them. Wait till I see them next and tell them they have two new grandkids to look forward too."

"They'll both be over the moon. They like grandkids."

"Why wouldn't they like grandkids. They already have the best two grandkids in the world." Brad gave her a big smile.

"You're not a little bias, now, are you?"

"Maybe a little. But seriously, they are great kids. They are polite and respectful. Compared to some kids I see, my kids are exceptional."

"Yes, I agree. I believe that kids need to be taught these things, and kids who spend hours every day in front of a

TV aren't being taught morals and values. That's why I limit our kids' TV time."

"I agree with you wholeheartedly. Kids need to be taught. I just wish they came with an owner's manual, like the ones you get with a new appliance or a new truck."

"Now that would be interesting. I would think it would be a very big manual. There'd have to be a huge section on why children are bad and what to do if they are."

"And each child is so different, with their own little personalities and traits. That's probably why there is no manual. It would be hard to write and too big to fit into a glove box."

"I'm happy with the kids we have. I think we should keep them."

TWENTY-SIX

The next morning, on the way to town to visit Jefferson and find a dress for Debbie, Brad chatted during the whole trip about the B&B and the architect who was adding two bedrooms to the plans. He was so excited about it all.

As he rambled on, Debbie's mind drifted. The trees were very pretty, and she enjoyed the sun shining on the empty branches and the ice hanging on them, sparkling with a rainbow of colors. She spotted a snow-white rabbit and wondered if it was expecting a baby, or six, and how a momma rabbit felt when they had a whole litter of babies.

"I think we will stop in to see Jefferson first, then go shopping and then lunch. How does that sound? Debbie?"

"What?"

"How does that sound?"

"Sorry, yes, that sounds fine by me."

When they arrived, Brad came around the van and helped Debbie get out. She kissed him for his efforts.

As they walked into the nursing home, Debbie was overcome with the sound of ringing phones and buzzers and bells going off all around her. There were people with walkers and some in wheelchairs coming and going. The main dining room was on the first floor, and some of the residents were already sitting there waiting for their lunch. A lady at the reception desk asked them to sign in and told them that Jefferson Penfold was in room three-sixteen.

When they stepped off the elevator, Debbie noticed how much quieter it was up on the floor. As they entered Jefferson's room, the first thing she saw was a huge bouquet of mixed flowers with a card from Janice. *We should have brought flowers*, she thought.

Jefferson lay with his eyes closed. "Jefferson, it's Debbie and Brad. We just wanted to stop in to say hi. How are you doing?" Debbie took his frail hand and rubbed it gently.

Jefferson opened his eyes and looked at her. He said nothing but kept looking at her as if trying to focus on her.

Brad came over and stood behind Debbie. "You remember Brad. He's here with me."

Jefferson looked up at Brad and tried to speak. It was baby jibber-jabber. Debbie's heart was breaking for him. A feeling of total helplessness washed over her. He looked so frail and lost. She didn't know what to say or do. There was absolutely nothing she could do to help him.

Brad leaned down and put his hand over Debbie's and Jefferson's. "You keep fighting to get your strength back, and before you know it, you'll be back home making us a beautiful dinner."

Again, Jefferson tried to talk but nothing was legible. After a few minutes, he closed his eyes and drifted off to sleep.

"I wonder if he even knows who we are or that we are even here?" Debbie asked as she stood up.

"I think he does. Somewhere in there, he knows who we are." Brad took her hand and led her from the room.

From there, Debbie and Brad went shopping. At the department store, Debbie went into the fitting room and tried on the white and red dress that she had seen there on her last trip. She stood in front of the mirror and turned to see the side and back views. Her belly was getting bigger by the minute. Soon, she'd be waddling.

She left the fitting room and twirled around in front of Brad. "So, do I look like a beached whale, or what?"

"No, you look very beautiful. I like it. That would be fine for the party on Saturday."

"I want to try on another one as well. I'll be right back." As she turned in the mirror, she decided that, yes, she would take this dress. She tried on the other one and again twirled in front of her husband.

"That is very nice. I like this one too. I think you should get both." Brad nodded.

"I'll be right out and then we can go for lunch. I don't know about you, but I am starving."

Debbie ended up buying the two dresses, as well as two maternity tops.

They walked hand in hand to the café and had just sat down at a table when Val and her friend Steve came strolling in.

"Hey, guys! Didn't expect to see you here. May we join you?" Val asked.

"Yes, of course. Please do," Brad offered.

"Brad, this is Steve, my coworker. Steve, this is Debbie's husband, Brad."

"Nice to meet you." Brad offered his hand, and Steve shook it before he sat down.

"Val's husband is Brad's best friend," Debbie stated, hoping for some type of reaction.

"What brings you guys to town? Did you have a doctor's appointment or something?" Val asked.

"No, we had that a couple of days ago," Debbie said.

"And I assume everything is fine with the baby?" Val asked.

"Babies." Brad grinned.

"What? Babies? As in twins again?" Val asked.

"Yes, we are having another set of twins. One boy and one girl," Debbie confirmed.

"How exciting," Steve added.

"They already have five-year-old twins at home. And now, another set. How crazy is that?" Val said.

"Very cool indeed," Steve agreed.

"Let's order. I am hungry, and we have to be getting home soon," Debbie suggested. Debbie was finding this lunch very uncomfortable. Val was her usual bubbly self, and she kept touching Steve. She was acting like they were lovers. Debbie decided that lunch could not get here fast enough.

As they waited for their food, they chatted about everything except babies. Steve wanted to know about the B&B and building homes in general, and Brad wanted to know about being a journalist for a small-town newspaper.

"So, are you ready for the party on Saturday night?" Val asked.

"Yes, I just picked up a new dress," Debbie said. "You and James are coming, right?"

"Yes, looking forward to it. James even bought a new dinner jacket."

"He would look good in anything. Have you decided what you are wearing yet?" Debbie asked.

"No, but I have a closet full of dresses. I am sure I'll find something to wear. What color is your dress?"

"It's right here. Want to see?" Debbie opened the bag and let Val look inside.

"Oh, pretty. White and red, good colors for a Christmas party."

"And I also bought this one, softer pink colors."

"Nice. Is that for the wedding?" Val asked.

"Not sure, either the wedding or another one of Brad's parties."

"Aren't you just the social butterfly?" Val said.

"In December, yes, I am. Brad holds two parties every year. Then, throw Janice's wedding in on top of that, and never mind Christmas, well, this is definitely a busy month."

As soon as they finished their lunch, Debbie couldn't get out of there fast enough. Watching Val flirt so openly with Steve was very unnerving. Debbie knew that Brad was going to have a million questions for her on the way home. Debbie made a show about gathering her bags and getting ready to go.

"I hate to be the party pooper, but if you are finished, we should get heading home," Brad said to Debbie.

"Yes, I guess so. Val, nice to see you as always. Steve, nice to see you again. Merry Christmas," Debbie said as Brad helped her into her coat.

Once they were back in the van, Brad started with the questions about Steve. "They looked very comfy with each other. She was finishing his sentences for him. Does James know what's going on with those two?"

"I don't know that there is anything 'going on.' According to Val, they are just coworkers who have the same lunch hour."

"Well, I think I need to talk to my friend James and tell him that his wife is getting cozy with this guy. You seem to know a lot more about this situation than I do. How long has this been going on?"

"I met Val for lunch one day a couple of months ago, and he came with her. That's really all I know."

"Have you asked Val what's going on between them?"

"Yes, of course, and she assured me that they are just coworkers, nothing more."

"Have you ever finished sentences for your coworkers?"

"No, but I'm not as outgoing as Val is, either."

"I don't want to get in the middle of Val and James's marriage, but he is my best friend, and I think I should at least give the guy a heads up."

"That is totally up to you. I have tried to talk to Val about it, but I haven't gotten very far. I know she is very unhappy at home."

"Unhappy, how exactly?"

"She has told me that James does absolutely nothing around the house. He cuts the grass and shovels the snow, but that's all he does. He can't even throw his dirty clothes into the hamper. And James never helps with Timmy. Val feels like she is a single parent and the family slave. She works all week, and on the weekends, she has to do laundry and housework, which she hates. Like I told you before, she is not happy with her homelife."

"So, she's not happy at home, and it looks like she might be having an affair with this Steve guy from work. Have I got it right?"

"I don't know about an affair. According to what she has told me, they are only coworkers who share the same lunch hour. As she puts it, some adult conversation, which she hardly ever gets at home because James always has his face in the TV."

"I think I should talk to James, just to let him know what is going on with his dear wife."

"If you remember, I asked you to do that months ago and you told me that you would absolutely not get involved in their marriage. And now, since you have met Steve, you're all gung-ho to talk to James?"

"Now that I have met the guy and I've seen how they interact with each other, I feel obliged as his best friend to give him the low down of what's going on behind his back. I am sure if he ever saw you out with another man, he'd tell me about it."

"When exactly do you think I would have time to be out with another man? I hardly have time for the man I have now."

"I was just saying." Brad scowled.

"I know, I'm just teasing. I think we are both happy in our marriage. I know I am. Sometimes, life gets so hectic that we lose sight of what's important. I like that we make sure to take the time to be a family. I love that you put family above all else."

"There is nothing more important to me than family. I love my kids and, of course, my wife. I love helping out with bath times and playing in the mud puddles with my kids. My parents are the same, and I can tell you that I have some great memories of the time I spent with my dad, tinkering on an old boat motor or going fishing. I hope one day that my kids will have the same great memories. My only regret so far is that our kids won't have the memories of a family dog."

"Oh, we're back to that again, are we? Well, with twins on the way, I think we should put that idea on the back burner for now. Maybe after the babies are potty trained."

TWENTY-SEVEN

Saturday morning, Debbie was showing the twins how to make their own beds. Ben was happy with just pulling the covers up over the mess, but Becky was a little more particular.

"Look, Daddy. I just made my own bed," Becky announced to Brad, who had just come up the stairs.

"Oh wow, you are such a big girl. Good job, angel." Brad picked her up for a bear hug, and she squealed with delight. "From now on, I am going to call you Mommy's little helper."

"I made mine too, Daddy," Ben insisted.

"You did? I don't believe it. Let me go see." Brad scooped Ben up and carried him into his room where he dropped Ben onto the bed and tickled him.

While Brad had the kids distracted, Debbie made Ben's bed, and Brad came up behind her and wrapped his arms around her. "I was just coming to see if we could have some fun before you got our bed made."

"You're in a silly mood this morning. Is this just excitement about the party tonight?"

"No, not really. I am just happy to see my kids and my wife." Brad smiled. "Can't that just be enough?"

"Sure, we're happy to see you too."

"Hey kids, don't forget to pack pajamas and your toothbrushes for Grandma's tonight," Brad said as he headed downstairs.

Debbie followed him down and put on a fresh pot of coffee. "Coffee will be ready in a minute. So, what is the final head count for the party tonight then?"

"Sharon confirmed seventy-two. Should be a good party. I think we should plan to be down there by four-thirty at the latest. If we are out of here by four, by the time we drop the kids off at Mom's, we'll be just on time."

There was a soft knock at the door, and it swung open. "Is anybody home?" Susan asked.

"Come on in, sis. How're things going with you?"

Susan sat down at the counter. "I could sure use a coffee."

Brad poured her a cup and set it in front of her.

"Thanks, Brad. Nice to see you. Guess with the B&B construction, you are home more often these days."

"Yes, exactly. Now, if you ladies will excuse me, I have work to do." Brad kissed Debbie on the cheek and was gone again.

"He's in a silly mood this morning. Tonight is his Christmas party for the workers and clients." Debbie took her tea and sat beside her sister.

"Oh, what fun. I am sure you will have a good time. Who's babysitting?"

"Brad's folks. They are keeping the twins overnight. Oh, and by the way, we had our six-month checkup and saw the ultrasound."

"And is it a boy or a girl?"

"One of each." Debbie shrugged.

"What? Twins again!" Susan grinned at her sister. "That's unbelievable. Congratulations, sis." Susan hugged Debbie.

"Thanks. Brad is ecstatic about it all. Me, not so much. I was hoping for only one this time."

"Obviously you two have the magic touch. Wow, another set of twins. So, one of each. How exciting. Wait till I tell Keith. He'll laugh his ass off."

"Yep, the joke's on us. Twins again! On a different subject, how's your dad? We stopped in to see him on Wednesday."

"That was nice of you. He's doing as good as he can do. He has no use of his legs and not enough in his arms and hands that he would be able to get around with a wheelchair. So, he's really limited to his room. It just breaks my heart to see him like this. I miss not seeing him at home, fussing over dinner or tidying up after us all."

"I'm sure you do miss him. How about you? How are you handling all this?"

Debbie couldn't help but notice that her sister was fidgeting with her coffee cup and the place mat it was sitting on. Susan didn't usually fidget, but she was today.

"I don't know. I guess I am okay. I just stay busy and try not to dwell on it too much. I stop in to see him every morning on my way to work. But there is no change, and as you know, he can't talk. So, I just sit there quietly with him until he falls asleep."

"Have you spoken with anybody about his future? Do they expect he can get any of his strength back?"

Susan was picking at a chipped fingernail. "The doctors all say that he will probably never get anything back. He will only ever have what he has now, which isn't much. I feel so helpless. After all he has done for us, now we can't do anything for him." Susan shrugged. "Anyway, I can't stay. I am doing the open house for Henry's place today, so I best be going."

"Well, always glad to see you. Good luck on selling Henry's place." Debbie walked Susan to the door.

The afternoon went by rather quickly. The kids had gone outside to play, and Debbie had packed them each a bag of things they would need at Grandma's house before she got dressed for the party.

By four o'clock, the kids were loaded in the van, and they all headed to Grandma's house. Once they were dropped off, Brad and Debbie headed to the resort.

When Brad and Debbie entered the lodge, Debbie was overwhelmed at how beautiful it all looked. The dining room was decorated with blue and silver everywhere. Janice spotted them right away. "Hi, guys. Are you ready for the party?"

"You bet. More importantly, are you ready for us?" Brad asked.

Gail came over and joined the group. "Hey, folks. Debbie, you look so nice tonight. Let me take your coats."

"Thanks, Gail. Before you run off, we have some news to share. We did an ultrasound this week, and guess what? We're having another set of twins, one boy and one girl," Debbie stated.

"What? Wow! Congratulations," Gail said as she took Brad's coat.

"Congratulations to you both. I am so excited for you," Janice said.

As they walked into the banquet room, Debbie was mesmerized. There was a beautiful, large, decorated tree in the corner that coordinated with all the decorations in the room. Garlands with flowers and bulbs all in reds and golds hung everywhere.

"Janice, the room looks amazing. You did a fantastic job," Brad stated.

"Thanks. I think I went a little overboard, but it was worth it. You didn't specify whether you wanted a head table, but there is one there at the top of the room if you prefer."

"No, with these guys, we don't need a head table. We'll just sit here. Thanks. I am going to wander out to the bar. Debbie, what would you like?" Brad asked.

"I think just a water for now, please," Debbie replied.

"I really like your dress. You complement my decorations. You could wear it to my wedding too," Janice suggested.

"No, I have a different dress for that and another dress for the Cedar Grove Sledder's party."

"You are just the little social butterfly, aren't you?"

"This month for sure," she replied before saying hello to Don.

"Hi, Debbie, the pleasure is all mine. Wow, it looks like a winter wonderland in here. Where's the boss?"

"Brad just went to get me a drink."

"I think that sounds like a wonderful idea. Be right back." Don excused himself.

"He seems like a good guy. You see more of him than I do. What do you think about him?" Debbie asked Janice.

"I don't know him well, but he is always friendly and pleasant to be around, and he seems to fit in good," Janice stated.

"Is he looking for a place to live, or is he just going to stay here?"

"I think he is looking to buy a small house around here."

"He should look at Henry's house. I know Susan was doing an open house there today. It would be perfect for a single guy."

"Here you are, my dear." Brad handed Debbie her water. "Ted said to say hi."

"I'll wander out there later to see him. Don, before I forget, I wanted to tell you that Susan was holding an open house today, just down the road. It's a small two-bedroom bungalow-style house. You should maybe take a look at it if you're planning to stay in the area."

"I have been looking, but everything seems to be a little out of my price range right now." Don shrugged. "I'll check it out," Don said as he sat down beside Brad.

Debbie joined them. For the next hour, Brad was up and down, greeting his guests as they arrived. By five-thirty, everyone was seated and the wait staff started bringing out the meals. Each guest was offered a choice of prime rib or baked chicken. Debbie chose the chicken, and although she wasn't hungry, it was good, so she ended up eating most of it.

Desserts were set out on tables at the back of the room, and the guests were encouraged to choose their own. Debbie wandered over to see the cake before it was demolished. It had Brad's logo on the front of it and was covered with red and gold icing.

When Brad looked her way, Debbie motioned for him to join her. "Hun, I wanted you to see the cake before it gets cut up. Actually, why don't you cut the first piece, and I'll get a picture." Debbie pulled her phone from her purse and took a few pictures. "That should do it. I'll have a slice, please."

Brad escorted Debbie back to the table but remained standing to start the speeches. He acknowledged all his workers individually and had something nice to say about them all, including Don, the new guy. He thanked them for their hard work and then made a toast to them all. He also acknowledged his secretary, Sharon. Next, he introduced several of his clients and explained what house or cottage he had built for them and some funny stories of things that had happened on some of the jobs. And finally, he thanked his wife. "Debbie, can you stand up here for a moment," Brad asked. "Ladies and gentlemen, for those that don't know her, this amazing woman is my wife, Debbie."

Debbie stood up, waved, and then sat back down.

Brad continued. "She's not only my wife, but right now she is also my client. She has me building a bed-and-breakfast onto the back of our house. I need to thank her most of all. She is the one that keeps me grounded and focused.

"As most of you know, we have five-year-old twins at home and are currently expecting another set of twins in the spring. So, as you can see, I do like to stay busy at home and at work. A company this size has lots of moving parts, and it takes a lot of people to keep it all moving forward. Tonight, this party is just my small way of saying thank you to you all for being part of it. So, eat, drink and be merry. Merry Christmas, everyone." Brad sat down to the sound of applause.

"How did that sound?" Brad asked Debbie.

"Just fine, hun. You did a great job."

The next few hours were busy. Clients and workers came to Brad's table to talk to him. He introduced them all to Debbie, and by the end of the evening her head was spinning with all the names that she couldn't possibly remember.

"If you will excuse me, I am going to go see if Ted is busy and say hi to some of the staff. I'll be back shortly," Debbie said quietly to Brad.

As she left the banquet room, she noticed the volume of the crowd diminish the farther she got away from the room. Debbie spotted Ted and asked if he was busy.

He looked up from the drinks he was making. "Oh, my goodness. It's so good to see you." Ted came around the bar and gave Debbie a big hug. "I was hoping I'd get a chance to pop in and say hi, but as you can see, I haven't been able to get away from here."

Ted helped Debbie onto the bar stool and then went back around the bar. "So, how are you? I just heard you are expecting twins again. Congratulations."

"Thanks, Ted. I heard that you have gotten yourself married. How are you enjoying married life?" Debbie asked.

"I like it just fine. Never thought it would happen to me, but here I am, living the dream. Can I get you a pop or a water?"

"Just a water, when you have a moment."

"No problem." Without hesitation, Ted set the glass in front of her. "You'll have to excuse me a minute. I have a tray of drinks to deliver. I'll be right back."

"Go do your thing. I'm quite content to sit right here," Debbie told him. She had an overwhelming urge to bus some tables for him. *Guess old habits do die hard.* As she looked around the busy bar, she had to admit that she missed the hustle and bustle of the resort.

Ted returned with a tray of dirty glasses. "You look deep in thought."

"Just remembering the good old days. I even had the urge to bus some tables for you." Debbie chuckled.

"Janice does a good job helping me with that now. She's not you, but she's doing a good job," Ted admitted.

A customer came up to the bar to order drinks, and Debbie didn't want to keep Ted from his job. "Well, I guess I should be getting back to the party. Just wanted to pop in to say hi. Ted, take good care of yourself and that new wife of yours." Debbie slid down from the stool.

"Go enjoy the rest of your party. We sure do miss you around here. So nice to see you, and good luck with the babies."

Debbie went back into the banquet room, and Brad pulled her onto the dance floor. "In case I haven't told you yet, you are the most beautiful woman here. I can't wait to get you home and out of that pretty dress."

"You do say the sweetest things, cowboy."

"I can still remember our first dance, back in high school. Do you remember?"

"Gosh, yes. You were so awkward. I remember you stepped on my foot."

"Guess it's a good thing that I have aged more gracefully than my old dancing moves have." Brad spun her around and she laughed.

"For sure. At least you don't step on my feet anymore."

There were still a dozen people left when Janice announced the last call for alcohol. "Last round is on me," Brad announced.

"Boss, the whole night's been on you," one of his workers said.

"What! Nobody told me that." Everyone laughed at the shocked expression on Brad's face.

Debbie heard one of his men thanking Brad for dinner and for the party. She also heard Brad tell him that he was happy to do it. He was proud of his workers and all the work they did. She was also proud of Brad. He was so sincere, so honest, and hardworking. She was proud to be his wife.

TWENTY-EIGHT

The next week flew by, and before she knew it, Saturday morning had dawned as a cold but sunny day. The kids were happily watching cartoons, so Debbie took her steaming tea over and sat looking out her bay window.

The fresh dump of snow the day before made for a winter wonderland, with tiny figures of ice fishermen far out on the lake. She loved how the sunlight shimmered on the fresh powdered snow, making it glisten like a sea of tiny crystals. She didn't mind winter, when she could observe it from inside, at least. Brad promised to take the kids tobogganing at the ski hill later, and Debbie was looking forward to the quiet. Ben already wanted to learn how to downhill ski. She thought about how he'd be their little athlete. He'd probably want to play hockey, baseball, and who knows what else.

Her thoughts were interrupted by a small voice. "Mommy, Ben is bugging me," Becky whined.

"Ben, stop bugging your sister," Debbie called out.

"I didn't do anything," Ben protested.

"We are not playing this game. Either you both behave, or you won't get to go tobogganing later with your daddy."

"Sorry, Mommy." Ben sat up straight, the excitement of the upcoming tobogganing enough to reign him in.

As Debbie's tea cooled in her hand, her mind drifted to the wedding she was going to later. Janice would be a beautiful bride. Sherry would be there to help her get ready. She prayed that this marriage would be the one that would last, but she was filled with hope and anxiety.

She liked Mark. He seemed like a very down-to-earth kind of man, very grounded, and he got along well with Zack. He could make Zack do what he was told, but they did have a lot of fun hanging out together. He brought a sense of calm that balanced Janice's craziness. Still, Debbie hoped she'd take her advice and wait a little bit to have more kids with Mark.

And Susan and Keith would be at the wedding, but without Jefferson. She felt so bad for her sister. She knew Susan was having a hard time adjusting to life without Jefferson at the house.

She heard Brad taking off his coat and boots. "Morning, family. How is everyone this morning?"

"Daddy, are we going sledding now?" Ben asked from his spot on the couch.

"In half an hour, buddy," Brad answered. "Daddy needs to make a few phone calls, and first, you need to get dressed and make your beds."

"Okay, Daddy," Becky offered.

"Let's all go upstairs and get ready." Debbie stood and turned off the cartoons.

When Brad and the kids left, Debbie took the opportunity to get some laundry picked up. She experienced another cramp and wondered what it was all about. She reminded herself to ask Doctor Barnes about it at her next appointment.

Since the kids were going to stay over with their grandma again, she packed them both an overnight bag, including clean pajamas and toothbrushes. Sharon had offered to babysit, but Linda had insisted that they wanted the kids to come spend the night.

It was going on two o'clock that afternoon before Brad and the kids came home. "Well, there are my little snow bunnies. Did you have fun on the hill?" Debbie asked.

"It was great, Mommy. We took our toboggan, but there was a kid there with a big inner tube. It was so cool. Man, could that donut ever fly down the hill." Ben's eyes sparkled with his excitement.

"What about you, Rebecca? Did you have fun?" Debbie asked.

"Yes, I guess so. Daddy even came down the hill with me one time."

"Daddy, you got in on the sledding too?" Debbie raised an eyebrow questioningly.

"You betcha, I sure did. Can't let the kids have all the fun. I might need a back rub, though." He rubbed his back for emphasis.

"I am sorry I missed all the fun. We have to leave for Grandma's in a little while. Why don't you kids have a snack and then get cleaned up?" Debbie suggested.

"Okay, Mommy. But can we have a cookie?" Ben asked.

"One cookie and a piece of fruit."

"What time do we have to leave?" Brad asked.

"The wedding starts at four o'clock, and dinner is scheduled for five. I need to go get dressed."

"I just need to make a quick call. I have been trying to reach this guy all day, but he's not answering," Brad said as he headed to the office while the kids were happily having a snack.

Debbie took the opportunity to get her dress on. As she

stood looking at herself in the mirror, she started to cry. She felt she looked enormous and that she'd grown inches over the past week. She collapsed on the bed in disgust.

Brad came into the bedroom and saw her sitting, shoulders hunched, on the edge of the bed, sobbing her heart out.

He quietly sat down beside her and took her hands in his. "What's wrong, hun?"

"I just put my dress on and saw in the mirror how fat I look. Brad, I'm getting as big as a house. The best dress in the world isn't gonna hide this big belly."

Brad tilted her face up gently. "Honey, you're not fat. You're pregnant. You are carrying two babies around in there. I think you look beautiful." Brad put his arm over her shoulder. "Now come on. We need to get ready."

"I know, I'm sorry. I just got overwhelmed when I saw myself in the mirror. I have grown bigger in the last week." Debbie reached for a tissue and wiped her face.

Brad put on the suit that Debbie had laid out on the bed for him. "How do I look?" he asked.

"Handsome as ever." Debbie sighed. "At least your clothes still fit you."

"Kids, are you ready to go? You got your backpacks and whatever you need for the night at Grandma's house?" Brad said as they headed hand in hand down the stairs.

"You look pretty, Mommy," Becky said.

"Thank you, baby. Mommy needed to hear that right now." Debbie gave her daughter a hug. "Let's get our coats and boots on. It's time to go."

In the van on the way to Grandma's, Debbie suggested, "We are running late. I think when we get to your parents' house, I'll just wait in the van while you drop the kids off. That might speed up the process."

"Sure, that sounds like a good plan," Brad agreed.

"You kids are going to be good for Grandma, right?" Debbie asked.

"Yes, Mommy," they answered in unison.

After dropping the kids off and taking the short ride to the lodge, Brad came around and helped Debbie out of the van. "You look beautiful, hun."

"Thanks, cowboy. You look handsome yourself."

When Brad and Debbie walked through the front door of the lodge, Mark greeted them warmly. "Hi, you two. We are all set up in the banquet room. This is Sam, my best friend and, today, my best man. Sam, this is Debbie and Brad Mumford. Debbie is Janice's sister."

"Hello Sam, nice to meet you." Brad shook his hand. "Should we just head on in then?"

"Yes, Susan and Keith are already in there," Mark said.

As they entered the banquet room, the smell of the flowers drifted out to meet them. The room was decorated with the same decorations they had seen last weekend for Brad's company party, with flowers added, predominately red roses, white carnations, and white lilies. And at the front of the room, the archway stood covered in greenery and cascading flowers.

"There's Susan. Let's go get seated." Brad took Debbie's arm.

Immediately, the sound of the wedding march started, and everyone stood and turned to watch as Sherry, then Zackery and Janice came down the aisle.

Zack looks so serious, so earnest about giving his mother away. Debbie wiped a tear off her cheek as she sat down.

"Dearly beloved," the preacher started.

Debbie was too busy looking around to pay much attention to what he was saying. She was distracted by the beautifully decorated room, and her thoughts drifted to all the people in attendance.

Mark kissed his new wife, and the small crowd applauded.

Brad and Debbie took turns hugging the bride and groom. "Janice, you look beautiful. I love your dress, and the flowers are absolutely gorgeous," Debbie said as she hugged her.

"Thanks, sis. You look very pretty yourself. I love the colors. The white and the soft pinks match my Christmas decorations very well."

Next, Debbie hugged Mark. "Welcome to our crazy family."

"Thank you. I like crazy, so I am sure I'll fit right in." Mark hugged her.

Brad took Debbie's hand and led her to the back of the room where the dinner tables were set up. Susan, Keith, Katie, and Jeremy were already seated. Brad and Debbie joined them.

There were bottles of white and red wines on the table and Susan was already sampling the red. Keith stood up. "I am going to the bar to get a beer. What does everyone want?" Turned out that everyone wanted something.

"I'll come and help you carry all that," Brad offered.

"Susan, you look very nice tonight," Debbie said.

"Thanks. I prefer pant suits to dresses."

"Katie, it's nice to see you, and you, too, Jeremy. How are the wedding plans going? Have you set the date yet?" Debbie asked.

"We are going to have a June wedding at the farm, and

we are definitely going to get Aunt Janice to do the decorating," Katie answered.

"I know, right? These flowers are gorgeous. She is just so talented. I wish I had even a part of the talent she does. But no, your mom and I got the brains instead," Debbie said.

"Janice got the creativity, I got the business sense, and Debbie, well, she got the baby-making gene," Susan added.

"I feel like an Easy-Bake oven these days. Katie, I am not sure if your mom told you, but we are having twins again."

"Yes, she did. Congratulations, by the way. I can't wait to meet my new cousins." Katie and Jeremy gave each other a quick look.

Brad and Keith delivered the drinks, and the announcement was made that dinner would be served shortly.

The waitress came with plates and offered a choice between baked salmon or chicken parmesan. Debbie chose the salmon and Brad chose the chicken.

They chatted while they ate their dinners, and the best man, Sam, asked everyone to please help themselves to dessert. Janice and Mark went over to cut the cake. It was a white flat cake that Janice had decorated with two entwined wedding rings. Once the cake was sliced, the staff offered it to anyone who wanted some. On the buffet table, there was also a selection of fancy desserts to choose from.

"Katie, you might also ask Janice to make your cake for you. I've seen her cakes, and they are beautiful," Susan suggested.

"Yes, I probably will."

As soon as the dinner was finished, the music started.

The DJ was playing the golden oldies, and after Janice and Mark had their first dance, everyone else joined in.

Brad stood and offered Debbie his hand. "Beautiful lady, could I have this dance?"

Debbie stood, took his hand and let him lead her onto the dance floor.

"Janice is beautiful, but not as beautiful as my wife," Brad said into her ear.

"Thanks, honey. You are, as always, the most handsome man in the room."

When they went back to the table, Debbie excused herself. "I need to go say hi to some people. I'll be back soon."

Debbie sat down at the table with James, Val, and Chef.

James stood up and announced, "I am going to the bar. Would anyone like anything?"

"I would have a ginger ale, please," Debbie said.

Val shook her head; she was drinking the white wine from the table.

"How's everything with you? I haven't seen you in a month," Debbie asked.

"Oh fine, same old, same old." Val shrugged. "I must say, I like your dress."

"Thanks. It's hard to look pretty when you're carrying around two kids in here." Debbie rubbed her tummy.

"You really are a sucker for punishment, aren't you?" Val chuckled.

James came back to the table with their drinks. "Come on, wife, let's dance."

"So, what have you been up to?" Debbie asked Chef.

"Not much. I tend to stay home more in the wintertime.

I don't like having to go out and clean the snow off the car before I go anywhere."

"Well, I am glad that you spend Monday mornings with me. If it is easier for you, Brad could run over and pick you up."

"Oh no, I'm fine. I can still do it, but I'd rather not. I was looking at buying one of those portable garages, you know, like the ones with a metal frame with a tarp over the top. But they want too much money for those things. And I would need to hire an army to put the damn thing up."

"Do you have someone to plow your driveway?" Debbie asked.

"Yes, but they don't clean my walkways like the last guy did."

Debbie made a mental note to ask Brad to clean off Chef's car and the walkways for him when it snows. "I'm like you. I would rather watch winter come and go from inside the house."

"So, when are the babies due?"

"The doctor says they are due in the middle of May, but I could go earlier." Debbie shrugged.

"They'll get here when they are ready. You are so impatient. With age comes wisdom, and you learn to slow down and take it all in. Things will happen when they are supposed to."

"Yes, I know. You are teaching me patience. This Monday, I thought perhaps you could teach me about Christmas cookies. I can do the standard peanut butter, chocolate chip, and sugar cookies, but I picked up some of those puff pastry sheets and was hoping we could do some fancy ones."

"Sure, we can do that."

James and Val returned to the table just as Brad sat in the seat beside Debbie.

"Here you are. I was wondering where my dance partner had wandered off to. Hey gang. How's everyone?" Brad asked.

"I'm fine but I think I have had enough fun for one night. I am going to head out." Chef stood up. "Brad, would you mind grabbing my walker for me, please. I parked it over in that corner somewhere."

"Sure, no problem." Brad brought Chef his walker.

"I'll walk out with you," Brad offered.

"Thanks, but I am good. I can get there by myself. I am parked at the back door, so I'll go out through the kitchen."

"Alright then, be careful," Brad told him.

"Val, could I interest you in a dance?" Brad asked.

"Sure, I like this song." Val stood and followed Brad onto the dance floor.

"So how is the new B&B coming along?" James asked Debbie.

"Good, the walls are up, and the electricity has been installed. Brad has a couple of other jobs on the go, and since I am in no hurry to finish, I am getting my job done last."

Debbie and James just sat chatting about his job and her homelife. She told him how Brad helped with bath time and reading bedtime stories to the kids. "Brad enjoys spending quality time with me and the kids, and I would be totally lost without him.

"Makes sense," James said as Val sat back down.

Brad put his hand out to Debbie. "Come dance with me, little momma."

"How can a girl resist an invitation like that?" Debbie

took his hand and followed him onto the dance floor. After a few minutes, Debbie asked Brad, "Would you be very upset if we went home now? I am not feeling the greatest, and would like to go home to lie down."

"Sure. Do you want to finish this song or go now?" Brad asked, his voice filled with concern.

"We can finish the song and say goodnight to everyone. I'm alright, just very tired all of a sudden."

"We can go anytime."

They finished the song and went around to say goodnight to everyone.

"You're leaving already?" Janice looked disappointed.

"Yes, I'm sorry, but I am wiped out. I need to go home to lie down," Debbie said as Brad helped her into her coat.

"Thank you both for coming and sharing this special day with us," Mark said.

"Thanks for having us. I wish you both years of happiness together." Debbie looked around. "I don't see Zack. Tell him goodnight for me when you see him." Debbie gave Mark and Janice both a big hug.

"Night all." Brad took Debbie's hand, and they left together.

TWENTY-NINE

Chef had been by on Monday morning, and they had made some fancy cookies everyone was excited about. Debbie and Brad even managed to get a day to go to the city to do some Christmas shopping, and while the kids were at school, she even got them all wrapped.

She felt good about being ready for Christmas. The tree was up and decorated, the stockings hung in front of the fireplace, and the cookies were all made. They only had the Cedar Grove Sledders party to attend. As the club president, Brad was responsible for arranging the party for the group. He commandeered Debbie to be his helper.

Personally, she couldn't care less about the whole Christmas season, but she knew Brad enjoyed it as much as the kids did, so she needed to make an effort. She used to enjoy Christmas, but nowadays it all just seemed to take so much effort. Even the Christmas dinner. She'd cook for days to be ready for the big feast, and in ten minutes, it was devoured and done with. Then there was the hour it took to clean up afterward. She didn't used to be such a scrooge, but every year, it seemed to be more and more work.

At least she could drink coffee again. She loved how the steam floated up from a fresh cup. And that aroma. Only a month ago, it had nauseated her, but now she could enjoy the strong aroma and taste coffee with pleasure. How pathetic was she? The highlight of her day was drinking a coffee. *I'm starting to sound like Val.*

Coffee in hand, she went to answer the knock on the door. "Well, hello John. Please, come on in." He sure reminded her of Henry.

"Hi. Is this a bad time?" he asked.

"No, not at all. Come on in. I just poured myself a fresh coffee. Could I interest you in a cup?"

"That would be nice." John set the bag he was carrying on the floor while he removed his winter coat and boots.

"Let's sit in the kitchen," Debbie suggested. He followed her in and sat at the counter. "How do you take your coffee?"

"Double-double would be perfect. Thanks. So, how have you been feeling? How are Brad and the kids?"

Debbie placed his coffee in front of him, then went around the counter and sat beside him.

"I am fine. Growing bigger every day. Don't know if you have heard, but we are having twins again."

"Yes, Susan told me the good news. Congratulations. You and Brad are both good parents."

"So, I understand that your dad's house has sold. I sure do miss Henry. He used to stop in here at least once a week, sometimes just for a coffee, and sometimes he'd stay for lunch. I think about him often."

"Yes, it has sold. The new owner, Don, seems like a nice fellow. He agreed to buy it furnished, so at least I didn't have to worry about getting rid of everything. I've cleaned out Dad's personal stuff, most of which will just be donated to charity. That's why I am here. I found a couple of Dad's things that I thought you might like to have." John reached down to the bag that was now sitting at his feet. He pulled out a picture frame with a picture of Henry and Debbie all dressed up. "I thought you might like to have this."

Debbie took one look at it and started to cry. "This was at Janice's second wedding. I remember teasing him that he looked so handsome in his suit and that I wanted a picture with him."

"Don't cry. I'm sorry. I thought you might like it." John was obviously flustered by her tears.

"Sorry, I love it. It's these damn hormones. These are happy tears," Debbie tried to explain.

"Oh, I thought I had done something wrong."

Debbie chuckled through her tears. "No, not at all. This is all Brad's fault." She rubbed her big belly.

John smiled. "Speaking of Brad, I noticed he likes hats. I brought him one of Dad's hats. I thought he might want to have it."

Debbie took the hat and smelled it. "I can still smell Henry on it. I can still see him standing there with it on. Brad will be honored to have it. That was so thoughtful of you, John."

"There, now I am done. Dad's house is empty of all his personal touches. Don is going to do some painting and hopes to be moved in by the end of next month. All that's left for me to do is to drop his keys off at the resort."

"I bet you're glad to be finished. You know, you don't know how much you will miss someone until they are gone."

"I think I miss our phone calls the most. Dad loved to talk on the phone, sometimes for an hour at a time. I miss that now." John finished his coffee. "I want to get on the road. I have a three-hour trip before I am home tonight."

"Well, thank you so much for the treasures, John."

"I know how important you were to my dad. You were probably his best friend, and I am glad he had you, always looking out for him."

"Knowing your dad was my great pleasure. The pain of losing him is hard, but knowing him has been such a joy for such a long time. I still remember the first day he walked into my life. Henry was truly one of a kind, and I, for one, will never forget him."

"You are such a kind person. I can certainly see why Dad thought so highly of you. Good luck with the twins and give Brad my best wishes." John pulled her into him for a hug.

"Thanks, John. You have a safe drive home." *Oh Henry, how I miss you, old friend.*

Debbie was upstairs making her bed and collecting laundry when Brad came up to find her.

"There you are." Brad carried the basket downstairs and into the laundry room. He brought a basket of clean clothes out, and set them on the coffee table. "Load is changed. Do you want me to fold these?"

"No, thanks, I can do that. I just made you a fresh pot of coffee." Debbie handed him a cup.

"Thanks. I am here waiting for the plumbers. They are installing the hot water tank and hooking up the plumbing for the washrooms and the laundry room."

"You know, I was thinking, why can't we buy the new washers and dryers now? I know it might be a while before the B&B opens, but with the mountain of laundry I do daily, I could be using them now," Debbie suggested.

"I don't see why not. If we had them now, the plumbers could have them hooked up. Why don't you go ahead and order them. The plumber will be here for a few days getting all the pipes run."

"I'll look into that today." Debbie touched his arm. "I admire how easily you can make executive decisions."

"If you can use them now, which I am sure you can, then why not get them now? I think it's a good idea." Brad kissed her. "Where did this hat come from? It's Henry's, isn't it?"

"John stopped in earlier. He thought you might like to have it as a keepsake. He brought me that picture of Henry and me as well."

"I imagine he was here cleaning out his dad's house. I know Don is quite excited about getting in there to paint. He hopes to move in by the new year."

"John was going to drop off the keys for Don on his way back home."

Brad filled up his takeaway coffee mug. "I see the plumber has just arrived. I'll go show him the lay of the land."

When Brad left, Debbie turned on the laptop and set about ordering two more washers and dryers from an appliance store in Clifford. They would all be delivered on Monday morning.

The next morning, the kids were both standing beside her bed when she woke up.

"Mommy, get up. We need to get ready for our ski lessons," Ben stated impatiently.

"Your lesson isn't until after lunch. You haven't even had your breakfast yet." Debbie pulled the blankets back, and Becky climbed up into the bed with her.

"We have already had cereal," Ben informed her.

"Did Daddy help you?"

"Nope, Daddy's gone to work. Becky and I got it all by ourselves."

"I hope you two didn't make a mess in my kitchen."

"Nope, we were careful," Becky offered as she snuggled up to Debbie.

"Well, as soon as Mommy wakes up, I will come down and see for myself."

Ben climbed up on the bed. "You'll see. We didn't make no mess."

Debbie waddled to the washroom. When she came back into the bedroom, both of the kids were hiding under the blankets.

"Where could my family be?" Brad asked as he came up the stairs. "I know, I bet some aliens came down and beamed them up into their spaceship."

Giggles came from under the blanket. Brad motioned to Debbie that he would go to one side and that she should go to the other. They reached under the blankets and tickled the kids, who both squealed with delight.

Brad helped the kids get dressed while Debbie grabbed a quick shower and got herself ready for the day.

She was pleased when she entered the kitchen, and the kids had not made a mess. The cereal box was still on the counter, but at least the kids had put the milk back in the fridge. Debbie had decided that it was unsafe for the kids to have to climb on a stool to reach the cereal, and as soon as she had a minute, she planned on moving the cereal down to a lower shelf.

Brad handed her a coffee and gave her a kiss. "Morning, beautiful. Are you ready for this day?"

"Ready or not, here we come," Debbie said as she rubbed her belly.

"Mom called to remind me to bring some coloring books for the kids tonight."

"I'll add a few to their backpacks." Debbie nodded. "You can tell her to keep them there at her house. They are getting new ones for Christmas."

The kids watched their cartoons and played quietly with their toys, but Debbie could feel their excitement over the upcoming ski lesson.

While they were gone, Debbie took care of some household chores and laid out the clothes they were going to wear for the party later. Her dress was white with a red stripe down the middle, both front and back.

When Brad and the kids came in, they were excited to tell her all about it.

"It was so cool. Mommy, we had to learn stuff and then we actually got to go down the hill. Becky fell over, but I didn't. I was skiing like a pro, the instructor said," Ben stated proudly.

"I liked the chairlift the best." Becky smiled.

"Well, I am glad you both had fun." Debbie brushed the hair out of Becky's mouth.

"And we get to do it again next Saturday. That's cool," Ben added.

"Yes, if you are good. Now, go wash up for supper and then we have to get ready to go to Grandma's."

By the time they dropped the kids off and arrived at the resort, it was going on seven o'clock.

"Hey, guys. Nice to see you both," Gail said as she took their coats. "I believe some of your party is already here, sitting in the bar."

"Are you ready for us?" Brad asked.

"Yes, everything is set up in the banquet room. The portable bar just opened."

"Thanks. I'll go see who's in the bar first. Deb, why don't you head into the room, and I'll be right in," Brad suggested.

"Sure, I can do that. Hi, sis. Are you all set for the party?" Debbie asked Janice, who had just come from the kitchen.

"Yep, right this way." Janice walked Debbie into the banquet room.

As they entered, Debbie noticed all the round tables set up. "Is there no head table?"

"Nope, Brad said he didn't need one," Janice answered.

"I thought he might for this party. But I'm really not surprised. He always just wants to be part of the crowd. So, how are you enjoying married life?"

"Fine. Mark and I just bought a house. We move in at the end of next month. I'm a little excited about it all. Now I will have to drive to work and that will be a bit of an adjustment." Janice shrugged.

"Congrats. How exciting. Where is the house?"

"Only twenty minutes away. My mailing address will be a rural route box from the Clifford post office. We will get the keys on January twenty-first."

"I am very happy for you all. What does Zack think about the move?"

"He's excited about having a whole room all to himself. It's a three-bedroom house, so one for us, one for Zack, and one for a nursery."

"A nursery?" Debbie was shocked. "Are you trying to tell me something?"

"Yes, ma'am. I am pregnant. About eight weeks."

Debbie faked a smile as she hugged her sister. "Congrats, sis."

"Congrats on what?" Brad asked as he came up behind them.

"Janice just told me that she has bought a house and is pregnant."

"I think it's something in the water." Brad chuckled. "Congrats, Janice. That's good news."

There was a steady flow of sledders, and by eight o'clock, over eighty people filled the room. The DJ had just started to play, and Brad asked Debbie to dance.

"Can you believe my sister is pregnant? I had hoped she'd wait for at least a year before they started having more kids," Debbie said.

"You have doubts about her marriage, don't you?"

This man knows me too well. "Well, she doesn't have the greatest track record, now, does she?"

"She has done a good job raising Zack on her own. I am sure that even if Mark doesn't stick around, she'll still be a good mom to this baby as well."

"Guess that's as good a way of looking at it as any."

When the song finished, Brad walked her back to the table. He told her he had to give a quick speech in a few minutes. He returned with the microphone, and when the next song finished, Brad stood up and asked for everyone's attention.

"I will keep this short. I just wanted to thank everyone for coming out tonight. I also want to thank the Cedar Grove Resort for letting us use their trails and hosting this great party. In case any of you don't know, we lost two members this year. John and his family have moved to Alberta, and Brian passed away a couple of months back. I would like to extend my sympathies to his family and friends. In case you are wondering, the club sent flowers for his funeral. Brian was a good man, and I am sure he will be missed by many of us.

"On a happier note, congratulations to Eric and his new wife, Jenny. May all your ups and downs be in bed and all your troubles be little ones.

"We will be putting some snacks out in a bit, so please help yourselves. The blue tickets in front of you are for a free drink at the bar, and the red tickets are for a door prize. You have a chance to win that bar fridge over there. Personally, I think it would look good in my house, but apparently, it's not up to me. So, that's all I wanted to say, other than Merry Christmas and enjoy the party."

The crowd applauded as Brad sat down.

"How was that?" Brad asked Debbie.

"Fine. You did a good job," Debbie assured him with a gentle squeeze of his leg.

The DJ was playing soft rock, with a bit of country music, and the dance floor stayed full all night.

Brad asked Debbie to dance a slow song and kept her on the floor for the next song which was faster. By the time she sat down, she was exhausted.

The next time Brad asked her to dance, she begged off. He asked another lady, and Debbie was quite contented to sit and watch.

Janice had taken Brad's empty seat. "How come you're not dancing? Are you not having fun?"

"I am fine, just tired. It's a lovely party."

"I try to keep Brad's work party more formal, with the dinner and all. I know he has clients there. But this party is much more casual."

"Yes, I can see the difference. Both parties have been wonderful. You are doing a great job here, sis. I am so proud of you."

"Thanks. You'll have to excuse me now; I am being hailed, and I have things to do," Janice said as she walked away.

A few minutes later, Janice and the staff brought out the food. There were trays of finger foods, an assortment of desserts, and a huge flat cake. She had decorated the cake with a pair of sleds and the Cedar Grove Sledder's logo. Debbie made sure to take some pictures of Brad cutting it.

Although Debbie was tired, she knew that Brad wanted to stay until everyone else had left, so she paced herself. She was quite happy when they announced last call, and she could finally go home to her warm, comfy bed.

THIRTY

As Debbie opened her eyes and glanced at the clock, she jumped out of bed and headed into the washroom. As she was heading down the stairs, she was surprised to see that the kids were already up, eating cereal and watching cartoons.

"Morning, you two. You do know it's Saturday and you don't have to go to school today, right?"

"But we woke up anyway," Ben told her.

"Well, Mommy needs a coffee." Debbie waddled to the kitchen. The kids had left the milk out on the counter. When she opened the fridge to put the milk away, she saw the big bowl of egg salad and the various cold cuts. She remembered that today was moving day for Janice and Mark.

Debbie knew that they were really doing two moves: one for Janice's meager belongings, and the bigger move for all of Mark's stuff, which included furniture. Brad had offered his truck, a trailer, and three of his guys to help with the moves.

Debbie had been to the new house, and she liked what she had seen. It was a nice bungalow, with a full basement and three bedrooms on the main level. It was on the back lot, on the next lake over from Brad and Debbie's. Debbie liked the fact that you could see the lake from Janice's front window. It wasn't a bay window like Debbie had, but a nice big picture window, which was the next best thing, at least in Debbie's mind.

She sat at the counter, trying to figure out how many people would be at the new house for lunch. She figured Brad and his three guys, Susan and Keith, and of course, Mark, Janice, and Zack, which made a total of nine for sure. And she didn't know about Katie and Jeremy or Josh. So, there could be nine to twelve people for lunch.

Debbie planned on making a tray of sandwiches that Brad would pick up around eleven o'clock. She couldn't physically help with the move because of her '*delicate condition*' as her mom would have called it. But she could make lunch. She calculated that she would need at least eighteen sandwiches. She would also send a couple of bags of potato chips and a big cooler full of water, juice, and pop.

She decided she wouldn't start making sandwiches until about ten o'clock. The egg salad was already made, and she just needed to spread it onto the bread. She wanted to put some lettuce on the ham and cheese, so she still needed to wash the lettuce.

Becky brought their dirty bowls back into the kitchen, set them on the counter by the dishwasher, and climbed up on the stool beside Debbie.

"What are you doing, Mommy?"

"I am just trying to figure out how many sandwiches I need to make for Aunt Janice today. Remember I told you that she is moving into a new house."

"Is Zack moving too?"

"Yes, Zack, Aunt Janice, and Uncle Mark."

"Can we go too?"

"Yes, but not today. Today they will be moving furniture and big heavy stuff, and we would just be in the way. But we will go another day for a visit, real soon."

"Alright then. So, what are we doing today?"

"This afternoon, at two o'clock, you and Ben have your ski lessons."

"Oh yeah, I forgot about that."

"Do you like your ski lessons?"

"They're okay, I guess. Ben is a good skier, but I fall down a lot."

"You'll get better the more you practice."

"I sure hope so because I stink now."

"You don't stink. Your daddy told me that last time, you came all the way to the bottom and didn't fall."

"I just got lucky that time, but the ten times before that, I fell every time."

"Oh, sweetie, remember, practice makes perfect. You keep practicing, and you'll start to have better results, I promise."

"Is Daddy coming home to take us?" Ben asked as he climbed up on the opposite stool.

"No, Daddy is busy today helping Aunt Janice move."

"So, who is taking us then?"

"Grandpa is going to take you."

"Why can't you take us, Mommy?" Becky asked.

"Because Mommy might slip and fall, and I don't want to hurt the babies." Debbie unconsciously rubbed her tummy.

"That's good thinking," Ben suggested.

"Grandpa is going to come pick you up and take you and wait to bring you home when your lesson is done."

The house phone rang on the counter beside them, and all three of them jumped. Because it was the business line, they let it ring and go to voice mail. They all laughed because they had all jumped when it rang.

Ben slid down from his stool. "Becky, the good cartoon comes on now."

"Coming." Becky slid down and followed him.

Debbie glanced at the clock. It was going on nine. She threw the lettuce into a sink full of water and then headed for the stairs. "Mommy is going up to shower and get dressed. You guys behave yourselves, please."

"Okay, Mommy," they said in unison.

When she came back downstairs a few minutes later, both kids were in the same position she had just left them in.

She headed to the kitchen to rinse and drain the lettuce. Then she cleared off the counter and wiped it. She would need the room to make these sandwiches. And she would need something to put them into once they were made. As she looked around, she found a box about three inches high that a case of juice boxes had come in. That could work, she decided. She took some tinfoil and covered the box to make sure it was clean.

At ten o'clock, the kids' cartoon was over. "You two should go upstairs and get dressed. And make your beds while you are up there, and tidy up your rooms, please."

"Okay, Mommy," Ben answered. "Come on, Becky."

Debbie got all the cold meats, mustard, and mayonnaise from the fridge, along with the egg salad she had already made. She spread out the bread and started making an assortment of sandwiches, some on white, some on brown.

By eleven o'clock, she had the sandwiches made and boxed up, the chips in bags, and the cooler refilled with new ice. She was still cleaning up her mess when Brad came in.

"Morning, family. How's everyone this morning?"

"Morning, Daddy," Becky called out.

"Morning, Daddy," Ben repeated.

Brad knocked the snow off his boots and came around the corner to see Debbie.

"Morning, hun. Are your sandwiches all made?" he asked as he leaned in for a kiss.

"Yep, ready to go. So, how's the move going?"

"Good, I think. We have already done three loads to get all of Mark's stuff moved." Brad grabbed an apple and took a big bite. "After lunch, we just have one more load to get Janice's personal belongings. Then we need to assemble Zack's new bed."

"Where did the bed come from?"

"Janice just bought it, and a dresser. They are at the resort so we will bring them with her stuff."

"So, by the end of the day, they'll be all set to sleep in their new house tonight?"

"That's the plan. I overheard Janice tell Susan they couldn't get the satellite hooked up until Tuesday but that it was alright, and they could just watch some movies."

"Good stuff." Debbie pointed to the sandwiches. "Everything is ready to go. That cooler is heavy."

"I got it. Thanks for all this, hun. I am sure we will all enjoy lunch. I best get going." Brad kissed her forehead and headed out. "Hun, can you get the door please?"

"Got it." He took the cooler first, and Debbie closed the door behind him. He was back in a minute to get the rest of the lunch.

"Thanks again, babe. Say hi to Dad for me."

"I will." Debbie closed the door behind him and watched through the window as he drove away.

She was a little sad that she couldn't be there to help, but she knew that she and her huge belly would be stuck in the way. She went back to cleaning up the mess. "Before I put all this stuff away, would you kids like a sandwich for lunch?"

"Coming, Mommy." Both kids bounced down the stairs. "What kind of sandwich is it?" Ben asked.

"Well, why don't you come see what I have?"

Debbie let them make their own sandwiches, and they sat together at the counter to eat.

"Are you guys ready for your ski lesson?" Grandpa asked as he came through the door.

"Hi, Grandpa." They both ran to give him a hug.

"I heard that you two need a ride to the hill for your lessons. Is that right?"

"Yes, please," Becky answered.

"You're a bit early, Grandpa. Have you had lunch yet?" Debbie asked.

"Yes, I did. Grandma made me a bowl of beef vegetable soup."

"We just finished lunch. Come on in for a few minutes. Would you like a coffee?"

"Now that I would agree to." Charles came in and sat at the counter.

"What is Linda doing? I half-expected that she might have come with you."

"She has picked up a cold somewhere and didn't want to come and share it with you guys."

"That was thoughtful of her. I'll give her a call later. How long has she been sick?"

"About four days, I think. I am keeping my distance, hoping I don't catch it myself."

"Better safe than sorry. Kids, are you both ready for your lesson?"

"Yes, Mommy, we are ready when Grandpa is," Ben answered back.

Debbie went to the door. "You both have gloves, hats, scarves, and goggles. Have fun, and be good for Grandpa."

Debbie watched them go and then stood in the kitchen and listened blissfully to the silence. She stood there for a minute, just enjoying it. Behind her, all she could hear was the clock ticking on the wall. Her cell phone rang and made her jump.

"Holy crap," she said out loud to no one. "Hello."

"Hey, sis. I only have a moment. We are waiting for Brad and the guys to bring my stuff over from the resort. I just wanted to say thanks for lunch. That was very kind and thoughtful," Janice told her.

"Well, I knew I couldn't physically be there to help, so I thought the least I could do was make lunch. Were there enough sandwiches?"

"Yes, I think there might be two left over. Anyway, I just wanted to say thanks."

"You are most welcome. So, how's it going?"

"Good. All the furniture is here, except for Zack's bed and dresser, which is on the way. Now it's getting all these boxes unpacked."

"You'll get there. Just do a few every day. It's usually a good idea to start with the kitchen and bathroom boxes."

"Susan told me the same thing. Anyway, gotta run. Just wanted to say thanks before it slipped my mind."

"Good luck with the unpacking."

As Debbie put the phone back on the counter, she chuckled at the thought of how it made her jump. She finished tidying up the kitchen and then took a fresh coffee over to her bay window.

As she looked out over the front lawn and toward the lake, she decided there had to be at least three feet of snow out there. Robert and Nancy at the ski hill would be happy about that. They had a snow-making machine but still needed real snow to make it work.

Debbie had learned to ski as a child, but it wasn't her favorite thing to do. Her favorite activities didn't involve snow, or being cold. She was more into swimming and baseball. Badminton and tennis were more her style.

But Brad enjoyed skiing, as did both her sisters, Susan more so than Janice. So, between the three of them, she used to get dragged out a couple of times each season. But not this year; she had gotten out of it because she was pregnant.

Debbie was tired, so she went to the recliner and kicked it back into a comfortable position. She involuntarily moaned when she found the perfect position. She closed her eyes, and the next thing she knew, the kids were home.

"Mommy, why are you sleeping? It's daytime." Becky pointed out the obvious.

"I guess I was tired." Debbie sat up. "So, how was your ski lesson?"

"It was alright. I came down the hill and didn't fall," Becky announced proudly.

"See, I told you, practice makes perfect."

"I didn't fall either," Ben added.

"And how about you, Grandpa? Did you have fun watching them skiing?"

"They are both doing really good. I think they have a good instructor."

"Do you have time for a coffee?"

"No, thanks. I think I should go check on Linda."

"Give her my best, and thanks for taking the kids."

Debbie forced herself to get up from the recliner. She put a movie in for the kids and went into the kitchen to start preparing the meatloaf they were going to have for dinner.

She decided that the half-hour nap she had didn't help. She was more tired now than before. She had the potatoes cleaned and cut into wedges, and opened a can of corn. She wrote out instructions for Brad on how to cook it all because she had decided that when he got home, he was going to have to take over while she went for a nap. She went back to the recliner to wait for him to get home. He arrived a short time later.

"Hello, family," he said as he removed his coat and boots.

"Hi, Daddy. I think Mommy is really tired," Becky informed him.

"You alright, hun?" Brad asked as he bent down for a quick kiss.

"Yes, but I am very tired. I need to go for a time-out." Debbie put the recliner back into the sitting position and tried to stand. She didn't have the strength. "Can you give me a pull, please?"

"Sure, let me help."

"Thank you. If you don't mind, dinner is in the oven and the instructions are on the counter. I need to go and lie down." Debbie headed for the stairs.

"Let me come tuck you in." Brad took her arm and escorted her up the stairs.

"So, Janice is all moved in?"

"Yes, she is. We also constructed Zack's bed, so they are good to go." Brad pulled back the covers for her. "Why don't you get into your nightie? You'll sleep better."

"Right this minute, I could sleep standing up." Debbie lay down, and Brad covered her up.

"Sleep tight, my sleeping beauty."

THIRTY-ONE

Debbie sat in her bay window, lost in her thoughts. She was so glad that Christmas was over and done with. Keeping the magic of Santa alive for two five-year-olds was getting harder and harder with each passing year. They had heard at school that there was no Santa, and Brad and Debbie had to reassure them that there really was. That he would find their house this year, just like he had last year, and all good little girls and boys could expect gifts from Santa.

Debbie had cooked the full turkey dinner for Christmas Day, with a lot of help from Janice. The kids were happy with their presents, and everyone had enjoyed the day. Linda's fruitcake was not so popular, but the pumpkin pie was a hit.

They missed having Katie with them, but she had gone to Jeremy's parents for Christmas Day. Brad was going to need to build a bigger dining room table for next year's dinner, Debbie decided. There would be three new babies with Janice also being pregnant again. Debbie couldn't help but wonder what her sister was thinking. She wasn't. That was the problem. She was in love and not thinking straight. Debbie prayed that the marriage would work out. Mark was a good guy, and hopefully, they could make it work.

She knew Brad was disappointed that they stayed home for New Year's, but she just couldn't handle another party. Three parties and Christmas Day were more than enough, especially for a woman in her condition. Susan and Keith, and Janice and Mark, had all gone to the New Year's party at the resort, but Debbie never even saw midnight.

She heard Brad in the kitchen all the way from the bay window and Debbie stood and stretched. Brad kissed her as she entered the kitchen. "How are you feeling? Are you still having cramps?"

"No, they have let up. But I am peeing a lot."

"Guess that's to be expected. The doctor even said so."

"Yes, hun. I know what the doctor said. I was there too."

"Well, take it easy. We don't want you on bed rest again, like you were the last time." Brad pulled her into his arms. "Have I told you lately how beautiful you are?"

"I don't know how you find me beautiful. I look like a beached whale, and I don't walk; I waddle." Debbie could feel tears running down her cheeks. She swiped them away in annoyance.

"Honey, don't cry. I was just trying to tell you that I love you."

"I can't help it. I am an emotionally exhausted wreck these days."

"You'll be fine once the twins are born. I am here to help you. If there's anything I can do, just ask."

"I will. I'm sorry for being so emotional. I blame it on pregnancy hormones."

Brad's phone rang. "Sorry, hun, I need to take this." He headed to his office to take the call.

Damn tears. I don't want to be crying all the time, but I can't seem to stop it. She wished the babies would hurry up and get there already.

"Sorry about that. It was a client asking questions. The

guys are almost finished with his house. They are building the fireplace today. I love it when the client chooses a rock face. And, he will also have the mantle made from rock. It's going to be beautiful when it's finished in a day or two."

"Sounds like there is a full crew working here today." Debbie nodded her head in the B&B direction.

"Yes, they are starting to put up the drywall now that the electrical and plumbing are all in. Have you picked out the paint colors or the light fixtures yet?"

"I was looking at that this morning actually. I was hoping you could take a look. I have it narrowed down to two sets of lights and would like your opinion." Debbie opened her laptop.

"They are both nice. I think I like this style better. I like that they have ceiling fans for the bedrooms. We will also need hallway lights. And I still think we should use pot lights in the bathrooms. I like the ones with the fans. That would be my choice. If you like it, I'm good with this one as well."

"Alright, this one it is. Let me write down the information you'll need to place the order."

"Is anyone home?" Val called from the doorway.

"In the kitchen," Debbie answered. "What are you doing home on a weekday?"

"I took a sick day today. Morning, Brad. How's life treating you?" Val asked as she sat down at the counter beside him.

"Good. Staying busy. How about you?"

"Fine, thanks," Val replied.

"And how's my buddy James doing?"

"Oh, he's fine. He's always fine. As long as he has a TV to watch and a cold beer in his hand, he's doing great."

Debbie set a coffee down in front of Val.

"I'll get a refill in my takeaway cup too, please, hun." Brad passed Debbie his cup across the counter. "If you ladies will excuse me, I need to go check on my guys."

"When is the B&B going to be finished?" Val asked.

"Probably another two weeks or so," Brad said as he took his coffee from Debbie. "Hand me that paper for the lights, and I'll go order them."

When Brad left, Debbie took his vacated seat beside Val.

"I am surprised to see you home on a workday. Is everything alright?" Debbie asked with a tone of concern.

"I had a doctor's appointment, so I took the day off."

"Now I am getting worried. A doctor's appointment? For what reason?"

"I had a checkup." Val started to cry. "I needed to have a pregnancy test. It's positive. Oh God, Deb, I'm pregnant. Twelve weeks pregnant."

"What? Wow, I didn't even know you and James wanted more kids."

"We didn't. We don't. At least I don't. Oh, Deb, I don't know for sure if it's James's kid." Val cried harder.

Debbie couldn't help but think, *I knew it. Damn, I just knew she would end up doing something stupid.*

"What exactly are you trying to tell me?" Debbie asked with a furrowed brow.

"It could be either James's or it could be Steve's."

"So obviously you and Steve have taken your friendship to a deeper level. How long has this affair been going on? I want details, damn it."

"It's over. Steve and I did have an affair for about a month, but I broke things off with him. And now, I am pregnant and don't know who the father is. How did I ever get myself into this mess?"

"Oh, Val. I warned you that you were playing with fire. I'm sorry that you are in this mess, but it's a mess of your own making," Debbie said. Debbie knew she sounded harsh, but she was right. What a stupid thing to do. And now, Val would forever pay for her deception. She wondered if her own mother had wrestled with this same problem when she found out she was pregnant with Susan. Had her mother been guessing, or had she known that Jefferson was Susan's father?

"I thought I might get some sympathy from my best friend, but I guess I was wrong." Val stood up to leave.

Debbie pulled at Val's arm. "Sit down! You just dropped a bomb on me! How did you expect I would react?"

"I thought you would be kind about it. I thought you would reassure me that it would all be okay."

"Sorry, of course it will be. You will figure it out. You have to tell James."

"I don't want to hurt him, and I know this will hurt him deeply."

Perhaps you should have thought about that before you decided to have an affair. "You'll still have to tell him."

"Not if I have an abortion," Val blurted.

"No, you can't be serious." Debbie was dumbfounded. Debbie wondered, why would she say that to me?

"I don't know what to do. That's why I came here." Val cried harder.

"I'm sorry, hun. But you know how I feel about abortions. I don't think that's your answer. I think you need to come clean with James, and with Steve for that matter."

"James will be disgusted with me, and Steve will be over the moon. Steve has no kids, but he desperately wants some of his own."

"Why did you start the affair, and why did you end it?"

"It started because Steve and I were so attracted to each other. We fought against it as long as we could, but the passion between us was like wildfire. We would go to the motel during our lunch hour a couple of days a week. The sex was fantastic, and compared to James, Steve was an excellent lover." Val wiped her face. "But that was the problem. I couldn't help but compare the two. Steve filled a need that I had. He satisfied my desires, which were not being filled at home by my husband. I was so ashamed and guilty about cheating on James that I just had to end it. Steve and I are still friends, but we don't go to the motel anymore."

"Oh, Val! James will be crushed. But you still need to tell him. You need to let him decide if he wants to raise another man's child. I still wonder if my father knew that Susan was not his kid. If he knew, he never let it show."

"This may very well end my marriage. What will I do then?" Val blubbered.

"You did the deed, and now you must face the consequences." Debbie rubbed Val's arm. "I think you need to put on your big girl panties and deal with whatever happens. Do you still love James?"

"Yes, of course I do. I love him with all my heart. That's why I don't want to hurt him."

"Then, you have to tell him. He is going to be hurt, for sure. You may even need to give him a couple of days to decide what he wants to do about it. If he decides to accept it, then I don't think you even need to tell Steve it could be his. Once that baby is born, you can do tests to find out for sure who the father is."

"Maybe I don't need to tell James either. I could just tell him I am pregnant, and in nine months, after I do the test, then if I have to, I'll tell him then," Val suggested.

"That's definitely an option. But won't the guilt eat away at you?"

"I think I could deal with my own guilt, at least for nine months. I just don't want to hurt him. I love him and want him to be happy. A new baby will no doubt make him happy. If I tell him the whole truth, he'll be so hurt."

Debbie handed her a tissue. "That's your decision to make."

"I think I need a few days to think about things. Damn, I wish James was more affectionate, more involved in my life. Most of the time, he's more like an annoying roommate than a husband or a lover. If he was more of a husband and father, this whole damn mess probably would have never happened. Know what I mean?"

"Sounds like you are looking for someone else to blame for your indiscretions, and James is a convenient scapegoat. I don't mean to sound harsh, but let's call a spade a spade."

"That's an awful thing to say, but there may be some truth in it." Val was crying harder.

Debbie handed her the whole box of tissues. "Maybe you and James should look into some marriage counseling. If you love him and want the marriage to work, then a counselor could help you both figure things out. Just a suggestion."

"I am sure in his mind, everything is perfect. He has a wife who cooks and cleans up after him and his son all the time."

"I think a counselor would be able to help you both with all of that. I think it would be worth a try."

"I need time to think about it all." Val wiped her tears. "Thanks for listening to me. If you could resist telling Brad about this for a few days until I can get it figured out, I would appreciate it. I need to tell James that I am pregnant at least. The rest of it, well, at this point, I think it may be best to stay a secret, for a few months."

"You know Brad and I don't keep secrets. We are both open and honest with each other. I'll try to keep this to myself, but they are both going to find out soon enough."

Debbie pulled Val into her arms for a hug and quietly whispered, "It's going to be alright. You will figure it out."

THIRTY-TWO

The shrimp ring was thawing in the kitchen sink, and Debbie was putting the vegetable tray together when she heard someone at the door.

"Hello, my beautiful family," Brad said as he kicked the snow off his boots.

"Hi, hun. Is everything alright?" Debbie wasn't used to seeing him home on a Saturday morning. He was usually at a jobsite or meeting with a client.

"Yes, everything is fine. There are only three guys working, and Don is with them." Brad snuck a carrot off the tray.

"You seem to be relying on Don a lot. Do you think you are going to promote him?"

"Yes, I think I will. He's good with reading the blueprints and good at calling me if he has any questions. The guys all like and respect him, and none of them want the job."

"At least now that he has bought a house, you know he's planning on sticking around for a while. I'm glad you have a supervisor to help you."

"Yes, because of that, I am planning on taking on a few more buildings this year." Brad popped a cherry tomato into his mouth. "Hun, I'm hungry. Do you have anything I could make a sandwich with?"

"The kids and I just had chicken salad. There's some left over in the fridge."

Brad came around the counter, made himself a sandwich, and came to sit on the outer side of the counter. "What time is this party tonight? What time do we have to go?"

"Not till four o'clock. After you all get back from the kid's ski lessons."

"Sounds good. And are Mom and Dad babysitting?"

"No. They are going to the party. Sharon is going to babysit tonight."

"I didn't know Mom and Dad were going. How did that happen?"

"I don't know. Janice invited them. They are part of our family, so I guess she decided to include them too."

"Who else is going?"

"I don't know. She said she was expecting about forty people. That's all I know."

"And what is a housewarming party about anyway? People move into houses every day. What's so special about that?"

"It's just a thing people do. It's a chance for everyone to see Janice and Mark's new home."

"We are expected to take them a gift, right? I think that's why people have housewarming parties, for the gifts. What did we get them?"

"We bought them a set of stacking stools. When they have extra company, they will have somewhere for them to sit. Susan and Keith bought her a set of stacking tables."

"Those little tables do come in handy." Brad took a slice of cucumber off the tray that Debbie was still creating. "Babe, could you grab me a glass of milk, please."

"I hope Janice and Mark are going to be happy in their

new home. I have decided that I like Mark. He seems like a real down-to-earth kind of fellow."

"Yes, I like him too. He's not afraid to get his hands dirty, that's for sure. But the main reason I like him is that he is bonding with Zackery. That young man needs a father figure in his life."

Debbie had the lid poised to put onto the veggie tray. "Do you want any more of this before I put it away?"

"No thanks, I'm good." Brad gave her his cheeky smile.

"So, if you are home for the day, I may go up and have a short nap while you and the kids are gone skiing."

"Why don't you go now? I can get the kids ready and off to their lesson."

"Yes, I will. Don't let them forget to take their goggles."

"Sure. No worries, Daddy has it covered. Do you want me to come tuck you in?" he said with a seductive grin.

"No, thank you. I am going for a nap, not to fool around with you, cowboy."

Brad pulled her into his arms for a sultry kiss. "Are you sure I can't change your mind? The kids are engrossed in cartoons and wouldn't miss us for half an hour."

"Thanks, but no thanks. I need a nap. But if you are a good boy at the party, maybe we could fool around when we get home."

"I'm going to hold you to that."

Debbie made it to the top of the stairs but had to stand and catch her breath. Carrying these twins around was getting to be a struggle. But she was still not ordered on bed rest, at least not yet. With the last pregnancy, she had done six weeks of complete bed rest, and it almost drove her out of her mind.

She pulled the covers back and climbed in.

A couple of hours later, she woke to Brad planting little kisses all over her face.

"Honey, I hate to wake you, but it's three-thirty, and you said you wanted to leave at four o'clock for the party."

"Oh my goodness. Is it really that late? I must have been tired. I haven't heard a thing since I lay down."

Debbie pulled the covers back and stood and stretched. "I still need to lay our clothes out. When you go down, could you please make me a coffee and tell the kids to come up to get ready, please?"

"I thought Sharon was coming to babysit."

"She is, but not till seven o'clock. Remember, we discussed it and decided to take the kids for a while and then bring them home for baths and bedtime."

"I'm sorry, yes, I had forgotten. I'll send them right up."

As Debbie waddled to the washroom, she thought about how strange it was that Brad forgot. *That man has a mind like a steel trap. Nothing ever gets by him.*

She then went into Ben's room and set out his good slacks, a clean shirt, and his suit jacket. In Becky's room, she picked out a white dress with pink accents on it and a pair of white leotards to wear under it.

As the kids came bouncing up the stairs, Debbie noticed how messy Becky's hair looked. "Sweetie, you need to tidy up your hair, please."

"Okay, Mommy, I will," Becky assured her as she bounced down the hall to her room.

Debbie was desperate for a coffee, but she detoured back to her own room. She decided that she might as well get dressed and save herself the trip back up those darn stairs. She put on the dress that she had worn for Brad's business party. She accessorized it with her good pearl earrings, quickly applied her lipstick, and then set out Brad's clothes.

"You look nice, hun. Is this what you want me to wear?" Brad asked as he walked in.

"Yes, it's casual. I thought maybe wear your blue jeans, a nice shirt, and your dinner jacket."

"Your coffee is sitting on the counter getting cold."

"Thanks. See you downstairs in a minute." Debbie held the handrail and carefully made it to the bottom as the kids came racing past her.

"You're getting slow, Mommy," Ben commented on the way past her.

"I'm trying to be careful."

"Is my hair better, Mommy?" Becky asked as she took Debbie's empty hand.

"Yes, it looks much better now. You look pretty, angel."

"Thanks, Mommy. I was going to ask you for some lipstick, but you were already gone."

They had reached the bottom of the stairs. "Do you want to share Mommy's?" Debbie asked.

"What? How can I share yours?"

"Give Mommy a kiss on the lips." Debbie bent down and kissed Becky. "There, now you have lipstick."

Becky giggled. "I need to go see." Becky ran into the washroom to look in the mirror.

"So, are we all ready to go then?" Brad asked as he came down the stairs.

"We have to take the veggie tray and the shrimp ring," Debbie said as she took a big drink of her now-cold coffee.

"Let me take those out to the van, and I'll come back to get you. Wait for me, please," Brad said to Debbie.

"Alright, I'll wait right here."

The kids were already in the van, and Brad held Debbie's hand as he walked slowly with her to the passenger side and helped her in. "This is why I don't go anywhere that I don't absolutely have to," Debbie said as she pulled herself into the seat. "I feel like a beached whale."

"You look beautiful and very pregnant, my dear." Brad gave her a quick kiss before he closed the door.

About twenty minutes later, they arrived at Janice's. Brad drove right up to the front door to make it as easy for Debbie as he could. He had come around and helped her out of the van and into the house. Then he carried in the food and the gift. The kids were already in the house. "I'm just going to move the van out to the side of the road so we don't get blocked in."

"Thanks, hun. That's a good idea." Debbie was in the process of removing her coat and boots at the doorway.

"Come on in here, please. Let me take your coats," Janice offered.

Mark came to the door and took the coats from Janice. "Please come in. It's nice to see you. What did you do with Brad?"

"He's just parking the van."

"What would you like to drink, sis?" Janice asked.

"I'd have a ginger ale if you have any, please."

"Coming right up! Go on into the living room and pick out the most comfortable chair."

"Thanks, I think I will. Hi, Val. James. Nice to see you

guys. I think I'll choose this big, comfy chair over here in the corner. I'll be less likely to be in the way over here."

"You look pretty. That's a nice dress," Val commented.

"Thanks. You look pretty yourself."

Janice brought Debbie her drink just as Brad came through the door with his mom and dad.

For the next hour, a steady flow of people arrived.

Ben and Becky were in Zack's room playing with his toys when Janice put all the food out. Brad was standing in the corner talking, and Debbie kept glancing his way until she caught his eye.

Brad came over to her. "You alright, hun?"

"Could you please give me a hand to get out of this chair? I need to go to the washroom," Debbie asked quietly.

Brad smiled as he pulled her up out of the chair.

Debbie excused herself from the crowd and went down the hall. She had to wait for the washroom. When she came back out, she went down the hall to find her kids. "Here you are. What are you guys doing?"

"Just playing. Check this out. This guy transforms into an army tank." Ben showed her how it changed.

"That's cool. How are you, Zack? Are you liking your new house?"

"I love it. This is so much better than being stuck in that little room at the resort," Zack answered.

"Your mom is putting the food out. Don't take too much on your plates, kids. You can always go back for more."

"Yes, Mommy," Becky answered.

When Debbie got back to the kitchen, people were already loading plates with food. Janice had put a smaller, shorter table on top of the larger table, so the food was on two levels. Debbie was impressed with Janice's idea. There were also desserts all down one counter.

Linda and Charles were in line, and Debbie joined them. "Hi, Debbie. How are you doing?" Linda asked.

"Good, but I am starting to need help getting out of chairs. Brad thinks it's funny."

"Yeah, he would. Men don't understand what women have to go through to give them the babies they want." Linda handed Debbie an empty plate. "Where are the kids? I thought you were bringing them."

"They are down in Zack's room, playing."

Debbie went through the buffet line and took her plate into the living room. Thomas was keeping her chair warm and stood up to allow her back her spot.

"Thanks, Thomas. You should go get some food. There's lots there to choose from."

When the kids had gotten their food, they came and sat on the floor at Debbie's feet.

After dinner, Brad took the kids home. Sharon would give them their baths and read them their bedtime stories.

Debbie was enjoying visiting with everyone. Because she stayed home most of the time, she hadn't seen much of other people. Around ten o'clock, people were starting to say goodnight.

Brad came over and suggested that he could get the van up to the door again. He wondered if she was ready to go home.

"Oh, yes, please. I am ready when you are."

Brad found their coats and boots and helped her get them on. They said goodnight to everyone and headed home.

In the van, Brad asked, "Did you enjoy the party? I noticed a lot of people coming over to talk to you."

"Yes, it was nice. But you must be tired. Other than when you sat on the arm of my chair to eat, you were standing the whole night."

"There weren't any places to sit. There were a lot of people there."

When they got home, Sharon was sitting on the couch knitting.

"How were the kids? Did they get their baths and stories?"

"Yes, they are both sound asleep. I'll see you Monday morning," Sharon said as she put her coat on.

"Thanks, Sharon. Night."

Brad watched to see that Sharon got away, turned out the lights, and locked the door.

Debbie was already halfway up the stairs. Brad joined her, and they walked the rest of the way, hand in hand.

THIRTY-THREE

The whole month of January flew by in a blur. Debbie had been so preoccupied with picking out paint colors, lights, furniture for the bedrooms, and then sheets, blankets, and comforters that the month was over before she knew it. Everyone who dropped in had been given the B&B tour now that everything was completed except for a few final issues.

She did miss Brad not popping in and out throughout the day, though.

Debbie heard someone at the front door. "Come in," she hollered back over her shoulder.

"You busy?" Nancy asked.

"No, but I need to use the washroom. Be right back. Help yourself to a coffee." Debbie waddled from the room. When she returned, she grinned. "Sorry about that, but when nature calls, I have to go. And go now!"

"I understand. I needed a break and have been hearing great things about your new B&B. If you feel up to it, I would love a tour."

"Sure, let's have our coffee first, and then I will show you around."

"Sounds good. How is the pregnancy going?"

"Good, I think. I keep getting cramps. They come and go, and the babies are very active." Debbie lifted her shirt, and Nancy could see the babies kicking. "See what I mean?"

"Oh, may I feel?" When Debbie nodded, Nancy put her hand flat against Debbie's stomach. "Oh, my goodness, that is so cool. Brings back fond memories way back when I was pregnant. I used to walk around with my hand on my belly just in case the baby kicked."

"These two are very active. They are kicking me all the time. So, how have you been? I know you were busy over the Christmas holidays. I was there for three events but begged off for New Year's. I was just telling Janice the other day that when we bought the place, there was no winter business at all. And now, what with the ski hill and the banquet rooms, I bet December is almost as busy as July."

"Nancy and Robert came in for dinner one day last week. We were talking about that very thing. They are looking forward to May when the skiing is finished so they can travel in their RV. The only problem with being a year-round playground is that we don't have downtime anymore. When the ski hill closes, the golf course starts to get busy."

"Gee, I feel so sorry for you," Debbie said mockingly.

"Yeah, I know, right?" Nancy laughed. "We had a party every weekend for six weeks straight. You did such a great job of building the business that we don't have any downtime, and I think our marriage is suffering because of that."

"Oh no. That is always tough for couples who work together all the time. You should plan a weekend away occasionally. Janice is quite capable of running the place in your absence. Why don't you plan a nice weekend away in May between the ski and golf seasons? Go to a nice hotel somewhere, with a swimming pool and a five-star restaurant. Get a couples massage, go sightseeing, or just sleep in. Spoil yourselves once in a while."

"That sounds funny." Nancy smiled. "Between ski and golf seasons. Most people have winter and spring, but we have ski and golf seasons." Nancy chuckled. "But I do like the idea of Phil and I having a break. We spend way too much time together."

"Take your breaks where you can," Debbie replied with a knowing look. "Some days it took me three hours to get back home from making the bank deposits."

"I know. I am doing the same thing. But I am thinking about going to the city and doing some shopping. Alone. Phil and I both need time alone, away from each other. I'd like to maybe see a play, or even a good movie."

"Then do that. You take a weekend away, and Phil can take the next weekend. What does he like to do in his spare time?"

"He used to like fishing, but he doesn't do that much anymore."

"Well, he should. Does he have a buddy that would go on a fishing trip with him?"

"Yes, he does. I just don't know that he would go. I am sure he thinks he has to be on duty all the time, or the place will collapse without him."

"Well, give it some thought. There's no one saying that you both can't have an occasional weekend away, either together or separately." Debbie stood up. "If you are ready, let's go do a walk-through of the B&B."

"Yes, let's." Nancy followed Debbie through the door and up the stairs.

"You'll notice the thick carpeting. There is also an under pad to help with the extra noise. The first door on the left is the full-size washroom."

"Oh my, this is nice. You could fit four people in that

shower." Nancy grinned. "I love the vanity. Very nice. And I like the wicker table and stand. And the wicker cabinet, I assume, is full of towels."

"Yes, of course. You can open it if you like."

"Then there are the six bedrooms, all the same," Debbie said as she opened one of the bedroom doors and let Nancy step inside. "Four poster beds, with homemade quilts. I found them online, believe it or not."

"They're quite nice. And I love the headboards. They look so majestic and regal."

"Thanks. Brad knows a good carpenter who did all the carving. They are quite exquisite," Debbie said proudly. "The matching nightstands are his work as well."

"Wow, I am impressed. And the sitting area is a nice touch. Those chairs look like they are leather."

"They are. Soft leather. Have a seat." Debbie sat down in one and Nancy sat down in the other.

"Oh my, this is comfy. I could see myself sitting here reading a book or having a nap, no problem."

"Come on, lady, let's get on with this tour." Debbie chuckled at the disappointed look on Nancy's face.

"Alright. I'm coming." Nancy reluctantly followed Debbie down the hall.

"All the rooms on this side have windows overlooking the pool, and on the other side, they overlook the woods." Debbie opened a door on the other side so Nancy could see the difference. "At this end is a smaller two-piece bathroom. It's in case the bigger bathroom is occupied."

"Good thinking. I like that idea." Nancy nodded in agreement.

"Now, let's head down to the lobby area. Brad has

thrown a rug down outside to control the mud, if you want to step out and see the apartments."

"Yes, please. I might as well see it all while I am here." Nancy smiled.

"There are two apartments, both with private entrances." Nancy followed Debbie into one of the apartments. "Well, hello, you two. I am just giving Nancy the five-cent tour."

"Come on in," Don said. "Hello, Nancy. Greg, this is my sister-in-law, Nancy. The guy covered in paint splatters is my buddy, Greg."

"Hello, Greg. Nice to meet you," Nancy said. "Sorry to interrupt your work."

"Not a problem. We're just doing final paint touch-ups today. You may want to avoid touching any walls," Don suggested.

"This is our two-bedroom apartment," Debbie said. "This is obviously the living room with the kitchen at that end. And on this side is the washroom and the two bedrooms, which both have windows looking out into the wooded area."

"Very nice indeed. When can I move in?" Nancy asked.

"I don't think Phil would approve." Don chuckled.

"Yeah, you're probably right about that." Nancy shrugged. "You guys sure have done a good job here. Don, how is the painting coming along at your new house?"

"Almost done. Brad came over for a few hours over the weekend and we got it all done except for the kitchen."

"When you get moved in, you'll have to have a house-warming party. I would love to see what you have done with the place," Debbie said.

"I'll have to give that some thought," Don replied.

"Well, sorry to interrupt. We'll let you get back to work now," Debbie said. "Nancy, if you want to follow me back, I'll show you the storage and the laundry."

Nancy looked shocked. "There's more?"

After the tour was complete, Nancy said, "Well, color me green with envy. Everything is amazing. I love the rooms upstairs, and those headboards with the poster beds are absolutely gorgeous. I am almost afraid to send my extra guests here because they will never come back to my little resort after spending a weekend here."

"I wouldn't worry too much about that. I only offer accommodations and breakfast. You offer so much more." Debbie refilled their coffee cups and took the seat across from Nancy. "I don't see us as competition. Guests who look for B&Bs are a different kind of people than those looking for a full resort experience. Honestly, I think the only thing that will happen is that I can accommodate your overflow guests."

"This place is incredible. Any idea when you will open?" Nancy asked.

"No, not yet. First, I need to get these twins delivered. I can't even walk normally at this stage. I am thinking maybe this fall. Or maybe next spring."

"Be sure to let me know when the big opening is so I can start sending you customers."

"I should tell you that I am going to specifically invite the Swansons for a free weekend as our first guests. They have been part of our extended family ever since we moved here."

"They are a super nice couple. They always ask about you," Nancy said. "I guess I should be getting back before the dinner rush. Thanks so much for the tour. Brad showed

Phil around when they were drywalling. He'll probably want to come see it now that it's finished."

"Tell him anytime." Debbie walked Nancy to the door.

"I will. Thanks again for the tour." Nancy pulled a handful of change from her pocket. "Here's your nickel."

"For what? Oh, my five-cent tour." Debbie gently slapped Nancy's hand away. "Don't be such a wise guy. Say hi to Phil for me."

As Debbie shut the door to the cold, she chuckled to herself at Nancy's silly gesture.

THIRTY-FOUR

Brad came home with a huge bouquet of flowers and a box of chocolates for Debbie. "Happy Valentine's Day, honey."

"Thank you. The flowers are beautiful."

Brad set the flowers and chocolates on the counter, and he pulled her in for a serious kiss. "I want you to know how much I love you. You are my whole world, and I am so thankful that you are my wife and the mother of my children."

"I love you too. Very much." Brad kissed her again, this time deepening the intensity.

"Look what else I brought you." Brad handed her a piece of paper.

Debbie read it and then looked at him. "What exactly is this? What does this mean?"

"It's your occupancy permit. The B&B is officially finished. You can move in, or open it, any time you want to. The apartments can be rented, and the rooms can be used at your leisure."

"That's great, hun. Oh, and the new beds and dressers for the kids' rooms were delivered and set up this morning. I will spend the next few days getting them moved into their new rooms. And Susan commented that maybe she and Keith could stay here for a few days while they redo their hardwood floors at the house."

"That is totally up to you. Whenever you want to officially open, you can do so. I won't interfere. But we are still in agreement that we won't hook up all the extra TV receivers until the actual opening, right?"

"Yes, you are right. I was thinking about what to call our new business. I have been kicking around some ideas and think I have found one I like. How does the Ben and Becky Bed-and-Breakfast sound to you?"

"Cute. It's kind of catchy. The B&B, B&B. The Ben and Becky B&B. Yes, I like it. Very clever of you. I figured you would have chosen something like the Cedar Grove B&B. But I do like the Ben and Becky B&B better."

"I decided that there are too many Cedar Grove businesses here already. The Cedar Grove Ski Hill, the Cedar Grove Golf Course, and of course, the Cedar Grove Resort. If you like it, then we are in agreement." Debbie raised her coffee cup in a cheer. "Welcome to the new Ben and Becky Bed-and-Breakfast."

"Have you given any thought to what we will name these little ones?" Brad rubbed her belly. "Oh goodness, I just felt a kick. That always freaks me out a little. Does it hurt when they kick you?"

"Not really. But sometimes I think they are both standing on my bladder."

"So, what about names for them? Have you given it any thought?" Brad asked.

"We could stay with B names. Like Brian and Bethany, or Barry and Beatrice. Or do something totally different like Nathan and Natalie. I don't know. Have you given it any thought?"

"I've always liked the name James and perhaps Jessica or Jasmine."

"I like Jasmine. But it would get shortened to Jazz. Jessica would get shortened to Jess. That sounds alright."

"James and Jess. I like that. James Christopher Mumford and Jessica Marie Mumford. What do you think?"

"Marie? Where did that come from?"

"I don't know. It just popped into my head." Brad shrugged.

"How about Jessica Ann?"

"I think I like Marie better. Let me think on it for a bit. What have we got for lunch? I thought I was meeting a client for lunch, but he postponed till next week, and I didn't make a lunch this morning."

"I was thinking about having tomato soup and a grilled cheese. How does that sound?"

"Perfect. What can I do to help?"

"You heat the soup, and I'll make the sandwiches." Debbie grinned.

After lunch, when Brad left, Debbie took a tea and sat in her favorite spot in the bay window.

James Christopher, she liked that. *How does that sound to you, little guy?* Debbie rubbed her tummy. Jessica Ann Marie. That one she liked. There was no law saying that she couldn't have two middle names, and Ann Marie went together nicely. She'd have to run that by Brad later.

She wondered what Janice and Val would call their new babies. There would be lots of baby showers and cakes with Janice due at the end of July and Val at the beginning of August.

She hadn't heard from Val for a couple of weeks. She wondered if she had decided how to handle the James versus Steve situation. Debbie still couldn't believe Val actually had an affair. She needed a good swift kick in the butt sometimes. Regardless, there was a new baby on the way.

Debbie also considered when to open the B&B. The twins would be arriving in a couple of months, and she wanted to give them at least six months of her full attention. So that would put them to the end of October at least. Maybe she'd plan on a fall opening. Or, she could hire staff and open now. Just the thought of that made her tired.

The phone rang and pulled her out of her thoughts.

"What are you up to today?" Val asked.

"Nothing too exciting. Are you coming over?" Debbie asked.

"Yeah, I could if you're home and not busy."

"I'll put on a fresh pot of coffee. See you soon."

A few minutes later, Val opened the door and hollered, "I'm here."

"In the kitchen. Come on in." Debbie poured them both a fresh cup of coffee.

Val slid onto a stool at the counter, and Debbie set her coffee in front of her.

"I was just thinking about you this morning. How are things going?"

"As good as they can be, under the circumstances." Val looked a tad embarrassed. "I think I owe you an apology. I shouldn't have dumped all my crap on you the last time I was here."

Val looked frazzled and not as put together as she usually was. "We are best friends. No apology needed. So, I assume you have told James you are pregnant by now?" Debbie said.

"Yes, I have told him. But that's all I told him."

Debbie couldn't help but ask, "And did you tell Steve?"

"No, I decided not to tell Steve until after the baby is born. He's a super nice guy, and I know he wants kids of his own, so I don't want to get his hopes up, only to disappoint him later."

"So, that decision has been made. And I assume James is excited about being a father again?"

"Yes, he couldn't be happier. I tried to talk to him about how unhappy I am at home and how I need him to step up and make more of an effort with me and Timothy. He said he would, but I have yet to see any evidence of it." Val hung her head. "I mentioned seeing a counselor but he thinks everything is fine and that I'm being overdramatic."

"How can he think that, when you have told him straight out how unhappy you are?"

"I wish I knew. According to him, everything is perfect. He wanted a wife and kids, and he has them."

"What if you threatened to leave him? Do you think that might get his attention?"

"That thought has crossed my mind on more than one occasion. I gave up a good job to move here and be his wife. I hate the thought of having to start all over someplace else. And now I have Timmy to think about as well."

"It's complicated," Debbie said quietly. "But at least I can tell Brad now. Congratulations, Val."

"Yes, thanks for keeping my secret. I know you and Brad tell each other everything."

"Yes, we are very open with each other. I think that is one of the reasons our marriage is so solid. Brad is a good-looking man, and women throw themselves at him all the time. Sometimes they even flirt with him right in front of me. But I don't worry. I know he only has eyes for me.

Even in this condition, he still tells me how beautiful I am."

"You don't know how lucky you are. It took you two a long time to be together, but at least now you know it's solid. I envy you and Brad. James and I are nothing like you guys. I can't even remember the last time he told me he loves me." Val shrugged.

"I have always liked James, from what I know of him. But they say that you never really know someone until you live with them. He seems like a good guy in so many ways."

Val bent over and smelled Debbie's flowers. "I suppose Brad bought these for you. Lucky lady. I will be surprised if James even remembers what day it is. I doubt I will be getting flowers or chocolates."

"I bought you flowers for your last birthday. Don't you remember?"

"Yes, I remember. I meant flowers from my husband. That never happens."

"I'm sorry that you aren't happy in your marriage. But you know me, if something isn't working, then fix it or forget it. Life is just too short to do anything else. Like with Brad and I, I used to hate when he'd climb in bed with prickly whiskers. We talked about it, and now he shaves every night before he comes to bed."

"Really, you trained him to shave every night?"

"I wouldn't say I trained him; I explained how much I disliked it, and he decided that it was something he could do to please me. When you have open and frank discussions, you can work on fixing the little things that drive you crazy. What is something James does that drives you nuts?"

"That is a very big list. Where should I start? Stupid things, like not putting the lid back on a jar he just opened. Or he'll take something out of the cupboard, use it, and leave it sitting on the counter. He may or may not even close the cupboard door." Val shook her head. "How hard would it be to put it away before he closes the door? And he can't hit the laundry hamper, no matter how hard he tries. Stupid little things that drive me crazy, and now Timmy is following his example."

"It's always those little things that get on your last nerve. I am sure you have tried to talk to him about it?"

"Of course. He may put his dirty clothes in the hamper for a couple of days and then it's like he has totally forgotten. But he's always on my ass for leaving my stuff around the house."

"I wonder what would happen if you got him one of those clothes butlers that men use. You know what I mean. It has a place to hang pants and shirts and a small shelf for wallets and jewelry. Maybe something like that might help. You could set it close to the hamper."

"That is not a bad idea. I could probably order one online."

"Would you like another coffee?" Debbie asked.

"No, I need to get home. Thanks for letting me vent. But I really should get going."

"Val, talk to James, honestly. Eventually, he'll start opening up to you as well."

"I'll work on that," Val said on her way out the door.

Debbie picked up the dirty cups and put them in the dishwasher. They were having spaghetti for dinner tonight and everything was ready. She wanted to go back upstairs to work on the kids' new bedrooms but knew that the bus would be there in about ten minutes.

She got a fresh coffee and sat at the counter, thinking about getting the kids to help move stuff from their old rooms into the new rooms. She knew they would be excited to see that their furniture arrived. For the past two weeks, the twins had been overly excited about moving into their grown-up rooms, and now they finally could. Then she needed to get a nursery ready for the new little ones who'd arrive in just two months.

Her thoughts were interrupted by the kids coming through the back door.

"Hi, Mommy. We're home," Ben announced.

"Welcome home, my little munchkins. How was school today?"

"It was okay. Becky got a star for a story she told. But I didn't want to tell a story."

"Why not?"

"Because he's shy in front of the class, and I'm not," Becky stated.

"Oh, I see. So, what was the story you told?" Debbie asked.

"I made up a story about a little dog who got lost in the woods, and a stray cat helped the dog find its way back home," Becky explained.

"Wow, that sounds like a good story. And you just made it up. Good job, angel. Why don't you both grab a piece of fruit and then we can go upstairs. I have a surprise for you both."

"What kind of a surprise?" Ben asked as he handed Becky a banana and took an orange for himself.

"You'll just have to wait and see. I'm going up now, and after you have your snack, wash your hands and then come up and find me." Debbie chuckled as she headed up the stairs.

Debbie had already moved their bedside lamps and some of their things into their new rooms. She was standing in the hallway when the kids came racing up the stairs. "Go look in your new rooms." Debbie stood back to let them pass.

"Holy crap. Our beds are here," Ben exclaimed.

"Benjamin, watch your language," Debbie scolded.

"I love it," Becky shouted.

"You can both help move your clothes into your new dressers, but carefully, please."

Becky threw her arms around Debbie's legs. "Thanks, Mommy. This is so cool."

"You're welcome. Now that you are both old enough to make your own beds and take better care of your toys, you deserve to have your own special rooms."

"We are getting older every day!" Ben announced.

"Yes, my son, you certainly are." Debbie smiled. "I guess you will both be sleeping in your new rooms tonight?"

"You betcha." Ben was grinning from ear to ear.

"Where is everybody?" Brad asked as he kissed Debbie.

"Setting up our new rooms, Daddy. Come see my new room," Becky called out to him.

"Oh, angel, look how pretty this room is." Brad sat down on her bed. "This is comfy. Maybe I'll sleep here tonight."

"No, Daddy. This is my room. You have to sleep with Mommy." Becky laughed at the silly expression Brad had on his face.

“Come see my room, Daddy,” Ben called out.

“Coming, son. Becky, your room is perfect for a little girl like you,” Brad stated.

“I’m not little anymore. I’m a big girl now!” Becky announced with one hand on her little hip.

“Yes, you are, but to me, you’ll always be my little girl.” Brad gave her a hug as he and Debbie made their way across the hall, to Ben’s room.

“Hey, buddy, I like your furniture. It looks manly,” Brad said as he sat on Ben’s bed.

“I’m a big boy now,” Ben stated proudly.

“Yes, you are. But how many teddy bears does a big boy need to have in his room?”

Ben thought about it for a minute. “I guess only one would do. I think I’ll keep this one.”

“I am proud of you, son. Good job.” Brad ruffled his hair and left the room.

After all the excitement, Debbie headed to her bedroom, and Brad followed. “You alright, hun?”

“Yes, I just need a little rest.” She leaned in for his kiss. “Val was here this afternoon. She said that she wasn’t expecting flowers or any special recognition, even if it is Valentine’s.”

“Sucks to be her.” Brad chuckled at the scowl on Debbie’s face. “My wife got flowers and chocolates. Guess I get the brownie points today and James won’t get any.”

“Seriously, if James doesn’t smarten up, he may lose more than just brownie points. Oh, and by the way, they are pregnant again.”

“That’s good news. I know he wanted more kids, but I am sure he told me that Val didn’t.”

"Well, my dearest husband, as we both know, sometimes, things just happen."

THIRTY-FIVE

Monday morning, as Debbie was making her bed, she stopped to smell Brad's pillow. She loved the smell of his cologne. She loved Brad!

Debbie remembered what it was like when Brad and his first wife had broken up, and he wanted to start a relationship with her. She had kept him at arm's length for a very long time, but when she finally gave in, and gave him her heart, she gave him all she had to give. And just look where that had gotten her. Two sets of twins.

Debbie noticed the time on the clock on the dresser and hurried and finished up then rushed back downstairs to the kitchen. Chef would be there anytime. Debbie was making beef stew for dinner and had peeled all the potatoes and carrots and chopped them up into a big bowl before it dawned on her that Chef was late this morning.

She glanced at the clock on the wall. He was half an hour late. That was unlike him. He hated it when people were not on time. Debbie got a nagging feeling in the pit of her stomach. Something must be wrong. She grabbed the phone, and with shaking fingers, she dialed his number. It rang, but no answer.

She decided that he must be on his way. Debbie needed something to do while she waited, so she dusted the living room. As she put the duster away, she checked the time again. It had been twenty more minutes and he still wasn't there. Now, she was certain something must be wrong.

Debbie didn't call Brad at work unless it was something urgent or important, but this was. Brad picked up on the first ring.

After Brad picked up, she said, "Chef isn't here yet. Did you clean off his car and walkways this morning?"

"Yes, did it first thing. It's not like him to be late. Should I go check in on him?"

"I think that would be a good idea. Can you do that now, please?"

"I am just down the road. I'm on my way. Do you have a key if I need to get in?"

"No, I don't. Brad, I am worried."

"Just pulling into his driveway now. I'll call you right back." Brad hung up.

Debbie paced, or rather waddled, the floors for the next few minutes, and she jumped when the phone rang. The call display showed it was Janice. She'd have to call her back later. The phone rang again.

"Brad, what's going on over there? Is Chef alright?"

"Chef has had a bad fall. I have called the ambulance, and I'll stay here with him until they get here."

"I knew something was wrong. He's never late. When you say a bad fall, how bad do you mean?"

"He fell in the bathroom, and the way he is lying on the floor, I think he may have broken his hip or something. I'll know more when the ambulance gets here. When I know, I'll call and let you know."

"I'll get ready to go to the hospital," Debbie said through her tears. "Are you busy, or could you drive me?"

"Remote start the van, and I'll come drive you. As soon as George goes in the ambulance, I'll come home."

"Thanks. I'll be ready. See you soon." Debbie grabbed

her cell phone and threw it into her purse. She also added a bottle of water and a handful of candies. While she waited for Brad, she decided to send a quick text to Janice.

It was only twenty minutes before Brad pulled in. Debbie already had her boots on and was getting into her coat when Brad came in.

"Let me help you. Chef George is on his way, and the doctor will have to examine him. He'll probably need X-rays, so we don't need to rush."

"I am scared for Chef."

Brad pulled her into his arms. "Everything will be alright. Let's just go, and we'll know soon enough."

Debbie took a tissue from her coat pocket and wiped the tears from her face. "Thanks for going to check on him."

"No problem. Now let's go." Brad held open the door and locked it behind them.

On the drive to the hospital, Debbie sat quietly, deep in thought. *Poor Chef. I know he's going to be alright. He has to be. I have already lost Henry and don't want to lose Chef. He's going to be okay. Dear God, please help Chef George.*

The phone beeped and made her jump. "It's just Janice," Debbie said to Brad. "She called earlier, just to chat, and now she wants us to keep her posted on Chef's condition."

As they entered the hospital, the constant ringing phones, the intercom making announcements, the floor polisher going down the long, polished hallway, and the beeping machines all bouncing around the gray-colored walls overwhelmed her senses. Brad took her hand and led her to the emergency nurse's station.

"You alright, hun? You look a little pale," Brad asked with concern.

"I think so. It just sounds like a three-ring circus in here."

They were told that George was in cubicle six and they could go in and see him. There was a big bandage around the top of his head, and Chef was propped up with his eyes closed.

Debbie laid her hand over his. "Chef George, are you awake?"

"Yes, I am. Hi."

Chef motioned for Brad to come closer.

"Thanks for coming to my rescue. I lay there for a long time because I couldn't move, so I couldn't call for help. Was there a reason you stopped by?"

"Debbie asked me to stop in to check on you. You were late for the baking lesson, and we all know how you hate being late."

"Thank you, child. You are my hero." Chef squeezed her hand. "In the heat of the moment, I had forgotten that today was cookie day."

"I'm glad it was, or I wouldn't have known that Brad needed to go check on you." Debbie leaned down and kissed his forehead. "I do worry about you living alone."

"I've been fine up till now. I remember stepping out of the shower and the bathmat slipping out from under my foot. Accidents do happen, and this time, it happened to me." Chef gave a shrug.

A nurse came into the cubicle. "George, we are going for a ride down for X-rays and a CAT scan."

"See you in a few minutes, big guy," Brad said as George was wheeled out.

"Probably half an hour at least," the nurse stated.

"Let's go down to the cafeteria and get a coffee and a donut or something," Brad suggested.

Debbie was quietly crying, sitting in a chair.

"What are you crying about?" He took her hand in his.

"Sorry, I was just thinking about Jefferson and Henry, and every time we have to come here."

"Let's go get you a coffee and take your mind off of it all." Brad took hold of her arm and led her out of the room.

When he got her seated in the cafeteria, he asked, "Would you like a muffin or a donut?"

"A carrot muffin, if they have any. Thanks." She hated this place. Even the cafeteria was painted in the same dull gray. The only difference was in the sounds: the buzz of many people talking, the bell on the cash register dinging, and the clinking of silverware on tables and trays.

Brad set the tray between them and sat opposite her. "You got the last carrot muffin."

"Good job, hun. Thanks. So, now, tell me what happened at Chef's house."

"I tried the front door, but he didn't answer. So, I waded in the snow around to the back door and thank goodness it was unlocked. I called out to him, but he didn't answer. I found him in the bathroom, sprawled out naked on the floor. I think his head must have hit the vanity, and there was a lot of blood pooling around his head. I called the ambulance, and when he heard my voice, he opened his eyes and looked at me with a dazed, blank look. I tried to help him up, but he couldn't move, so I covered him up with towels and waited for the ambulance." Brad took a bite out of his donut.

"So, there is a big mess that needs to be cleaned up?" Debbie asked.

"I cleaned up the worst of it with a rag I found," Brad stated. "Floor probably needs to be scrubbed now, but I did wipe it up."

"You are a good man, Mr. Mumford. You know, I am thinking that Chef should move into one of the apartments. I could keep a closer eye on him then."

"He would still be living alone. I don't think location is going to change that unless he moves into a retirement home."

"Guess you're right. I have been thinking about putting an ad in the newspaper to see about getting some tenants."

"And which snowbank do you suggest they park in?"

"Never thought about parking. Good point. Guess I will hold off on that for now, then."

"I think you should, at least for a couple of months. Eventually, there will be lots of parking. And a swimming pool."

"Will the tenants be allowed to use the pool?"

"I would think so, but they will need to respect our other guests," Brad said. "I think we should be very careful who we rent those apartments to."

"Oh, I agree. I am in the process of drawing up an agreement. I don't want anything lying around outside. No loud noise after eleven p.m., that kind of thing."

"Good idea. It's been half an hour, so if you are finished, we can head back upstairs." Brad put his empty plate and cup onto the tray.

"Yes, let's go."

When they entered the cubicle, it was empty, so they took seats on the two chairs up against the wall.

Debbie shivered. “I hate this place. I can’t help but think about Henry when I am here. He took his last breath right here in this same cubicle.”

Brad took her hand. “I know. But Henry is gone now. And Chef George is going to be alright.”

Debbie’s cell phone dinged, and she pulled it out of her purse.

“It’s Susan asking if we know how Chef is doing.” With shaking fingers, Debbie punched in an answer to her text and dropped the phone back into her purse. “She has obviously been talking to Janice.”

“It never ceases to amaze me how close you three sisters are.”

“We are now, but only since we lost our mom. Before that, we only spoke maybe once a month.” Debbie noticed the baffled look on Brad’s face. “They called, but they usually talked to Mom.”

A different nurse pushed Chef’s bed back into the room. “There we go, back safe and sound. Once the doctor gets the results, he’ll be in to talk to you. In the meantime, I am going to put an intravenous in your arm so we can give you some fluids and medication. I’ll be right back.”

“Gosh, that was hard work. Glad it’s over.” Chef yawned.

“We are going to stay here until we see the doctor, but if you are tired, feel free to close your eyes and have a little cat nap,” Debbie instructed him.

“Don’t mind if I do,” Chef said.

“Let’s get you hooked up.” The nurse quickly had the intravenous in his arm with a bag of solution dripping. “The doctor should be in shortly.”

“Thank you.” Brad nodded at the nurse.

Chef closed his eyes, so Brad and Debbie both checked on their cell phones. It was only about ten minutes later that the doctor came in.

"George, is it? I have some information for you. You have indeed broken your hip and will need surgery to fix it. There doesn't seem to be anything else broken other than your hip." The doctor flipped papers on the clipboard he was holding. "Your head injury shows some internal bleeding, but we suspect it will resolve on its own. I suggest we do some stitches to the gash to help speed up the healing. We can do your surgery probably later today, and you will be admitted overnight for observation." The doctor put the clipboard under his arm. "Do you have any questions for me?"

"No, I can't think of any," George answered.

"Do you know what his recovery time will be?" Debbie asked.

"Usually about three months," the doctor answered.

"George lives alone. Will he be allowed to go home, or will he need to go to a retirement home for the three months of recovery?" Brad asked.

"That is totally up to him. Personally, I would prefer that he not be alone, but the decision is up to him. We can arrange some home care for him as well," the doctor answered.

When the doctor left, Debbie went over and kissed Chef's cheek. "We are going to go now and let you rest. But we will come back later after your surgery."

"Don't be silly. I'll be all groggy and stuff. I appreciate you coming, but there is no need for you to come back later. But maybe tomorrow, I will need a ride home."

Brad put a hand on Chef's arm. "No worries, big guy,

we've got you covered. We'll see you tomorrow morning then."

"Sounds good. Thank you both for everything." Chef smiled.

"I think I should call Kathy and Ben to let them know what happened and that you are having surgery later today," Debbie suggested.

"You'll just get them all upset. I wish you wouldn't. I'll tell them both after I get home."

"Alright then. We'll see you in the morning." Debbie kissed his cheek again before they left.

As they walked out into the cold, brisk March air, Brad took her hand. "That sun feels nice. It won't be long before spring will be here, along with our two new babies."

"That will be another trip to this damn hospital." Debbie shivered.

Brad kissed her before he opened the van door and helped her in. "Yes, but for once, it will be for a good reason."

THIRTY-SIX

The following Monday morning, Chef didn't come to give Debbie her baking lesson. He had come through the surgery fine, and was now recovering at home with lots of home care coming in.

Debbie couldn't help but miss him. She picked up the phone and gave him a call. "Morning, Chef. I just wanted to call and see how you are doing. I miss you not being here with me."

"Yes, child, I miss you too."

"How are you? Are you getting around alright? Do you need any help? Would you tell me if you did?"

"Goodness sake, girl, slow down. I am fine. Moving slowly and carefully but still able to get around my house just fine. I have nurses and home care all checking in on me. Actually, I am expecting a lady to help me with a shower any time now."

"Well, I won't keep you. I just wanted to check in. Call me if you need anything. Brad could go grocery shopping for you if you need anything."

"Got that covered, Debbie. Thanks for thinking about me, but please don't worry. I am fine. I am getting stronger every day."

"Alright, but if you need anything, don't hesitate to call. I am sure either Brad or I could help you out."

"I know. My shower lady just pulled into the drive. I have to go. Thanks for checking in on me."

He sounded good. Debbie didn't want to be a nuisance, but she did worry about him. He was very special to her and had been like a surrogate father most of her life. He was such a kind and generous man and had spent the last few years looking after Debbie and her mom at the resort. Now, since he had officially retired, he was coming by once a week to give her baking lessons. Debbie believed that if you could read, you could follow a recipe and bake anything. But she loved spending this time with Chef George. He had taken such good care of her over the years, and now it was her turn to take care of him.

Debbie sat drinking her coffee remembering when she first met Chef George. He was retired from the army and had lost his wife. In his career, he cooked in some very swanky places all over the world. But he liked Cedar Grove and had bought a small house, not too far from the resort. He had come, hat in hand, one day and talked to Debbie's mom about cooking part-time. He was a certified red seal chef and was definitely overqualified to cook at a fishing lodge, but he was bored and needed to find a purpose. She had hired him on the spot.

For the next fifteen or twenty years, he worked as much as he wanted to. He took great pride in his cooking abilities, and the quality of the food increased tenfold. Like most long-term employees of the resort, he became one of the family. When Debbie's mom passed away, he just stayed on, taking care of Debbie and her sisters.

He had trained Trevor, the new chef, who had taken over when they sold the resort, and Chef George officially retired. Because Chef was registered, Trevor could work under him as his apprentice, which would benefit him later when he went to write his own chef's exams. Trevor was young and eager, and Chef turned out to be a good teacher.

After they sold the resort, and Debbie and Brad moved into the house, Chef had suggested that he could come by occasionally and bake some bread and treats for Debbie and her family.

Debbie remembered how humble he had been when he offered to teach her how to bake and even to give her some cooking lessons. Debbie loved and respected Chef George. He had been like a father figure to her for a long time. He even walked her down the aisle and gave her away when she married Bradley. She remembered how proud he was and how handsome he looked in his new suit.

Debbie decided that she would bake some sugar cookies and some apple strudel, which were Chef's favorites, and drop them off at his house.

She turned on the radio in the kitchen, put on her apron, and got busy baking without Chef there to guide her.

By the end of the afternoon, she had made what she wanted to for Chef, as well as cookies for the kids' lunches. Her apple strudel was not as good as Chef's, but it was good enough. She decided that she just needed more practice working with the puff pastry. She noticed that she got tired easily and had to take many breaks, but she got it done just the same.

It was going on three o'clock by the time she got the kitchen tidied up and started supper.

Tonight, they were having oven-baked chicken, baked potato wedges, and frozen veggies. She had the chicken coated and the potatoes washed and cut, all in the oven, by the time the kids got off the school bus.

She was exhausted and sitting having a coffee when the kids came charging in.

"Mommy, look! We both got stars today on the pictures that we painted." Becky handed her a picture that looked like a mommy, a daddy, and four kids of various sizes.

"Is this a picture of our family?"

"Yes, see, that's you and Daddy, me and Ben, and two new babies. They are the little ones in the blankets. We were all asked to paint our families."

"And what did you paint, Ben?"

"I didn't put the babies in my picture 'because they aren't here yet," Ben stated matter-of-factly.

"You mean because, not 'cause," Debbie corrected him. "Can I see it?"

Ben pulled it out of his backpack and handed it to her. "That's a nice painting. Too bad it's so rumpled up. I want to put them on the fridge, where I can see them every day."

"Yeah, I don't like painting too much. I'd rather color or draw," Ben explained.

"Well, the teacher must have thought you both did a good job. I see you both got a gold star. Congratulations to you both."

"What can we have for a snack?" Ben asked.

"How about some apple strudel and some fruit," Debbie suggested.

"That sounds good."

"Let me get you both a piece." Debbie went around the counter and gave them each a plate with a small piece of strudel.

The kids took their snacks into the living room to watch their after-school cartoons.

A short while later, Brad came home. "Hello, family.

How was everyone's day? Oh my, look at the pretty pictures. Good job, you two. And how's Mommy?" Brad asked as he reached over to give her a kiss.

"Mommy is very tired," Debbie said. "I decided to bake today. I want to drop off some apple strudel and some sugar cookies to Chef tomorrow and see how he's doing."

"You look tired. What's for dinner? Do you need any help?"

"Dinner is in the oven. It will take forty-five minutes to cook. Do you think we could eat then? I'm exhausted and don't know if I'm going to make it till bedtime tonight."

"Absolutely. That's no problem. So, if I turn the oven on now, we can eat as soon as it cooks. Why don't you take your coffee and go watch cartoons with the kids? Go put your feet up for a while. I'll cook dinner."

"Bless your sweet heart. Turn the oven on at three-fifty, and don't forget to set the timer. If you think of it, in half an hour, you could stir the potatoes," Debbie said as she dragged herself into the recliner in the living room.

"I got it," Brad said to the back of her head.

Debbie got comfortable in the recliner, with her feet raised, and fell instantly asleep. When she woke, she was momentarily disoriented. For a moment, she wasn't sure where she was or why she was there.

"Hey, sleepyhead. You zonked out on us. The kids have had their baths and stories read, and both are sound asleep. I tried to wake you for dinner, but you didn't want to wake up."

Debbie made a mad waddle to the washroom and splashed some cold water on her face. When she came out, Brad had her supper sitting on the counter for her. "Come have something to eat, babe."

"Thanks. Could I get a glass of milk, please?"

Brad sat beside her. "You really were exhausted. Do you think maybe you overdid it today and played yourself out?"

"Guess I must have. Thanks for dinner."

"As soon as you're finished, I think we should just call it a night."

Debbie leaned her head against him. "I think that sounds like a wonderful idea.

THIRTY-SEVEN

The next morning, Debbie was up and bopping around, getting her chores done. She planned to go visit Chef George as soon as the laundry was finished. She had to admit that she really enjoyed having the three washers and dryers. Now she only had to do laundry once a day, not all day long.

As she was folding the last load, she had some cramps, and they weren't going away. She carried the laundry up the stairs and when she reached her bedroom, she stretched out on the bed to see if changing positions would lessen the cramps. The next cramp felt like a contraction. She decided it couldn't be; she wasn't due for another six weeks. Debbie rolled over onto her other side. Another cramp hit her hard. *That was definitely a contraction.* She had better call Brad.

Debbie got to her feet and carefully went down the stairs. She headed straight to the kitchen and grabbed her cell phone.

Brad picked up on the second ring. "Morning, hun. What's up? Everything alright?"

"I don't think so. I am having contractions. Can you come and take me to the hospital, please?"

"Yes, start the van, and I'll be right there." She could tell by the tone of his voice that he knew she was scared.

Debbie pushed the remote to start the van, then slipped into her boots and put her coat on. Before she could get back to the kitchen to sit down, Brad came flying through the front door.

"Are you ready? How far apart are the contractions?" he asked with concern in his voice.

"They have just started. I don't know how far apart they are yet. Probably ten minutes or more. I have only had two so far, but I think they were more than just cramps. I think they were contractions. I think we should go get things checked out just to be on the safe side. It may end up being nothing, but it may be something. Can you grab my little suitcase from our bedroom closet? And you should also grab a couple of towels in case my water breaks before we get there."

"Suitcase and towels, coming right up." Brad dashed up the stairs and quickly came back down. "Can we go already?"

"Yes, Brad, we can go." She suddenly realized that he'd never even kissed her when he got home. "I think we have lots of time. I'm just wanting to go get checked out."

"Alright, let me help you." Brad threw the suitcase into the back and laid the towels down on the passenger seat before he helped Debbie in.

While he was walking around the van, another contraction hit hard. *There's no doubt about it. That was definitely a contraction.*

"You alright?" Brad asked when he opened his door and saw the look on her face.

"Yep, you drive, and I'll make some phone calls." Debbie opened her phone's clock and set the stopwatch. When the next contraction hit, she would be able to tell how far apart they were. Then she called the doctor's office and explained that she was having contractions and that they were on their way to the hospital.

"You should also text Janice and Susan," Brad suggested.

"Yeah, I guess I should. But it could be false labor," Debbie said. "I would hate to get them all excited for nothing."

"It's up to you. But if it was happening to one of them, you would want to know, wouldn't you?"

"I guess you're right. I'll do it now." Debbie sent a text to both her sisters and was just about to set the phone in her purse when another contraction hit. When she could breathe again, she checked the stopwatch. Eight minutes and thirty seconds from the last one. She reset the timer.

"So, how far apart are they?"

"Eight and a half minutes. We have lots of time. Babies don't usually come until you're down to five minutes or so."

Brad pulled the van right up to the emergency door, got out, grabbed a wheelchair, and helped her out of the van. "I'll just wheel you over here out of the way while I go find parking. I'll be right back."

"Brad, we're fine. You can slow down before you give yourself a heart attack."

As Brad was parking the van, Debbie thought about how the nursery wasn't ready. Brad had set up the cribs and the other furniture, but she hadn't gotten all the baby clothes moved into the dresser yet. She hadn't even bought diapers. What kind of a mother was she?

"What's wrong?" Brad asked as he knelt down in front of her. "Why are you crying?"

"I'm a terrible mother. I'm not ready for these babies to

be born yet. Holy crap!" she blurted out as another contraction hit. "That one really hurt."

Brad wheeled her into the nurse for triage and gave them all the necessary information. The nurse took them straight into a cubicle. "How far apart are your contractions?"

"Seven minutes. But my water hasn't broken yet. I'm not even sure they are contractions."

"Well, let's get you into a gown and into bed. I will be calling the portable ultrasound tech so we can have a look-see. I'll be right back," the nurse informed them.

Brad helped Debbie get dressed into her hospital gown and then helped into the bed. He was just figuring out the controls to raise up her head when the technician arrived. "Let's take a look." She put the gel on Debbie's belly. "Yep, one baby is heads-down in the birth canal." She pointed to the screen. "You are about to have your babies."

Debbie sat up with her feet hanging over the side of the bed. "I need to pee. Hun, would you grab my slippers out of the suitcase for me, please?"

Another contraction hit, and Debbie cried out in pain. She lay back down for a minute until it subsided. "Brad, help me up. I really need to pee."

Brad helped her out of bed, and still in her bare feet, she waddled to the washroom.

"Holy crap," Debbie called out. "My water just broke. Could you get the nurse?"

"Oh, my goodness, let's get you into a dry gown and back into bed. We will be moving you down to the birthing room. I understand Doctor Barnes has just arrived."

Once they were in the room, Brad texted Janice and

Susan to update them on Debbie's delivery. They both responded back with best wishes.

"Brad, I never even got our bed made this morning. I don't have the nursery stocked. I am not ready to have these babies yet," Debbie said through her tears.

"Honey, don't worry about the bed. I can stock the nursery, and ready or not, the twins are coming today."

It wasn't long until the doctor arrived. "Good morning, you two. I understand you are going to be having these twins today," Doctor Barnes said as he came into the room.

"Isn't it too early to be delivering? I still have six weeks to go."

"Early delivery in women your age is not uncommon. I understand that your water just broke. That's good. Things are progressing normally. I'll have to see how far dilated you are. Now let's have a look." Doctor Barnes put on his gloves. "Shouldn't be long now. Maybe another ten minutes or so. When you have a contraction, try not to push just yet. I'll be back shortly." He removed his gloves and left the room.

A nurse came in. "I am going to put an intravenous in, just in case we need to give you some fluids or meds."

Debbie hated needles, but she knew that once the intravenous was in, they could put any needed medications in that line. So, one needle was better than several more.

The needle hurt and Debbie started to cry. Tears ran down her face, and Brad took a tissue and wiped them away. "It will all be over soon. Hun, it's going to be okay."

Debbie couldn't answer him at the moment. *Easy for him to say. He isn't having his body stretched to the limit. He's not the one who has to deliver these two babies.*

Another nurse came in with a jug of water, a glass, and

a straw. "You should try to drink some water; we don't want you to get dehydrated."

Doctor Barnes came back in and put on a fresh pair of gloves. "Let's see how far along we are." He lifted the sheet up as far as Debbie's knees. "I can see the baby's head. When you have your next contraction, I need you to push as hard as you can."

The first baby came after three good pushes. "Congratulations, you have a fine-looking son." Doctor Barnes held up the baby so Debbie could see before he handed the baby over to the nurse. "Now we just have to wait for the little lady to make an appearance. I expect it might take a few minutes. In the meantime, I would like to do another ultrasound just to see where she is."

The ultrasound showed that the baby had turned and was just entering the birth canal. "She'll be here soon. Debbie, I have some concerns that because your water has broken and your son is born, there may not be enough fluid, and the next delivery could be a lot more painful." Doctor Barnes patted her hand. "But we'll keep a close eye on you. In the meantime, try to rest as much as you can and don't push until I tell you to."

Debbie put her head back and closed her eyes. *What if he's right and there isn't enough fluid for the next baby? What if something goes wrong? What if I can't deliver the baby? What if they have to cut me open to remove her?*

She closed her eyes, and when she opened them again, Doctor Barnes was telling her that she could push hard with the next contraction.

When the contraction hit, she yelled out in pain as she pushed with all her might. After six hard pushes, their baby girl was born. Debbie sobbed and Brad tried his best to console her, stroking her hair. "It's all over, hun. Both our babies are perfect. Good job, little momma." Debbie was so distraught that she pushed his hand away.

"Leave me alone. Please, just leave me alone." Debbie sobbed harder.

Brad didn't know what to do so he just stood at the top of the bed and let her have a moment. He had never seen her cry this hard before. The nurse brought over their son. "As soon as you are ready, you should try to feed this little fellow, all six-point-four ounces of him. Dad, would you like to hold your son until Mom is ready?'

Brad stepped forward and took the baby from her. "Well, hello, James Christopher. I am your daddy. Welcome to our little family. Are you a hungry little guy?"

Debbie pulled herself together, the best she could, and wiped her face. When Brad handed James to her, she took him to her breast. She gave Brad an apologetic look. "Sorry, I just needed a moment."

"It's okay. I understand. I'm sure that wasn't easy. Guess he is hungry. He's taking to that boob like a man on a mission." Brad chuckled at his own joke.

Debbie switched breasts, and when he slowed down, she put him on her stomach and gently rubbed his back. The nurse came and took him back to the crib and brought their daughter over.

"Meet your new daughter, weighing in at six pounds, one ounce."

Debbie took the baby to her breast, but she didn't seem interested in eating. She tried her on the other breast, but again, Jessica Ann Marie wasn't interested. Debbie called the nurse over. "She's not eating. Is there something wrong?"

"No, not necessarily. You can try to feed her again in a few hours. I suggest now that you try to get some rest," the nurse stated.

"That's my cue to leave. I'll be back in a couple of hours. Can I bring you back anything?" Brad asked.

"No, I'm good, thanks. Just need some rest, I think."

Brad kissed her forehead. "I am so proud of you. I love you so much. Now get some rest."

When Brad left, Debbie tried to fall asleep. She was totally exhausted, but the pain she was feeling outweighed her need for sleep. She finally relented and pushed her buzzer to call the nurse.

"Yes, Mrs. Mumford? What can I do for you?" the nurse asked.

"You can start by calling me Debbie. I am in a lot of pain. I was just wondering if there is anything you can give me?"

"Yes, I can give you some pain meds. But we don't want to give you too much because you are breast-feeding."

"I know that, but anything you could give me would be appreciated."

"I'll be right back." The nurse left the room, and Debbie rolled over, trying desperately to get comfortable.

The nurse returned and injected some pain medication into her intravenous. "There, that should help with your pain. Now, you need to get some rest," she said as she pulled down the blinds, putting the room into a semi-darkness.

"Thank you," Debbie said quietly. As she lay there, hearing all the chatter and the ringing phones coming from the hallway, the medication finally started to help, and she finally fell asleep.

THIRTY-EIGHT

The next morning, Debbie had just fed the babies and had settled back into her hospital bed when she glanced at the clock and realized the time. She immediately thought about Brad and wondered how he was making out without her. She imagined him sitting at the counter, wondering what he had to do to get the kids ready for school. She decided that she had better give him a call. "Morning, hun. How's everything going at home?" Debbie asked.

"Fine. How are things there? How are you and the babies?"

"Good. I just finished feeding them and realized the time. I thought you might need me to walk you through the morning routine."

"Oh, yes, please. I have been sitting here wondering what I need to do."

"That's what I figured. Well, I usually make their lunches, which consist of a sandwich, usually jam or jelly. There is a big bag of chopped veggies in the fridge, and they both get a small bag of those, along with one cookie and one piece of fruit. I also give them juice in their thermoses. It's in the big jug in the fridge. All of this goes into their lunch boxes at the back door.

"At quarter to eight, I go upstairs and wake them up. They need to get washed up and dressed for school. I let them dress themselves, but I have the final say on what they wear. Becky has some strange fashion sense, so she may need some help. She may also need help braiding her hair. They are to make their beds and then come down for breakfast. Today, they can just have cereal, which they can get themselves. By eight twenty-five, they need to have coats and boots on, and I walk them down to wait for the bus. When it arrives, I hug and kiss them both, say good-bye, wish them a good day at school, and wave to the driver."

"I am so glad you called. I knew you would have a routine. Thanks, hun. How are you feeling? Have they said anything yet about when you, and the babies can come home?" Brad asked.

"No, not yet. I expect the doctor will be making rounds sometime this morning. I'll know then. Brad, you will need to pick up some diapers, newborn ones."

"Yes, I know. I managed to get the babies' dresser filled last night and the crib sheets on."

"Oh, thanks. That was so nice of you. You might as well get about six bags of diapers. That will at least get us started."

"Is there anything I can bring you?" Brad asked.

"No, I think we are good. The car seats are in the van. If you could find the box marked winter clothes, you could bring the two bunting bags."

"You mean those things that look like sleeping bags with hoods?"

"Yes, please." Debbie chuckled at his description of the bags. "I know it's April, but I don't want them catching a cold going home."

"I'll go see if I can find them. I need to check in on my guys and then I'll come see you."

"Did you tell the kids where I am?"

"Yes, they wanted to come see you and the new babies. I told them that if you didn't come home today, I would let them come see you after school."

"What did you do for dinner last night? I didn't even have anything planned before the labor started."

"Mom and Dad took us to the resort for dinner."

"Lucky you. Speaking of your mom, did she mention wanting to help with the twins like she did last time?" Debbie asked.

"She did mention that she is available if you think you will need her. Maybe you could give her a call later. I know she'd be pleased to help."

"Yes, I definitely will. She was amazing the last time. I really like your mom. We can spend hours just sitting and talking about anything and everything. Sometimes, we even talk about you."

"About me, that can't be good. My two best ladies comparing notes about me. Now I'm scared."

"It's all good. She thinks you are a saint, and I think you are my hero." Debbie chuckled.

"Well, you should probably be resting, so I'll let you go, but thanks for calling and giving me the rundown on the morning routine. I'll see you later this morning. I love you, hun."

"Love you too. Bye for now."

Debbie settled back and fell instantly asleep. About two hours later, she woke to the sound of babies crying. At first, she thought she was dreaming, but as the crying persisted, she came fully awake and remembered that it was her babies who were crying.

A nurse had come in to help her change and feed the

babies. Once they were settled, the nurse helped Debbie have a shower to clean herself up. Debbie was happy to put some lipstick on. She just never felt dressed until she applied a little lipstick.

When she went back to her bed, she noticed that they had delivered a breakfast tray. She gingerly picked at the offerings, but she wasn't hungry enough to try the bowl of mushy porridge or the rubbery eggs. She removed the juice and coffee from the tray and pushed it aside.

She was just about to fall asleep when Val came charging into the room. "Good morning, Deb. How's every little thing?"

"Morning. Good, I guess. I just had my breakfast, if you can call it that." Debbie rearranged herself on the bed. "I didn't expect to see you this early."

"I thought I would stop in on the way to work. I wanted to meet the new additions to your little family." Val had walked over to the plastic crib. "So, have you picked out names yet?"

"Yes, James and Jessica," Debbie stated proudly.

"James. So, is he named after my James, then?"

"I think so. Your James is Brad's best friend."

"And where is the Jessica from?"

"Just a name we liked. Jessica Ann Marie." Debbie went over and stood beside Val. "Would you like to hold her?"

"No, they are sleeping. I wouldn't want to disturb them." Val stepped back. "Is there anything you need? Anything I can get for you?"

"No, I think I'm alright. Thanks for asking." Debbie went back over and sat on the edge of the bed. "How are you feeling? Are you still having morning sickness?"

"Yes, but at least not every day now. I don't enjoy being pregnant any more than I like delivering babies."

"No one enjoys the delivery part. I didn't mind being pregnant, except for the morning sickness and having to give up coffee."

"I don't care for either option. I'm not even that crazy about kids, to be perfectly honest."

"It's too bad you don't have stronger motherly instincts. My kids are my whole world."

"Yes, I know they are. You always knew you wanted kids, even growing up. Me, I never had that wish."

"But yet, here you are with a great son and another baby in the oven. Funny how life works out sometimes, isn't it."

"Funny, I don't think I see much humor in it. Other than you being blessed with two sets of twins. Now, that's funny."

"Yes, that is a big joke. It's all Brad's fault. Twins run in his side of the family," Debbie said with a big yawn.

"You look tired. I guess I should get going. I just wanted to pop in and check on you and the babies. If you think of anything, just shoot me a text. I can stop on my way home if you need me to. Do you think you'll get out of here today?"

"I don't know. I haven't seen the doctor yet."

"I know you need your rest, and I need to get to work. I'll talk to you soon. And Deb, congratulations."

"Thanks, Val."

As Val walked away, Debbie smiled to herself. *It won't be long till she'll be in here, having a baby of her own.*

THIRTY-NINE

Debbie opened her eyes and saw Brad sitting there looking at his phone. She smiled at him.

“Morning, little momma. How is my family this morning?”

“Good, I guess. Doctor Barnes was just in, and says I will be here at least another day.”

“Is anything wrong?” Brad asked, his voice full of concern.

“No, I don’t think so. It’s just that because they are so small and they haven’t gained enough weight, he wants to keep us a while longer. He suggested that maybe I could go home, but the babies would have to stay. I told him that I wasn’t going anywhere without them.”

“That’s my girl. You tell him straight.” Brad smiled at his stubborn wife.

“Did you get the diapers and the groceries?”

“Yes, I did. They are all in the truck. The kids and I are having lasagna for dinner. I bought it at the store.” Brad smiled. “I don’t expect it will be as good as yours, though.”

“Probably not. How did you make out with the kids last night?”

“Fine. We went out for dinner, watched a movie, then baths and bedtime stories. It was cute. Becky went into the nursery by mistake, I think. Anyway, she spotted the mobile and asked me to turn it on.” Brad smiled as she shifted positions on the bed.

"I sat in the rocking chair, and she climbed into my lap. The 'Twinkle, Twinkle Little Star' and the memories of when she was a baby made a tear roll down my cheek. She gently wiped it away for me, and I had to explain how happy I was. Ben climbed into the other rocking chair, and I explained how they started out as tiny little babies, but now they were big kids, and able to take care of themselves."

"That must have been a memorable moment." Debbie squeezed his hand. "It's going to be a busy house when we all get home. With the new babies taking most of my time and attention, we need to make sure Ben and Becky don't get lost in the confusion."

"Maybe I could get them each a new toy so they can each have a present when you come home," Brad suggested.

"Yes, that would be good. Something age appropriate for a five- to ten-year-old."

"There is a transformer thing that Ben comments on every time he sees it on TV. It turns from a robot guy to a big truck. I'll see if they have anything like that. And as for Becky, I have no idea."

"Maybe something for dressing up. She likes anything pink and sparkly."

"Got it. I'll stop at the store when I leave here. I'll stick around for the next feeding if that's alright with you. If you need to nap, I can just sit here quietly," Brad suggested.

"No, I'm good. It's almost time to feed the babies anyway."

"Morning, you two. I just wanted to come meet your new family." Susan smiled as she laid flowers and a gift bag at Debbie's feet.

"Thanks, sis. You always know how to cheer me up."

"You can leave them for the nurses when you get to go home. Will that be later today?"

"I don't think so. Doctor Barnes says it might be another day or two."

"So, who do we have here?" Susan asked, looking into the crib.

Brad went over and explained, "This little man is James Christopher, and this angel is Jessica Ann Marie."

"James and Jessica, how cute." Susan grinned as she sat down on the edge of Debbie's bed and handed her the gift bag. "Here, open this."

There was a box of cigars with pink and blue bands, just like the last time Susan had given Brad cigars. She also had a care package for Debbie, with things for her to have a home spa.

"Thank you, Susan. This is so very thoughtful of you," Debbie said as she handed Brad his box of cigars.

"Morning, all." Janice came in with another arm full of flowers. "I see Susan has beat me to it."

"Come on in and meet our new family," Debbie said. "Brad, could you do the honors?"

Brad walked over to the crib and introduced James and Jessica to their Aunt Janice.

"James and Jess. I like their names. Good job, momma. So, when can you get sprung from here?" Janice asked.

"Probably a day or two. Doctor Barnes says they need to gain more weight before they can go home. And I'm not leaving without them." Debbie shrugged.

"Well, I am going to leave you three beautiful ladies. I have some shopping to do. Hun, I'll bring the kids by after school for a little while." Brad leaned down and kissed her.

"See you later then," Debbie said with a touch of panic.

"How are you all liking your new house?" Susan asked Janice.

"Good. Zack is thrilled with having his own bedroom, and Mark is enjoying finally having a family. He treats me like a fragile doll. He's afraid if he touches me, I might break. It's kind of cute and kind of annoying all at the same time," Janice explained.

"At least now, Zack will have room for all his toys. And he's happy having Mark around?" Debbie asked.

"He hasn't really said. He's old enough now that he's busy with his own things. Right now, he is crazy for transformer toys."

"Brad is going to buy one of those toys for Ben right now. We'll give both the kids a little gift when we bring the babies home, if they ever let me out of here." Debbie rearranged herself in the bed. "Thanks for the bag of toys you dropped off for the kids. Any time you are downsizing Zack's toys, we'll be glad to take them."

"And any newborn clothes and toys that you are getting rid of, I'll be glad to take them," Janice answered.

"Look at you two, swapping baby stuff. I am so glad that my two kids are beyond all that. Katie will be coming by this weekend to meet her new cousins. Keith said he'll wait till you get home, and he'll come see the babies then."

"Keith doesn't like hospitals very much, does he?" Janice asked.

"No, he doesn't. He was here when Dad had his stroke, and it gives him great anxiety," Susan explained.

"How is Jefferson doing?" Debbie asked.

"The same. He can't move at all, and he can't speak

either. But we do have a blinking thing figured out. One blink for yes and two blinks for no. But most times, he can't even manage that. It's truly heartbreaking. And I miss him at home. The house just isn't the same without him there."

"Sue, I'm so sorry. This must be unbearable for you," Debbie said.

"Yes, but there is nothing I can do about it. I go see him every day and he seems to recognizes me. I think he's happy to see me, but it's like he has just given up, and I can't say that I blame him. I just feel so helpless."

Debbie was having a hard time keeping her eyes open, so Janice and Susan both said their goodbyes. When they left, Debbie rolled over and went sound asleep until she was woken by crying babies.

She fed the babies again and had another nap.

A short time later, lunch was served, and even though Debbie was hungry, she only picked at her food. She called Brad and asked if he could make her a sandwich or bring something when he came later with the kids. He said he could do that.

Later that afternoon, after school, Brad brought the kids to see her.

"Mommy!" Becky came running into the room and right up onto Debbie's bed for hugs and kisses. Ben followed her lead.

"Hi, guys. It is so nice to see you both. I have missed you so very much." Debbie plastered them both with kisses.

"Doesn't Daddy get a kiss?" Brad leaned down and gently gave her a quick kiss.

When everyone was settled down, Brad took Ben and

Becky over to meet James and Jessica. Debbie got up, put her slippers on, and joined them all at the crib.

"What do you think, guys?" Debbie asked. "This is your new baby sister and brother."

Ben leaned in to get a closer look. "They're so little."

"You two were that little when you were born," Debbie explained.

Becky nuzzled up to Debbie. "Mommy, what happened to your tummy?"

"You remember me telling you that the babies were in my tummy. Well, now they are here, so Mommy's tummy isn't that big anymore."

"That's cool," Ben said. "You're not fat anymore."

"Mommy wasn't fat. She was pregnant. Ben, there is a difference," Brad tried to explain as he picked James up. "If you two get up on those chairs, you can hold your brother."

"Me first," Becky said as she climbed up onto the chair.

Brad laid James into Becky's arms. Her eyes were big in pure wonderment. She never said a word, just sat there studying his little face.

Ben had climbed into the chair beside her and waited his turn. "Ben, this is Jessica. Would you like to hold your sister?" Brad asked as he placed her into Ben's arms. They both sat there mesmerized by the small little babies.

James was starting to fuss. Brad explained, "I think he is waking up because he has a wet bum and is probably hungry. Let me take him to Mommy."

Debbie took James, changed his diaper, and then sat on the bed to nurse him. Becky was speechless and watched the performance with complete concentration. When James was finished eating, she handed him to Brad. He put James back into the crib and took Jessica from Ben's arms for her turn.

Becky was still sitting quietly, totally mesmerized. Ben, on the other hand, was full of questions. He watched as Debbie changed her and then fed her. Debbie had to explain to them that the babies were getting milk from her breast, and when they got older, they would get milk from a bottle instead.

"I would like to get some pictures of you all together," Brad suggested. "When Mommy is done with Jess, I would like you all to get on the bed beside her and you can each hold a baby."

While they were getting the pictures taken, the nurse came in to check on them. "Let me take a few pictures with Daddy in them." She took the camera and Brad got on the bed behind his new family.

"Thank you so much. I appreciate that," Brad said as he took his camera back.

"No problem. So, who are these big kids?" the nurse asked.

"This little man is Benjamin, and this young lady is Rebecca. Better known as Ben and Becky," Brad said.

"Ben and Becky, nice to meet you. How are you doing, Mommy? Is everything okay?"

"Yes, thanks. The babies are changed and fed."

"Then I'll leave you to it. But don't visit for too long. Mommy needs to get some rest while the babies are sleeping." The nurse gave them a big smile and left the room.

"We better put the babies back in the crib." Brad took one baby, and Debbie took the other and laid them down.

"When are you coming home?" Ben wanted to know.

"Soon as I can. As soon as the doctors say it's alright, Mommy and the babies will come home."

"We miss you, Mommy," Becky said with a sad look on her face.

"I miss you too, angel. We'll all be home soon."

It's going to be alright. It will be hard, and there are bound to be a million questions from the big kids, but it will all be alright.

FORTY

The next morning, Debbie had just finished changing and feeding the babies when the doctor stopped in.

"Good morning, Debbie," Doctor Barnes said as he glanced at her chart. "How are you feeling?"

"Fine, thanks. Just waiting for the twins to put on a couple of ounces before I can take them home."

"How are you feeling?"

"I'm alright, just anxious to get out of here. You know I have a great support system at home. Brad is a great help, and his mother will come over every morning to help with the babies' feedings. And I have two five-year-olds that will be helpful if asked."

"That's good to know. Ben and Becky are both strong, healthy kids. And I am sure these two little ones will be as well. I am going to take them now for an examination and give them some needles. What are their names?"

"James and Jessica," Debbie said proudly.

"Well, James and Jessica, let's go for a little ride. We won't be gone long," Doctor Barnes said as he wheeled the portable crib out of the room.

Above all the ringing phones and intercom, Debbie could hear the babies crying, and had to force herself to stay in bed. It seemed like an hour had passed when the nurse wheeled the crying babies back into the room.

"I know they just ate, but perhaps if you nursed again,

they would settle down," the nurse said as she handed James to Debbie.

Sure enough, it did settle him. Within a minute, he was starting to fall asleep, and the nurse took James in one arm and handed Jessica to Debbie, from her other arm. Jess lasted a couple of minutes before she lost interest. Debbie wrapped her up and cuddled her to her cheek. Jess fell asleep, and the nurse gently took her back to the crib. "You try and get some rest now; the doctor on call will be awhile making his rounds."

"Thank you for all your help," Debbie said as her eyes closed.

When she woke from her cat nap, Brad was sitting there with a baby in his arms.

"Morning, beautiful. James was starting to fuss, so I cooed to him, and he settled back down."

"Morning, hun. You'll have to excuse me for a moment." Debbie made a mad dash to the washroom. "Sorry about that. I'll take James and change him if you like."

Debbie changed James's wet diaper and then sat beside Brad to feed the baby. "So, how are things going at home?"

Brad gave her a smile. "Everything is going fine, but we all miss you not being there."

"I miss being home as well. Doctor Barnes was here earlier, and he examined them and gave them their first needles."

"So, are we going home today?" Brad asked.

"I'm not sure. I'm just waiting for the doctor on duty. He's making his rounds, and he'll get around to me eventually."

Jessica was starting to whimper, so Brad picked her up and changed her wet diaper.

"Perfect timing. I think James is done." Debbie wrapped him back up and handed Brad his son. "You can burp James, and I'll feed Jessica."

"Well, now, isn't this a picture," the doctor on call said as he came over to stand in front of them. "Teamwork makes the dream work." He chuckled.

"So, doc, what's the good news?"

"The good news is that you can take your new family home today. Both babies are eating and gaining weight. I'm happy about that, and I see from Dr. Barnes's notes that you have a lot of help at home. So, I just signed your release papers. A nurse will come in with a pile of paperwork for you. Debbie, according to this note, Doctor Barnes would like to see you, and the babies in his office in a week."

"We'll all be there. Oh, and doc, these are for you." Brad handed him two cigars. "Thanks for taking such good care of us."

"Thank you, doctor," Debbie said.

Linda and Charles walked in just as the doctor was walking out.

"Good news, doc says we can go home today." Brad stood and handed James to his father. "Grandpa, meet your new grandson, James Christopher."

"Look at you, young man. Aren't you a handsome little guy!" Charles was talking to James, who was sound asleep.

Debbie stood and handed Jessica to Linda. "Grandma, I would like to introduce you to Jessica Ann Marie."

"Oh my. Jessica. I like that name. So, James and Jessica. Very clever," Linda said.

"When can you leave?" Charles asked.

"We still have to do paperwork. I think we should stay here for the next feeding, and then maybe they will sleep all the way home," Debbie suggested.

"My wife is so smart. I would have never thought of that." Brad beamed with pride.

"You call me when you get home, and I'll slip over and help you get settled," Linda stated.

Brad put his arm around his mother's shoulder. "Mom, you are absolutely the best. I love you so much."

"I love you, too, son. And now, I have two more babies to love." Linda snuggled Jessica to her cheek. "I just love how soft and smoochy babies are."

Charles handed baby James back to Brad. "Congratulations, son. Your family is now complete."

"Thanks, Dad. I couldn't be happier if I tried," Brad said as he lay James back into the crib. "I have something for you." Brad reached into his coat, pulled out two cigars, and handed them to his dad.

"Thank you, son. That's very nice." Charles turned to Linda. "Are you ready to go, Grandma?"

"Yes, Grandpa, I'm coming." Linda took the baby over and lay her down beside her brother. She turned to Debbie. "Now, you call me when you are on your way home."

"Thanks, Grandma, I will," Debbie assured her.

Brad sat beside Debbie and put his arm around her. "Are you excited about going home?"

"Absolutely. I can't wait to have a nap in my own bed." Debbie leaned her head on his shoulder.

"Should I go now and let you have a rest?" Brad asked.

"That's probably not a bad idea. Or you could just sit here quietly if you don't have anything more pressing to do."

"I think I'll stroll down to the cafeteria and get a coffee. Would you like anything?"

"You could bring me back a coffee, and a carrot muffin if they have any." Debbie got into bed and Brad helped her cover up.

"Close your eyes, pretty lady. I'll be back soon." Brad kissed her forehead. Debbie was asleep instantly.

A while later, Brad came back. "Coffee and muffin delivery for the pretty lady." Brad set them on the table in front of her bed. "I see you have the suitcase packed. What else has to happen?"

"You need to take this out to the van and bring in the car seats, please," Debbie said as she pulled the wrapper off her muffin.

"Have you already fed the babies then?"

"Yes, just finished. So, as long as we don't bounce them around too much, they should stay sleeping until we are home."

"That sounds like a wonderful plan. I'll be right back."

Brad was back before she had finished her muffin. He sat down in a chair across from her. "I can't seem to wipe this smile off my face."

"Smiles suit that handsome face. I'm happy too. A little nervous, but happy."

"Nervous? Really? What are you nervous about?"

"Being a new mother, again. Taking care of these precious little ones." Debbie shrugged as she threw the muffin wrapper into the garbage can.

"Honey, you will do just fine. Besides, you have done all this before, and you are a great mother." Brad sat beside her on the bed.

"It's hard to explain. A new mother has a lot of things

to worry about, most importantly that the babies are gaining weight and getting stronger every day."

"And they will. You are a good mother." Brad pulled her into his arms. "We'll be just fine. James and Jess will be just fine. You are worrying for no good reason."

"I know. I'm just trying to tell you how I feel." Debbie started to cry.

"And I'm just trying to let you know that I understand and am here to support you and the babies with everything I have."

Brad held her while she cried. When she was all cried out, he handed her a tissue. "It's okay, hun. We are going to be just fine. You'll see."

"I know, I'm sorry to be so emotional. I don't know what's wrong with me." Debbie wiped her face.

"There's nothing wrong with you. You're just overwhelmed with it all. You'll feel so much better once you are home." Brad stood up. "Are we ready to go then?"

"I guess so. Let me get the kids into their bunting bags and then we'll be ready." Debbie took the blue bag and gently placed James inside it and then into the car seat. Brad followed her example, and had Jessica dressed and strapped into the other car seat.

"So, have we got everything then? Do you want to take the flowers, or do you want to leave them?"

"No, we'll leave them for the nurses." Debbie took a final look around as she put on her winter coat and boots. "I guess we are ready."

Debbie called Linda to let her know they were leaving and would be home in thirty minutes.

They had just pulled into the driveway when Linda pulled up behind them.

"What can I carry?" she asked.

"I have the suitcase, and Brad has both the car seats. Maybe you could take my key and go ahead, and open the door."

Once everyone was inside, Debbie opened the bunting bags and just let the babies sleep. Brad carried them upstairs, and when they woke up for their next feeding, they were put into their new crib.

As Debbie happily climbed into her own bed, As Brad tucked her in, her last thought was, *that was a smooth transition. It feels so good to be home.*

ABOUT THE AUTHOR

Deloris Packard grew up in Harcourt, a small town at the base of Algonquin Park, in Ontario cottage country.

She is the youngest of eight children, having two brothers and five sisters.

Now retired, she currently lives in another small town, in Stirling Ontario.

Her personal knowledge of sibling rivalries, along with her vast experience in the hospitality industry, has given her the capability to tell her stories, from an inside perspective.

For more info, check out her YouTube channel https://www.youtube.com/@delorispackard

Made in the USA
Columbia, SC
31 March 2025

185c5faf-89bb-46b5-b1b1-8d388d5ebbb4R01